THE NATION'S MISSING GUEST

AN AMOS LEE MAPPIN MYSTERY

THE NATION'S MISSING GUEST

AN AMOS LEE MAPPIN MYSTERY

Hulbert Footner

Coachwhip Publications

Greenville, Ohio

ISBN 1-61646-271-X
ISBN-13 978-1-61646-271-0

Cover: Arabic avatar © Natalia Kulinich; Locomotive © Vertyr/Fotolia; Hulbert Footner (George H. Doran Co., 1921)

CoachwhipBooks.com

CONTENTS

CHAPTER ONE

To Luke Imbrie it seemed as if he were being forced to mark time while the parade of life marched by with bands playing. He had all the education in the world, but no money. Upon being graduated from Harvard he had been awarded a Rhodes scholarship at Oxford, and after returning to America had gone through the Harvard Law School with flying colors. The day after he was graduated he went to work for Dunning, Dunning, Heberden, Colfax, and Porter, the number one New York firm engaged in the practice of law. They took their pick each year from among the honor men of Harvard and Yale.

The job proved disappointing; Luke found himself one of the least among the two hundred and odd lawyers employed by the firm, with duties scarcely more than those of an office boy, and pay miserably insufficient to support a life of elegance in the big city. Among themselves the younger men referred to their office as "the factory." As Luke put it, it had taken a mountain of preparation to produce a mouse of a job.

Even so, he could have had a good time if he had been willing to do as others did. The whole glittering, fantastic, extravagant show of New York life was open to a handsome, well-born young man whether he had any money or not. But Luke had an unconquerable repugnance to letting the papas and mammas of debutantes or bored wealthy wives slip him the wherewithal to pay for an evening's fun. It became known that he would not accept gifts of tickets to the opera or the theater, or subscriptions to dances, or "loans," and as a result he spent more evenings than he liked at the Harvard Club (the one extravagance he could permit himself) playing contract with other young men in a like situation. Luke was not crazy about contract. Bored with his job, and bored with his evenings, he asked himself what the hell kind of a life is this when you're twenty-seven?

One alleviation that Luke enjoyed was his friendship with Amos Lee Mappin, the celebrated amateur criminologist and author. It was only Lee who termed himself "amateur"; for the keenest minds in the profession acknowledged him as their equal. The astute and humorous little man had been a classmate of Luke's father. He had a flair for youth, and Luke in his company was never conscious of the difference in their ages. Lee occasionally invited the young man to his little dinners where one was sure of meeting personalities, whether fashionable or not; and, better still, he encouraged Luke to drop in of an evening to sit by the fire and chew the fat. Unfortunately, Mr. Mappin did not spend many evenings at home.

As he entered the Harvard Club one night, Luke was handed a fat envelope which bore an English post-mark and was inscribed in a sprawling, unformed hand that he did not recognize. It contained several closely filled pages of writing. There was also a bank draft, always a welcome discovery. He turned first to the signature—"Meddy." Luke stared at it blankly. Who the heck was Meddy! Then it came to him. Of course! Meddy was the nickname applied to the little Arab at Oxford who was said to be the son of a Sultan somewhere in the East. Luke had never been intimate with him, and he wondered greatly what Meddy could have to say to him that ran to such length. He read:

> My dear Luke Imbrie:
> It's a beasly fag to have to write a letter myself, and I cant spell right, but I cant trust this to a seccertary. You wouldn't believe the trouble I had to get by myself long enough to write it. The problem of posting it without being seen is still to be met. You will be surprised hearing from me. Perhaps youve forgotten

me. You never paid much attention to me at Oxford, but you made a lasting impression on me, you were so dam big. I'm very glad now that I know you, because I need a friend in America. You're the only American I know. Americans are so natural! They can afford to be because they're free. As for me, I am surrounded by a net of intreag. I can trust nobody.

My whole name, in case you have forgotten it, is Ahmed bin Said. My father died two years ago and I am Sultan of Shihkar which sounds very grand, but isn't so imperssive when you examine into it. My country is so small you would have a hard time finding it on the map, and I am only the ruler by permission of the British who pays me £50 000 a year to allow a British resident to run things, and like a European monarch you have heard of, the only thing I am allowed to stick my nose in is my handkerchief. However, the £50 000 per annum is very nice, and the Sultan manages to amuse himself. The respectable British are continually trotting out different dark-eyed houris as suitable wives for me, but I have made up my mind to choose for myself, and to date I am still unmarried.

These canny British authorities, my gides, phisolophers and friends, have been urging me for some time past to pay a visit to America in semi-state; twenty-one gun salutes, lunch with the President, military escort and so on. Exactly what they expect to gain by this I don't know—certainly they are not offering to pay all expenses for the sake of my bright eys—but I imagine it is some thing like this. By showing the world how considderatly one of their wards is treated by the wealthy United States, they hope to persuade other small potentates in the East to accept their subsidies. Well, I don't mind letting myself be used as a paun in the game if there's any fun in it. So I have consented, and all the arangements have been made.

I will arrive in New York on June 21st per S.S. *Queen Mary*, and I hope this is where you come in. Will you meet me and acompanny me on my tour? I feel I *must* have somebody close to me that I can trust; somebody who knows America and can advise me how to act. I want to win the good will of the American people. More about this when we meet. I beg you not to let any other engagements interfere. You were planning to be a lawyer, I remember. By this time you must have completed your edducation. So let it be arranged on a professional basis. I pay you a retainer for your services. Ask what you please; it can all be charged to the British!

Now I come to a more personel matter. On the *Normandie* which will arrive at New York a week before me, I am sending two ladies. For obivus reasons they cannot come on the same ship as me. They are Miss Diana Morven and Mrs. Morven, her mother. Mrs. Morven is American born, the widow of a British diplomat. She has been absent from her country so many years she will be like a stranger. Will you please engage acom—can't spell it—rooms for them at the Hotel Conradi-Windermere (where a suite has been reserved for me) and meet them at the ship? They will wait for you in their cabins. And if you will watch over them until I come, you will be putting me under an internal obligation. Please see that their rooms are filled with flowers every day, and any other attentions may occur to you. This will not be charged against the British!

There is one more small service I am asking of you. I am consining to you in care of the Harvard Club, twelve cases of a Scotch whiskey called "Glenardrey." Will you please attend to clearing it

through the custom house? Accept a case for yourself and keep the rest for me. When you see me do
not mention whiskey until we are alone together. I
will explain then. This Glenardrey is something very
special, a straight whiskey produced by a small dis-
tillery in 1904. When you taste it you will agree that
there is nothing to equal it anywhere. My dear Luke,
there is noboddy I would want to share it with more
than you.

All this in strick confidence. I look on you from
this moment as my legal adviser. I am writing in
haste. I will explain everthing when I see you. Please
acnowlege receet of this by cable to Grosvenor
House, London. I am enclosing a draft for £200 to
cover pre—you know—expenses. I shall be on ege
until I hear everything is aranged.

With my best,

Ever your friend,

Meddy.

Luke dropped in a chair, staring before him while all this
revolved in his mind like a Catherine wheel in showers of sparks.
To a man chafing at the dullness of his life it sounded too good to
be true. A hoax, perhaps, evolved by one of his ingenious British
friends. However, the bank draft had every appearance of being
genuine. He would find out when he tried to cash it.

Meanwhile, he gave himself up to delightful visions of the fu-
ture. Fifty thousand pounds a year! A quarter of a million dollars.
Boy! . . . And offering Luke a retainer, the first he had earned, any
amount that he cared to name! . . . To be the intimate of a ruling
Sultan! Visit in state to Washington. Fascinating suggestions of
mystery, intrigue, and international politics! . . . Not to speak of
romance in the person of one Diana Moryen! What a lovely name!
How could a Diana fall for a shrimp like Meddy? . . . Still, of course,
if he was a ruler! . . . And to top off, a case of the best Scotch whisky
in the world! Oh, boy! it had everything!

Luke excused himself from the bridge game, and wandered out into the street, dreaming still. He went into the first Western Union office he came to, and chewing a pencil, debated on the proper form of address to be used to a reigning Sultan. He finally decided on this:

His Highness Ahmed bin Said
Grosvenor House
London, England
    Letter received. Accept with pleasure.
    Imbrie.

Feeling the need of a steadying influence, he taxied to Lee Mappin's apartment overlooking the East River. He was lucky enough to find his friend at home. Lee's rotund little form in smoking-jacket and slippers was sunk in an easy-chair with his feet on another. In appearance and style Lee belonged to the early nineteenth century, and it pleased him to dress the character as far as he could without causing a riot; a black stock with his evening clothes, and always on fine days a white or lemon-colored waistcoat, ditto spats. He carried a snuff-box which he was fond of tapping for emphasis; and at psychological moments he would inhale a pinch with two emphatic sniffs.

At this moment Lee was reading the Newgate Calendar. His eyes twinkled in friendly fashion at Luke through his glasses, and Luke handed him the Sultan's letter to read without comment.

"Well, I'm damned!" said Lee, cheerfully, when he had come to the end. He blew on his glasses and polished them. One of his watchwords was, Always keep your specs bright.

"Do you think it's a hoax?" asked Luke, anxiously.

Lee shook his head. "Not with the draft inclosed. It wouldn't be worth all that trouble unless the draft is good, and if the draft is good, what do you care?"

Luke was relieved.

"Help yourself to a cigar and sit down," said Lee.

"What do you suppose my firm will say to this?" asked Luke. "After all, I can't afford to jeopardize my job for a month's junket with the Sultan."

"Don't say anything about it until he arrives," Lee advised. "The papers will give him a front-page spread. You can then tell your firm that the Sultan wishes to engage you as his personal counsel for the duration of his visit, and they'll give you leave of absence in a hurry."

"He is God's gift to a starving lawyer!" murmured Luke.

"It seems to be customary for English girls to marry these Eastern princes," said Lee.

Luke shrugged. "Meddy's lineage goes back for six hundred years. In European clothes he would pass for an Italian. He's a handsome little lad, scarcely five foot tall. More like an English schoolboy than anything."

Lee got out a bottle of Scotch.

"You shall have half my case of the Sultan's whisky," said Luke. "It's little enough return for all the good liquor of yours that I have drunk."

"Not more than one bottle!" said Lee, wagging his hand.

Opening Lee's big atlas, they found Shihkar a tiny patch of red on the Persian Gulf. A chain of lofty mountains separated the sea coast from the desert behind. To the north lay the French sphere of influence. The Britannica supplied a few details about the country and its history. Shihkar camels were famous throughout the East. It was true that Ahmed bin Said was of very ancient lineage. For a while during the eighteenth century his ancestors had been driven out of Shihkar by the Portuguese, but Ali ibu Achmed, the hero of the family, had returned in 1755 and reconquered the country. The present Sultan, it was stated, lived abroad.

CHAPTER TWO

LUKE IMBRIE AWOKE in his bed, and lay frowning at the ceiling. Another routine day! Suddenly the recollection came to him that today he had not to shut himself up in a windowless office to read dull briefs by electric light. Springing out of bed, he went to the window. It was an exquisite blue-and-white morning in June; just the sort to beckon a young man to adventure.

He shaved, bathed to the accompaniment of song, and dressed with a particular care, grinning at himself meanwhile for his own folly. This is another fellow's girl you're going to meet, he told himself; there's nothing in it for you! But an excitement was running in his blood; he felt that life was beginning today. He stopped at a florist's and bought a knot of cornflowers because some girl had told him that blue was his color. In the florist's shop they served him like a king because of the order he had given for flowers to be sent daily to the Conradi-Windermere.

After breakfast he was driven to the French line pier, armed with a pass. As he entered the long shed the incredible ship with her three gargantuan funnels was coming into view downriver, attended by a whole flotilla of tugs. Luke went out on the uncovered end of the pier where the friends of the passengers were waving to the oncoming ship before there was any possibility of being recognized.

The monster filled the whole river; she was not like a ship, but a section of the city which had become detached. Sixteen tugs were required to swing her around and head her into the slip. As the black steel cliff slid by, Luke searched the crowded rails for a face which looked as if it might belong to a Diana. Diana! the name bewitched him. There were too many faces; they blurred before his eyes.

As soon as he was permitted, he boarded the ship. Upon applying to a steward he was informed that Mrs. and Miss Morven had the Fécamp suite, number 134 on the main deck. A moment later he was knocking at the door. A fretful voice told him to enter, and he found himself in a beautiful little sitting-room facing a stout, smartly dressed woman with waved and hennaed hair. There was nobody else in the room. The stout woman, in a great state of fluster, immediately burst out with:

"So here you are at last! I suppose you're Mr. Imbrie. What has kept you? The ship has been here for hours and I didn't know what on earth to do!"

Her complaints were so perfectly unreasonable Luke could only grin. He wondered anxiously if by some chance daughter had been left behind. A voice from the adjoining room reassured him—the voice of a Diana with a husky drawling quality that laid a spell on him:

"For goodness' sake, Mother, Mr. Imbrie isn't equipped with wings. He couldn't light on the deck until they ran up the gangplank."

"Well, I'm sure!" said Mrs. Morven. It was her stock remark when she had no other answer. Luke recognized the type. She had had everything done to her that was fashionable at the moment, but all the beauty aids in Paris couldn't disguise the fact that she had put her fiftieth birthday behind her and was thirty pounds overweight. "All the hand baggage has been carried away!" she cried, tragically. "I don't know where they've taken it. I have no receipt, no check of any kind. I'm sure something will be lost or stolen!"

"No danger," said Luke, soothingly. "They do this every day. You'll find everything waiting for you under the letter M."

She wasn't listening. "Well, let's go ashore," she said. "We've been ready for hours. Where's my pocketbook?" She searched wildly. "Diana, I've lost my pocketbook!" she screamed.

"It's here on your bed," said the unhurried voice from the next room.

She appeared in the doorway, tall, slender, blonde; Paris to her finger tips. As exquisite and exotic as the pale cattleyas that flowed over her corsage, she was the embodiment of the dream that a man hides even from himself. She had a remote, uncommon air such as home girls do not acquire. Luke felt as if she ought to be slapped for looking so superior, but it maddened him just the same. Glancing at him levelly, she drawled:

"So this is what you're like!" Luke could say nothing. She went on: "Meddy told us so much about you that it was merely confusing. We couldn't form any picture except that you were ten feet tall."

"Not quite," said Luke. "I'm surprised that Meddy should remember me so clearly. We weren't very well acquainted at Oxford."

Diana said: "Meddy is crazy about everything American."

"I wish you wouldn't refer to His Highness so familiarly," said Mrs. Morven.

"He likes it," said Diana.

"Well, I'm sure!" said her mother. ". . . Come on, do let us go ashore and find the luggage."

Luke followed them off the vessel in a dream.

A small mountain of expensive-looking luggage waited for them under the letter M. Mrs. Morven, having checked it a dozen times, reluctantly admitted that it was all there. Word had come from Washington that Mrs. Morven was entitled to diplomatic privileges, and their bags were expeditiously passed. They were already being wheeled off the pier while envious ordinary passengers stood about, waiting for an inspector.

The baggage completely filled a taxicab. Luke and his two charges set off ahead of it in another. During the whole journey Mrs. Morven sat with her neck craned, watching the following cab through the rear window. When she lost it in the traffic she was perfectly sure the driver had run off with her belongings. Luke heartily wished that she had accompanied them.

Diana looked out of her window at the town she had never seen. To Luke, watching her from the little seat in front, it was marvelous that something so rare and exquisite should be enframed in a commonplace New York taxi. She was disappointed in what she saw.

"One expected a wonder city," she murmured. "But it looks very shabby."

"You're seeing the worst of it," said Luke.

Driving through Forty-eighth Street the soaring R.C.A. tower suddenly came into view. "That comes up to promise," said Diana.

Luke accompanied them up to the suite he had engaged in the Conradi-Windermere. It was one of the best in the house; designed by a master-decorator and filled with fine antiques. Mrs. Morven looked around her.

"Just like any other hotel," she said. "After all I've heard about the Conradi-Windermere, I expected something different. . . . Will H. H.'s rooms be on this floor?"

"His Highness," explained Diana, dryly.

"No," said Luke. "They're giving him an apartment in the tower."

"Oh," said Mrs. Morven.

"Apartments in the tower are hard to get," said Luke, "because most of them are leased by the year. But I'll see what I can do."

"Not at all," said Diana, quickly. A hint of color had crept into her pale cheeks. "These rooms are very nice. There's no earthly reason why we should be lodged on the same floor with Meddy."

"But if we dine with him," objected her mother.

"Well, I suppose there are lifts," said Diana.

"I must have a personal maid while we're in New York," said Mrs. Morven. "I'm sure I don't know why Diana refused to bring the excellent woman we had in London. American servants are terrible. Her recommendations must be carefully looked into."

Diana's fine brows drew together. "Mother, Mr. Imbrie is not a servant."

Mrs. Morven shrugged impatiently. "H. H. said he'd get us anything we wanted."

Luke hoped Mrs. Morven would go on being rude to him if Diana took his part. "The hotel will supply a personal maid," he said; "and they take the responsibility for her honesty. I'll speak about it on my way out."

"Thanks for the flowers," said Diana, glancing around the room.

"Meddy's orders," said Luke.

"H. H. is so thoughtful!" murmured Mrs. Morven.

"But you chose them," said Diana to Luke.

Luke addressed Mrs. Morven politely. "After you're settled a bit, I hope you'll give me the pleasure of lunching with me. So we can talk over what you'd like to do in New York."

"I'm exhausted," said Mrs. Morven, raising her shoulders.

"I'll come," said Diana.

Luke went down the corridor, walking on air.

Mrs. Morven found herself sufficiently rested to join them at lunch, and she did most of the talking. Earlier, Luke had spent half an hour in consultation with a *maître d'hôtel*, and between them they had settled upon the most perfect luncheon that the great Conradi-Windermere could produce that day. It cost Luke half a week's salary. Mrs. Morven spent her time in pointing out how much better the various dishes were served at Meurice's in Paris or the Berkeley in London, and Luke wondered why nobody had strangled this woman before she reached her fiftieth year.

This was Monday. For Luke, six enchanted days followed. Advance notices of the coming of the Sultan of Shihkar had appeared in the press, and when Luke had asked for a month's leave of absence "to attend to business of His Highness," it had very willingly been granted. Consequently he had nothing in the world to do this week but to wait on the beautiful Diana. Unfortunately, her mother was always present and always talking, but at least he could look at Diana. He felt as if he could look at her his whole life long without getting his fill.

As long as they were together Luke was lost in this pleasure, and made no attempt to think. When he was alone, the inevitable question presented itself. What was to come of it? And the answer was: Nothing! His days were heaven and his nights hell. Almost from the first moment he realized that the bell had rung for him.

This was the sort of thing that didn't happen twice to a man. But how could he ask a Diana to share seventy-five dollars a week? It wouldn't buy her orchids.

Furthermore, he had the consciousness that he was not playing a very good part. True, he had not yet taken any of Ahmed's money for his own use, but he had accepted the job of looking after Ahmed's girl—only to fall in love with her! A hundred times a night he told himself that the little Arab was nothing to him; in a case of this kind it was every man for himself; but it did not quiet his conscience. Obviously it would be impossible for him to go on tour with them. Six short days of happiness to be followed by a lifetime of regret!

Only once or twice did Luke get an hour alone with Diana. For the most part she put up with her tiresome mother equably, as if after so many years she had learned not to hear her complaints. But occasionally with a word she shut up Mrs. Morven with startling effectiveness. Generally it was too much trouble.

As to Diana's feelings toward himself, Luke could never be sure. Probably not very strong one way or the other. When, because he was young and in love, he was impelled to pour out the story of himself, she listened with friendly mockery—but she listened; she asked questions. He could not, however, beguile her into telling him anything about herself. It tormented him to think of what her life must have been during the past ten years; hundreds of men must have been ready to die for her.

Sometimes he felt like a wave dashing against the wall of her smiling indifference. Then he would rage against her in his mind— she had no heart; she wasn't worth a man's love. And then a hint of piteousness in her lovely, guarded eyes would strike him down again.

Sunday night came all too soon for Luke. The *Queen Mary* was reported a hundred miles east of Nantucket lightship, and would dock at nine next morning. As usual, Luke dined with Diana and her mother at the Conradi. As Mrs. Morven sailed out of the room in advance of them, Luke whispered to Diana:

"Will you fix it so that we can have a little time together to-night?"

She looked in his eyes. "It won't do any good."

Luke set his jaw. "I know. I have no expectations."

"Then what's the use?" she murmured.

"I must talk to you once . . . to clear the record."

"Very well," she said, lowering her eyes. "On your own head!"

They had brought their wraps downstairs. In the lobby Diana said, coolly, "Mother, Luke and I want to prowl around by our-selves tonight."

"Well, I'm sure . . . !" Mrs. Morven began indignantly, but Diana was looking at her levelly, and she dried up.

Waiting on the step for a taxi, Luke said: "No dancing, no floor shows, no hot-spots tonight, eh? But a quiet little place where we can talk?"

"Is there such a place in New York?" asked Diana.

He nodded. "If you want to be by yourself at night you choose a restaurant that is popular at lunch time." He gave the taxi driver an address near by.

In the cab he picked up her hand and pressed it to his lips. She drew it away. "Please, Luke, don't force me to be on my guard against you. I want to be myself tonight."

"Sorry, Di."

They entered a quiet restaurant with shallow alcoves around the walls where a couple might sit unobserved. The place was al-most empty. There was no music. Luke gave himself up to the pain-ful pleasure of gazing at Diana.

"Don't look at me like that," she murmured.

"You know I love you," he said.

She nodded.

"It's not this cheap feeling that is talked about and sung about till you gag at the word," he said. "It's a knockout."

"Is it my fault?" she murmured.

"No. You can't help being what you are."

"It's hopeless, isn't it?"

"Quite."

"Then why did you have to speak it? I wanted to save you pain."

"I had to tell you," said Luke. "There's something in a man that forces him to testify, no matter how hopeless his case is."

Diana was silent.

"Are you going to marry Meddy?" he asked.

She nodded.

"O God! how that galls me!" he muttered. "A little shrimp like that! At Oxford he was a joke."

"He's young," she said, stubbornly; "he's gay and good-hearted. He's very much in love with me."

"And he has quarter of a million a year!" added Luke.

She faced him out defiantly. "Well, why not? We're not children. We're dealing with realities."

Luke shrugged.

"Believe me," Diana went on, "Meddy is a great improvement on the other recent candidates that Mother has brought forward."

"Why should that be?" asked Luke. "A woman like you has only to choose."

Diana smiled bitterly. "Unfortunately, Mother's method is wrong. It is so obvious that we are out for a rich husband, that the more desirable sort of men sheer off."

"It's horrible!" he cried. "Why do you stand for it?"

"It has been going on for too long," she said. "It has sapped my character. I came out at fifteen, twelve years ago. Ever since I've been dragged around Europe and shown off."

"It's a crime!" said Luke. "You should get rid of such a mother!"

"How?" she asked, smiling.

He was silenced.

"We haven't any money," Diana went on in her indifferent voice. "My father had a good income once. He was of the type that is always chosen as minister to Luxembourg or Liechtenstein, never the big posts. He always spent more than he had and he speculated in American securities which went up so fast. In 1929 he was cleaned out. He killed himself. Since then Mother and I have been put to one shift after another to keep going. I had never been taught anything useful. And our only friends belong to those European circles where ladies are not supposed to work."

"But *Meddy!*" groaned Luke.

"It's useless to talk about it. I'm committed to this marriage a hundred times over. He's been supporting us for the past year. I couldn't get out of it now, even if I had something else in view."

"Why did you wait a year?"

"Because the British told Meddy there would be a revolution in Shihkar if he married an unbeliever. His brother, Abu Daud, who's the next in line, was just watching for such a chance."

"Well, why won't there be a revolution now?" asked Luke.

"There will be," she said, coolly. "But now it is known that Abu Daud has sold himself to the French, consequently the British will have to stand by Meddy whomever he marries. If the people rebel, the British will put it down."

"He's a Mohammedan!" said Luke. "What does marriage mean to them?"

"He has promised to become a Christian. We will be married in a Christian church."

Luke gloomed at the tablecloth.

"Don't grieve," she said, softly. "I'm not worth it."

Jerking his head up, he said, harshly: "I don't know what you're worth, and I don't care. I only know I want you! . . . What do you think about me?" he demanded.

"I like you ever so much," she said, quickly, "or I wouldn't be talking to you like this."

"Sometimes it has seemed as if it was more than liking," he said, searching her face. "If I thought you cared for me . . ."

Diana laughed lightly. "There's nothing in it. I'm incapable of loving anybody."

"I don't know whether I believe you or not."

Diana lowered her eyes. "It's only your vanity that makes you think I care for you," she said. "You're not *very* vain, but of course you have your share."

"O God! I love you so!" he murmured.

She kept her eyes down. "Please, Luke . . . forget me quickly. It hurts me to see you suffer."

"I shall never forget you," he said. "What the hell am I to do when his Royal Crispies comes tomorrow? I have engaged myself to accompany him on his trip, but that would be more than flesh and blood could stand!"

"Aren't you coming with us?" she said, in dismay.

He leaned towards her warmly. "Would you miss me, Di?"

She recovered herself. "No. I was counting on you to look after Meddy. He's so imprudent. He needs somebody like you to keep him straight. . . . Why shouldn't you come? This will never be brought up again. It shall be buried between us."

"You said you didn't want to make me suffer," he said, looking in her eyes.

She turned her head away.

"I ought not to come," said Luke, gloomily. "But I reckon I will. . . . The truth is I haven't the strength to pass up the opportunity of being near you."

CHAPTER THREE

ON SUNDAY LUKE GOT UP at an ungodly hour and went down the Bay on a cutter to meet the *Queen Mary*. Early as it was, the reporters and press photographers were before him, and a long time passed before he was able to work his way to his client's side.

The scene in the lounge of the vast ship was like something out of Hollywood. On a little sofa at the end of the long room sat the diminutive figure of Ahmed bin Said, Sultan of Shihkar, clad in flowing robes of gold and brown, on his head a turban of gold cloth with a snowy aigrette fastened by a ruby the size of a half dollar. Meddy had grown fat, Luke saw, but he was not lacking in royal self-possession. His pleasing oval face with its silky mustache was wreathed in a good-humored smile.

Ranged in front of him in a semicircle was a wall of press photographers, lying on the floor; squatting; perched on chairs; on tables; even on chairs planted on top of tables; each with his box trained on the little robed figure on the sofa. Their bulbs flashed blindingly. "Hold your head higher, Sultan," they were crying. "Look this way! . . . Stand up now! . . . Sit down! . . . Give us your profile!" And so on. His Highness among the conflicting orders good-humoredly obeyed as many as he could.

His entourage, in Arab dress, was grouped near by, alternately stepping forward to be included in the picture, or stepping back at command. In the forefront Luke recognized from Diana's description, Ahmed's half-brother, Abu Daud, a sleek, olive-skinned youth of twenty, as beautiful as a girl. But the glitter in his long-lashed velvety eyes was all male. Luke guessed that this precocious stripling was already old in wickedness. The other principal figure was a tall, seamy Arab with a swath of green in his turban. A pair of thick-rimmed glasses lent an incongruous touch to his make-up. This would be Shihab al Zuri, the Sultan's secretary. He was nervous; his expression was tense and his prominent Adam's apple moved up and down.

Between and behind the photographers and grouped at either side was a throng of reporters. When the cameras gave them a chance they pressed up to the sofa with their questions. "How do you like America, Sultan? . . . What's the first thing you want to see in New York? . . . Is that ruby in your turban the biggest you've got? How much is it worth? . . . What is your object in visiting our country? . . . Are you looking for an American wife?"

Shihab al Zuri was scandalized by the freedom of their questions. "Gentlemen, I beg of you!" he protested, waving his hands.

The Sultan took it all smilingly. "I can't talk to fifty men at once," he said in a pleasant English voice without a trace of accent. "If you'll write down your questions I'll answer as many as I can. I suggest that you appoint a committee of two or three from among you and let them wait on me at my hotel."

By this time Luke had worked his way up between two photographers, and Ahmed caught sight of him. He jumped up with a cry, holding out his hands. "Luke, my dear fellow!" He drew Luke towards the sofa, and instantly the photographers gave voice again, and their bulbs flashed.

"Turn around, Big Boy! . . . What's your name, mister? . . . What are you to the Sultan?"

Luke faced the cameras with a strained smile. He pictured how absurd the photographs would look in the evening papers, because Ahmed's big turban scarcely came to his shoulder. Ahmed answered for him.

"This is my dear friend Luke Imbrie. We were classmates at Oxford. He's a lawyer and a member of the firm of—what is it, Luke?"

"Dunning, Dunning, Heberden, Colfax, and Porter," said Luke, dryly. "But I am not yet a member of the firm."

"Mr. Imbrie will be my attorney and counselor during my stay in America," Ahmed went on, "and hereafter you had better apply to him for the news." He slipped his hand under Luke's arm. "Come on, let's go some place where we can talk in peace."

Cries of protest were raised. "One more picture, Sultan. Turn around so we can take the two of you. . . . Here's my list of questions, Sultan. . . ."

Ahmed, though small, was unperturbed. "Happy to receive you at any time, gentlemen, but just now I have a little business of my own. I'll see you later."

He led Luke down a stairway and through a corridor with all the reporters streaming after. Other passengers pressed back against the wall of the corridor, staring. Ahmed pushed Luke into his suite, and politely and firmly closed the door in the faces of their followers and locked it.

"Let me look at you," he said to Luke. "By God! what a figure you would make on horseback with a turban and an Arab lance!"

There was an agitated knocking on the door, and a hurried voice speaking Arabic. "Damn!" said Ahmed. "That's Shihab. We'll have to let him in, because he mustn't suspect that you and I have any secrets from him. We'll get together later."

The secretary was admitted. His sallow face was greenish with agitation. "Oh, these Americans! these Americans!" he wailed, holding up his hands.

"Where's my brother?" asked Ahmed.

"They are questioning him now."

"Fetch him in here," said Ahmed. "There's no knowing what he might tell them."

The sulky, smooth-faced Abu Daud was brought in. "What do you want?" he asked with ill-concealed insolence.

"To remind you," said Ahmed, sternly, "that no member of my party is to give information to the press excepting myself or Shihab al Zuri or Mr. Imbrie. This is Mr. Imbrie."

Abu Daud nodded coolly to Luke, and sat down on a sofa, where he lit a cigarette and, letting the smoke drift through his nostrils, stared idly through the window. His good looks were extraordinary. A good deal taller than his brother, he was as lithe and dangerous as a black leopard.

"Is Diana all right?" asked Ahmed.

The youth by the window never turned his head, but Luke saw his face change. Abu Daud was listening sharply. Luke said, with a wooden expression: "Right as rain. You gave me no instructions, and it seemed better, under the circumstances, to let Mrs. and Miss Morven wait for you at the hotel."

"O Lord, yes!" said Ahmed. "We mustn't let the reporters get hold of Diana! . . . But it's so long to wait!"

Abu Daud smiled insolently and flicked the ash from his cigarette. Shihab turned his head away, but Luke could see his Adam's apple working convulsively. Luke felt that he was in the middle of a tense situation with the disadvantage of not knowing what it was all about.

An hour later Luke and the Sultan entered a taxi at the door of the Cunard line pier. They had one medium-size suitcase which Ahmed insisted on taking with him. "My jewels," he said, carelessly. Shihab al Zuri was to bring along Abu Daud, the servants and the rest of the luggage.

All the effects of the party had been franked without examination. Ahmed settled back with a sigh of relief. "My God! it's good to be alone with you, Luke. I can trust you; you have no ax to grind. How I regret the old happy days at Oxford when I hadn't a care on my mind! I am naturally an outspoken, impulsive sort of fellow, and to have to be on my guard all the time is like being shut up in a prison. I am the center of a net of intrigue!"

"You had better tell me something about the situation," said Luke, "so I can act intelligently."

"My little country is controlled by the British, as you know," said Ahmed. "To the west and north of me lies the French sphere of influence, and the French covet Shihkar because it would give them an outlet to the sea."

"But the French and the British are allies," interrupted Luke.

"Surely. Surely. But that doesn't prevent them from jockeying for position in these out-of-the-way corners of the world. There are plenty of unscrupulous native agitators to be bought, and you may be sure that the respectable British and the polite French never appear openly in these matters. In my charming brother, Abu Daud, the French have an instrument exactly suited to their needs."

"Your own brother!"

"That's one of the evils of the harem system. Abu is my half-brother, the son of a different mother. He dreams of filling my shoes. Abu is a natural-born—what is the English word?—dema-gogue. . . ."

"Rabble-rouser," suggested Luke.

"Excellent! He represents me to the people as a traitor who has sold them out for English gold, while his slogan is 'Shihkar for the Shihkarri!' The poor fools do not know, of course, that if they turned me out they would merely be exchanging one foreign master for another."

"The English would never allow you to be deposed," said Luke.

"Quite right," said Ahmed, "but Abu purposes to solve the problem by presenting me with a dish of poison. That's a brotherly custom in the East, you know. It's very difficult to guard against because servants are venal."

"Horrible!" said Luke. "Why don't you lock him up?"

"That would only make him a hero in the eyes of the people. My ancestors used to strangle their younger brothers and cast them into the sea in sacks, but public opinion is against it nowadays."

Ahmed grinned delightfully and Luke was obliged to grin, too. He couldn't hate Ahmed; he was too little; it would have been like hating a schoolboy.

"I brought Abu along with me to keep him from stirring up trouble in Shihkar," Ahmed went on. "I feel safer when I have him under my eye. He is not likely to try to poison me while we are in America. It would be too difficult to get away with it."

Luke was forced to give the tiny man credit for a kind of cool courage. Ahmed, it seemed, was a fatalist. "How is it all going to end?" asked Luke.

"The thing for me to do is to get married as soon as possible and have an heir," said Ahmed, cheerfully. "That will put an end to

Abu's pretensions. At first the British were strongly opposed to my changing my religion on account of the effect in Shihkar, but as I have positively refused to marry anybody but Diana, they have finally come around."

Luke with a wooden face said, "Abu Daud is in love with Diana."

Ahmed glanced at him in surprise. "You have sharp eyes," he said.

Luke didn't feel it necessary to explain why his eyes were so sharp in this instance.

"Say that Abu *desires* Diana," corrected Ahmed. "He couldn't love anybody. His heart is as black as gall."

They were silent for a while.

"Now that I have reached America," said Ahmed, "my dream is to stay here. To let politics go to the devil and settle down with my lovely wife like any ordinary citizen." He sighed. "But I suppose it would be a low trick to let the British down after all the money they have spent on me. . . . And fifty thousand pounds a year is an awful lot to give up!"

"What else would you have to live on?" asked Luke, bluntly.

"Oh, I wouldn't be exactly a pauper," said Ahmed, with a secret smile. "I inherited a fortune in jewels. That is, they were mine if I could get hold of them. By the exercise of cunning and patience I have succeeded in bringing them out of Shihkar. It's a long story. I won't go into detail now. My brother knows nothing about it. My jewels have never been appraised, but according to our methods of computation their value much exceeds a couple of million dollars your money. I have deposited the greater part of them in the Midland Bank of London, and the rest I have with me." He kicked the suitcase at his feet.

"You have them with you!" cried Luke. "My God! this must be kept out of the papers!"

"Why?"

"Nearly a million in jewels! If that was known, every bandit in the country would start licking his lips!"

Ahmed chuckled. "Bandits are an old story to me."

After a moment Luke asked: "How about Shihab al Zuri? Can't you trust him?"

"Oh, sure!" said Ahmed. ". . . I trust him, but I don't tell him everything," he explained. "Shihab is a good deal more than a secretary. At home in Shihkar he is my wazir, or vizier, as the English say, my right-hand man. Shihab is an able and a conscientious man. He's very religious. He belongs to an ancient Mohammedan sect called the Shi'ites, great sticklers for the old forms and ceremonies of our religion."

"Like our fundamentalists," suggested Luke.

"Fundamentalists, exactly. Shihab himself is revered by the Faithful as a descendant of Muhammad Ali. I'm not referring to the Prophet, but to the Twelfth Imam, who disappeared a thousand years ago and is supposed to be still living somewhere in the desert, waiting to appear at the proper time. That's why Shihab wears green in his turban. . . . It's very inconvenient to have such a holy man in my service. I dare not let him see me take a drink. Hence the secrecy about the whisky."

"Does he know you are going to marry Miss Morven?" asked Luke.

"I've never told him," said Ahmed, "but of course he must suspect it. I dread the day when Shihab learns that I am forsaking his religion."

By this time the taxi had reached the middle of the city, and Ahmed was staring out of the window as pleased and excited as a small boy. "My God! what a town!" he said. "I'll have to go right down to Washington to present my respects to your President, but I'll be back! I'll be back! . . . Anyhow, we'll have tonight here," he went on. "Let's you and I and Diana sneak out of the hotel after dinner without any guards or servants, and see the town!"

Luke shook his head. "I couldn't take that responsibility, Meddy. Not after what you told me."

"Damn!" grumbled the little man. "You're as bad as the British."

"Think how conspicuous we'd be."

Ahmed chuckled. "Little me, big you and beautiful Diana, eh? . . . Well, if I can't go out, I'll give a party in the hotel. I met some amusing people on the ship. I have their telephone numbers."

"You'd better be careful whom you take up," warned Luke.

"Damn! I'm not going to live every minute in fear of my life!" cried Ahmed. "Certainly not in free America! I might as well be dead already."

The little Sultan in his flowing robes and jeweled turban created a sensation in the lobby of the Conradi-Windermere, and Luke hustled him through as quickly as possible, and up in an elevator to the magnificent state apartment that had been reserved in the tower. Diana and her mother were waiting for him in the salon, and Luke, not wishing to be a spectator of that meeting, hastily turned back at the door of the room, muttering that he had business down in the lobby.

In the corridor outside the state suite Luke ran into a well-dressed little man with a dusky complexion and a wall eye that immediately excited his suspicion. "What do you want?" he asked.

The man smiled and bowed repeatedly from the waist. "To present my respects to His Highness," he purred. He was too smooth, too oily.

"You should send up your name through the usual channels," said Luke. "Come down to the lobby with me."

The man showed his teeth. For a second he was inclined to defy Luke. But he thought better of it, and, shrugging deprecatingly, spreading out his hands, he preceded Luke to the elevator.

In the lobby Luke said to him: "Wait here with me. His Highness' secretary will be here directly."

One of the assistant managers of the hotel brought two stalwart, soberly dressed men to Luke. They introduced themselves as Officer Mahony and Officer Cutler, Secret Service men assigned by the State Department to guard the Sultan of Shihkar; and offered their credentials. Luke looked behind him for the little dark-skinned man, but he had slipped away. He said to the detectives:

"I will take you up to His Highness' apartment. Already I have found a suspicious-looking character loitering in the corridor."

In the salon of the state suite, Ahmed and Diana were sitting on a sofa. Diana, in heliotrope chiffon, looked as lovely and expensive as an orchid, and Luke turned his eyes away with an inward groan. Ahmed was holding her hand.

Ahmed's face fell like a child's when Luke presented the two Secret Service men. "Do I have to submit to being followed wherever I go?" he cried. "Here in America? I came here expecting to be free!"

"The Secretary of State's orders, sir," said Officer Mahony, respectfully. "He looks on you as the guest of the nation."

Cutler glanced at the glittering ruby in Ahmed's turban. "It would hardly be safe for you to go out alone, sir."

"Well, wait outside somewhere," said Ahmed, waving his hands. "Keep out of my sight as much as you can!"

When Shihab arrived at the apartment he questioned Luke anxiously as to the points of the compass. Luke, wondering somewhat, pointed to the north, the east, the south, the west. Ahmed said, with a sly grin:

"He has to know where Mecca lies so that he can face in the proper direction when he prays."

CHAPTER FOUR

THE ROBED, TURBANED, SOFTLY STEPPING SERVANTS attached to the Sultan's party gave Luke no little anxiety. There were six of them, all so strange-looking he had difficulty in telling them apart; dark-skinned, humble-seeming, ready to fall on their knees and salaam at the slightest excuse; it was impossible to tell what their dark faces might hide. Some time passed before he could get their uncouth Arab names straight in his mind.

By degrees he made out that three were attached to Ahmed's person, one being his cook; two to Abu Daud and one to Shihab al Zuri. The last was a snuffy little scribe wearing horn-rimmed glasses like his master. Presumably he was harmless. Abu Daud's servants were young men like himself, too sleek, too watchful, too bright-eyed for Luke's taste. He watched them as well as he could.

The Conradi-Windermere is well supplied with house detectives. In addition to these, and to the Secret Service men, the Police Commissioner of New York sent a plainclothes man to patrol the corridor outside the state suite, and notified Sultan Ahmed that a motorcycle escort would be supplied whenever he went out. The Sultan was disgusted. Luke reflected that all these precautions would be of little avail against treachery within. The fact that Luke knew deep inside him that he would not be exactly heart-broken if Ahmed were removed from the picture, made him doubly determined to protect the man who had given him his trust.

In the middle of the afternoon an important functionary arrived from Washington in the person of Mr. Emory Branscombe,

Chief of Protocol of the State Department. It was his job to direct the forms and ceremonies in connection with the visits of distinguished foreign visitors. He had come to escort the Sultan to the capital. As might have been expected, Mr. Branscombe was a faultless gentleman with elaborate manners, and Ahmed, who hated formality, did not take to him.

Meanwhile the afternoon papers were out with sensational accounts of the Sultan of Shihkar's arrival in New York, illustrated with a wealth of photographs. They had got hold somehow of the story of the near-million in jewels and it was played up to the limit. In the salon Mr. Branscombe was explaining the details of the next day's arrangements to Sultan Ahmed, Luke, and Shihab al Zuri, when young Abu Daud strode in unannounced, clutching a newspaper in his hand. His eyes were blazing.

"Ahmed, is this story about the jewels true?" he burst out.

"As you see, I am engaged," said Ahmed, coldly.

"Is it true? Is it true?" cried Abu, shaking the paper.

Ahmed's own temper began to rise. "Yes, it's true," he said. "What of it?"

Abu Daud broke out in a storm of passionate Arabic. Shihab turned pale with alarm.

"Speak English!" commanded Ahmed. "Let my lawyer hear you!"

"All right!" shouted Abu. "You've played me false! Those jewels are not your property! They belong to the Sultanate!"

"Well, I'm the Sultan, am I not?" retorted Ahmed.

"You have no right to dispose of them!"

"I haven't disposed of them!"

"The reversion belongs to me!"

"Stuff!" said Ahmed. "In all that pertains to Shihkar I am the law! Leave the room!"

"You have no right . . . !"

Ahmed sprang up. "Leave the room!"

Abu, with a poisonous glance, turned and strode out. Luke bit back a smile. Royal brothers, he was thinking, quarrel just like common folk. Ahmed turned to the scandalized Chief of Protocol with his sweetest smile.

"Please pardon this intrusion of my domestic affairs, Mr. Branscombe. You were saying . . . ?"

"A private car for Your Highness will be attached to the train leaving the Pennsylvania Terminal at one-thirty A.M. The car will be ready to receive you at any time after ten P.M."

"Well, we won't go to bed at ten o'clock," said Ahmed, winking at Luke.

Mr. Branscombe bowed. "The train arrives in Washington at seven A.M. Your car will be placed on a siding in the Terminal. At ten-thirty A.M. the Secretary of State, the Private Secretary of the President, officers representing the Army, the Navy and the Marine Corps, a troop of cavalry and a band will arrive at the Terminal to welcome you and to escort you to the White House."

"I'm glad I don't have to get up early," put in Ahmed. "I hate it. Don't you?"

Mr. Branscombe cleared his throat. "I have here a plan of the private car to enable you to make your sleeping arrangements. Additional rooms will be available in the regular bedroom car ahead."

Ahmed looked over the plan. "Four staterooms," he said; "one for me; one for Mrs. and Miss Morven; one for Abu Daud; one for Shihab al Zuri. The servants can sleep on the floor. They're used to it. I'm afraid I shall have to ask you to take a room in the car ahead, Mr. Branscombe."

"That will be quite all right, Your Highness. In any case, I should have to leave the train early in order to complete my arrangements in Washington."

"Luke," said Ahmed, "there seems to be no room for you. Would you mind sharing my room? There are two beds marked in it."

"Certainly, if you wish it," said Luke.

"Mr. Branscombe," said Ahmed, studying the plan, "what's this little square thing adjoining my room?"

Mr. Branscombe looked over his shoulder. "It appears to be a shower bath, Your Highness."

"A shower bath in a railway car! Fancy that, Luke!"

After the newspapers came out, the telephone in the state suite rang almost continuously. Luke borrowed a young woman from the hotel to take the calls. All kinds of people called up the Sultan, to get him to subscribe to something, to buy something or to go to something. Some very fine people invited him to dinner. The young woman was instructed to decline all invitations on the score that His Highness was unable to make any private visits until after he had paid his respects to the President of the United States.

Meanwhile, in spite of Luke's remonstrances, Ahmed began to do some telephoning on his own account. His shipboard acquaintances were invited to come to the hotel at nine o'clock. Shihab al Zuri was horrified at the amount of liquor that was sent up for the party.

"They're only unbelievers," said Ahmed, provokingly. "What do we care if they drink themselves black in the face? You know I never touch the stuff."

"Such a bad example to put before young Abu Daud," murmured Shihab.

"Abu Daud!" cried Ahmed. "Don't make me laugh. Young Abu Daud, as you call him, could give us all lessons!"

That night a great throng was attracted to the different restaurants of the Conradi-Windermere for dinner, in the hope of catching a glimpse of the exotic little ruler of Shihkar. Ahmed, however, chose to dine in his own suite. Seven persons sat down to the table, including Mr. Branscombe of the State Department. It was an uneasy party; Abu Daud was sullen; Shihab worried. The Chief of Protocol hardly knew how to behave in the company of a potentate so extremely casual and outspoken as Ahmed. Only Mrs. Morven appeared to enjoy the meal. As she and her daughter were the only ladies present, she was sure of receiving plenty of attention from the other sex.

The Arab gentlemen came to dinner in conventional evening clothes. Abu Daud's London-cut suit showed off his slim figure to perfection, but little Sultan Ahmed was not helped by his. He looked like the Fat Boy in tails. Shihab was as self-conscious as a man finding himself at the dinner table in a bathing-suit. When he stood up, it was evident that his new, American-made shoes pinched his feet cruelly.

They were still at the table when the guests of the evening began to arrive. It was a strangely assorted lot; a pair of vaudeville performers no longer in their first youth; a Georgian Prince decidedly the worse for wear; a Jugo-Slavian millionaire and his bediamonded wife; a bevy of young girls in tacky evening dresses who constituted a dancing-troupe; a grinning old woman in a white satin gown trimmed with monkey fur and yards and yards of purple malines wound about her almost bald head; various unidentifiable, hard-faced young women and boozy men. Soon they came so fast Luke could no longer single them out.

"Good God, Meddy!" he said when he could get the Sultan's ear. "Did you invite all these people?"

"Not all of them," was the cheerful reply. "My friends have brought their friends. It's all right. There's plenty of champagne."

The guests lapped up champagne as if they had only an hour to live, and the party soon exhibited an unnatural gaiety. Ahmed was never seen to take a drink, but he was visibly keeping pace with his guests. Luke knew that he had a bottle of Glenardrey hidden in his bathroom. Abu Daud drank like a fish without showing the least effect. Shihab stood unhappily against the wall of the salon, the only strictly sober man present. Mr. Branscombe, finding himself very much out of his element in such a second-rate crowd, soon took his leave. He would be waiting for them on the train, he said.

Luke drank plenty of champagne to keep himself going; it did not make him happy. For Diana in a black dress that defied the laws of gravity was so beautiful that it made his heart ache. The dress had no straps or visible means of support; her bare arms and neck were lovelier even than he had expected. Moreover, he was worried on Ahmed's account. There were infinite possibilities of danger in this disorderly mob. Too many servants were about. Luke had an ugly suspicion that additional Arabs had been introduced to the apartment; he could not be sure because they were never together at the same time. All were dressed in identical black-and-white-striped caftans and white turbans, and he could not tell them apart.

Every moment the party became noisier and more unrestrained. Ahmed had engaged an orchestra which was stationed in the foyer, and there was dancing of a sort. Diana declined to dance. Amongst that rabble the tall, calm Diana stood out like a goddess. Abu Daud had not approached her, but Luke noticed that his eyes scarcely ever left her. Luke hated to see Diana in such surroundings. He succeeded in separating her for a moment from the flushed gentlemen who pressed close, and murmured:

"You are beautiful enough to drive a man mad!"

She answered coldly: "If you continue to say such things it will make the situation impossible."

"I know," he said, miserably; "I'm sorry. But every time my eyes fall on you you seem more beautiful. . . . Look, are you ready for the journey?"

"Yes."

"In another hour this will be a shambles. Can't you persuade your mother to go on to the train with you, and go quietly to bed?"

"What would Meddy say?"

Luke glanced at the little Sultan where he stood in the midst of the dancing girls. "He won't notice your departure. When he asks for you I'll tell him you've gone on."

"Are you going to be on the same car?" she asked.

"Yes," said Luke, dryly. "The Sultan has honored me by asking me to share his stateroom."

"Tell him," said Diana, "that we've gone to the train, but that we won't go to bed until after we have seen him. He said he had something important to tell me tonight."

"You and Meddy!" he said, bitterly. "O God, Di, if you and I could only hop on a plane and fly away from all this!"

She left him without answering.

A few minutes later he had the satisfaction of seeing her and her mother make an inconspicuous exit. It was then about eleven. Later, when Ahmed started looking for her, Luke gave him her message. Far from resenting her early departure, Ahmed was relieved. He said:

"You're a good fellow, Luke; you think of everything. This is no place for Diana. Come into my room and have a spot of Scotch."

"No, thanks, I've had too many," said Luke.

"Meaning that *I've* had too many," said Ahmed, laughing. "'S all right, Luke, old boy. I'll be married in a few days and then I'll have to toe the mark. I'll be more particular then in choosing my friends." He drifted away.

The old woman trimmed with monkey fur went about with her purple toque on one side of her head, spilling champagne out of a glass and telling everybody how she had been cleaned out at Monte Carlo; the Jugo-Slav millionaire was making passes at one of the dancing-girls, and his wife had annexed a gigolo; the vaudeville couple obliged with one song after another from their repertoire, each one rowdier than the last. The whole company joined noisily in the choruses. Afterwards the dancing-girls gathered up the skirts of their evening dresses and went through their routine. During this number the blushing Shihab left the room.

Diana had been gone for about an hour when one of the soft-footed servants approached Luke. He said in good English:

"Please, you are wanted on the telephone, Mr. Imbrie."

"Who is it?" asked Luke.

"Miss Morven, sir."

Luke's heart leaped. "Where?"

"Please, I had the call switched to one of the bedrooms, sir, where you could talk in quiet."

"Good boy! Show me the way."

The state suite which had been put at the Sultan's service was larger than his party required. On each side of the reception-rooms, a corridor led away, with numerous bedrooms opening off it. The Arab in his striped gown led Luke to the far end of one of these corridors and opened a door. The noise of the party could scarcely be heard at this distance.

No thought of danger to himself entered Luke's head. He went into a luxuriously furnished bedroom with softly shaded lights. It was evidently one of the unoccupied rooms. Afterwards he had an impression that the servant had closed the door and remained out in the corridor. The telephone stood on a console between the two windows. As he put out his hand to take the instrument, a crashing blow descended on his head from behind, and he knew nothing more. He never saw his assailant.

CHAPTER FIVE

WHEN CONSCIOUSNESS RETURNED to Luke Imbrie, he found himself lying on a stone floor with his ankles bound together, his wrists bound behind him and his lips expertly sealed with surgeon's tape. His first bitter thought was: All according to the best American practice! His head ached consumedly; it was difficult to collect his wits. In the thick silence he could hear far-off, the hum of the city that is never stilled.

Under his hands he traced the pattern of a mosaic floor, and he guessed that he had been dragged into the bathroom adjoining the room where he had been struck down. He tried to cry out, but only a hollow groan issued between his sealed lips. Immediately a door opened beside him, and a voice with an Eastern accent said, softly:

"Keep quiet or I'll knock you out again. If you keep quiet you won't be harmed."

Luke decided to keep quiet. He had no expectation, anyhow, of being able to make himself heard through the solid walls of the Conradi-Windermere. The footsteps retreated. The man left the door open. In the room outside Luke presently heard the sound of whispering. So there were more than one of them.

Luke's thoughts were very bitter. The boldness of these foreigners was appalling. In spite of Secret Service men, police, hotel detectives, they had dared to strike him down in the Conradi-Windermere, which one might have supposed to be one of the safest spots on earth. Luke apprehended no further danger to himself. Ahmed was their mark, of course. How much time had passed? What had they done to Ahmed? He burned with a helpless rage.

By cautiously shifting his position, an inch at a time, he was able to look further into the room outside. The window curtains were closely drawn, and it was as black as your hat. From the occasional whispering he established that there were two men seated at a table. They had a bottle. Luke heard a faint glug as one of them put it to his lips, and the rap of glass on wood when it was set down again. One of the men pushed his chair back and came towards the bathroom. Coolly stepping over Luke, he felt around in the dark and drew a glass of water. The sky reflected a faint light through the bathroom window, and by the fact that the man's legs separated, Luke knew that this one was not in Arab dress. He went back to his companion.

Luke applied himself patiently and silently to the task of loosening the bonds around his wrists. A long time passed. The men outside ceased whispering. Judging from the little sounds which came to his ears, Luke guessed that one of them had thrown himself on the bed. The other had left the table.

Later the second man went out of the room, closing the door softly behind him. In a minute he returned and the aroma of a cigarette was carried to Luke's nostrils. The man with the cigarette came to the bathroom door and looked down at Luke; prodded him with his foot; dropped to one knee to test the ropes. Luke pressed his wrists apart to tighten the bonds, and the man was satisfied. He held one hand cupped over his cigarette so that the spark would not shine back in his face.

More time passed. Luke had no means of measuring its passage. In the stillness the ticking of his watch sounded loudly. It seemed to him that the ever-present hum of the city had increased a little. If so, morning was near. Apparently the man on the bed had risen and joined his partner at the back of the room where Luke could not see them. After hours of patient working he had succeeded in loosening the ropes around his wrists a little, but he was still far from freedom.

Suddenly Luke saw that morning was really at hand. Out in the bedroom it was as dark as ever, but the bathroom window was definitely paling. For some time past he had heard nothing from the two men. He hunched himself forward until his head stuck out of the door. As the light increased he saw that the room was empty. They had stolen away unheard.

He then made all the noise he could; groaning, bumping his head against the wall. Nothing happened. Foot by foot he worked himself towards the console between the bedroom windows, with the object of pulling down the telephone. But upon reaching it he hesitated, feeling a curious reluctance to giving an alarm which would set the whole city, the whole country, by the ears. After all, his hands were nearly free. Better find out first what had happened, if he could.

There was now no need of being silent. He succeeded at last in getting one of his thumbs over a strand of the rope, and the rest was easy. It was now full day. His first act upon getting his hands free was to glance at his watch. Quarter past six. He freed his lips, his ankles. Flinging the curtains back, he saw his own hat and top-coat lying on the bed, and smiled grimly at this evidence of somebody's thoughtfulness.

He washed his face and tidied up as well as he could. With his hat and coat on he was sufficiently presentable. His face was lividly pale, but that was perhaps not remarkable in a young man in evening clothes at six o'clock in the morning. Running out of the room, Luke searched all the rooms opening off the corridor. None of the doors was locked; every room was empty; the beds had not been slept in. The hotel servants had not been about and everything was just as it had been left by the departing Arabs.

The great salon presented the usual squalid appearance of the morning after; champagne bottles; broken glasses, bits of apparel dropped by the merrymakers of both sexes, and a litter of cigarette ends. The dining-room was worse. Luke proceeded to Ahmed's own room with his heart in his mouth. Empty; likewise the rooms beyond. He searched every closet and bathroom. Satisfied, at least, that Ahmed had not been attacked in the apartment, Luke pressed his aching head between his hands, trying to figure what to do next.

At such a moment the thought of his friend Lee Mappin was like a cool spring in the desert. Luke went down in the elevator. The hotel servants glanced at him curiously, but after all he looked like a patron of the Conradi-Windermere only a little the worse for wear. He left the building and, hailing a taxi at the door, had himself carried to Lee's apartment overlooking the East River.

Lee's establishment was not given to early hours. Luke had some difficulty in getting Jermyn, Lee's man, to the house phone. At last a sleepy voice answered. "Jermyn," said Luke, "I'm sorry to disturb you, but I must see Mr. Mappin on a matter of urgent importance."

"Very well, sir. My master's still asleep. But come right up, sir."

A minute later Luke was standing beside Lee's bed. The little man sat up, bald and blinking, feeling for his glasses on the bed table; perfectly unruffled and serene. Luke, pressing his head between his hands for clearness, told him briefly what had happened.

Before he had finished Lee's plump legs were out of the bed. He looked at his watch. "Five minutes to seven. The train has already arrived in Washington. . . . Jermyn!" he called, "lay out my brown worsted suit and a yellow waistcoat. I have to go to Washington." Then to Luke: "You've told me sufficient. Details can wait. Go home and dress quickly. Take a taxi to the Newark airport. Offer the driver a bonus. First plane for Washington leaves at eight. Got enough money on you for the cab?"

Luke nodded.

"Then get along with you. Meanwhile I'll be getting in touch with Inspector Loasby. I'll be at the airport as soon as you are. On second thought the regular plane's too slow; it has to come down at Camden and Baltimore. We'll charter a special if there is one."

Luke hastened away.

In less than an hour he was at the airport. Lee Mappin drove up immediately afterwards. Lee said:

"I've talked to Inspector Loasby. He'll take care of everything at this end, and keep the story out of the papers until we find out what's what. Loasby's secretary was calling the Union Station in Washington while I was there, but I didn't wait for the result. I'll call him from here."

The business of chartering a plane was accomplished in a few minutes, and while the pilot was warming up his engine Lee went away to telephone. When Luke saw him coming back he could read nothing in his bland face.

Lee said: "The word from Washington is that they had an uneventful journey. All is quiet aboard the Sultan's private car. Nobody up yet. The car is lying on a track in Union Station, guarded by detectives."

Luke let out a breath of relief. "Fine! Evidently the plan to get the Sultan has slipped up somewhere. Maybe there's no need now for you to go down there, Lee."

"This report from Washington is not exactly conclusive," said Lee, dryly. "Let's get going."

During the flight Lee was putting Luke through a searching cross-examination as to the events of the past few days. Lee was nothing if not thorough. Luke gave him a painstaking description of every member of the Sultan's party, and told him of his suspicion that additional Arab servants had somehow been introduced into the hotel.

"But surely," said Lee, "if there were any strange servants the Sultan would have taken notice of them."

"I'm not so sure," said Luke. "It would have been easy, in that crowd, for them to keep out of Ahmed's way. Ahmed has a lordly disregard for servants. Moreover, he was a little drunk."

"Where are his jewels?" asked Lee.

"He has them on the car with his other baggage."

Lee went into many details that to Luke had no bearing on the situation. He couldn't follow Lee's line of thought. Luke told Lee frankly of his love for Diana and, as far as he could remember, everything he had said to her, and what she had said to him. His heart sank, thinking how, if anything *had* happened to Ahmed, it would appear in the newspaper stories as if he, Luke, had an excellent motive himself for putting the Sultan out of the way. He couldn't tell what Lee was making of it. His friend's face was as smooth as wax. He was making copious notes.

In Washington they lost time getting from the airport to Union Station. There was considerable excitement outside the private entrance to the station—a squadron of cavalry, a mounted band, and a great crowd; police everywhere, both in uniform and in plain clothes. Inside the station they found the usual brigade of press photographers lined up with their paraphernalia, and a score of reporters. The general public was roped off at a suitable distance.

Simultaneously with the arrival of Lee and Luke, the official welcoming party drove up to the station in several cars escorted by screaming motorcycles. They came out on the concourse; the Secretary of State and the President's private secretary in gleaming silk hats; a general and an admiral in full regalia, besides lesser officers. The Chief of Protocol, as director of the show, was waiting for them. He shook hands with his chief.

Luke contrived to catch Branscombe's eye, and introduced Lee to him. The official glanced disapprovingly at Luke's rough tweeds in that fine company; Lee's natty attire was more to his taste. Amos Lee Mappin was well known to him by reputation and he was affable. Lee offered him his snuff-box, which he hastily declined, whereupon Lee took a pinch with two loud sniffs. Glancing at his watch for the dozenth time, the harassed official said:

"Ten-twenty-nine. It's almost time for His Highness to appear."

"Let's go to the car," suggested Lee.

They walked down a long platform, leaving the official party lined up behind them in their dignity. The luxurious private car, Gaillardia, occupied a track to itself. Several detectives were patrolling the platform alongside. A grinning negro porter in a snowy coat opened the car door for them. In a passage just beyond they came upon Douban, Sultan Ahmed's middle-aged valet, grave and deferential.

Mr. Branscombe was in advance. "Where's His Highness?" he asked.

"He has not yet rung for me," said Douban. "He gave orders that he was not to be disturbed."

"It's ten-thirty!" said the scandalized Mr. Branscombe. "The Secretary of State is waiting on the platform!"

Douban was not at all put about by the mention of a Secretary of State. "I will arouse His Highness," he said, courteously. He turned and led the way further into the car. "These Easterners have no sense of time!" grumbled Mr. Branscombe.

They passed an open door through which Shihab al Zuri, the secretary, and his servant could be seen in their little stateroom, packing their things. Shihab greeted them in his usual agitated manner and was introduced to Lee.

"How did you get here so soon?" he asked Luke.

"I'll explain later," said Luke. "Just now we have to get His Highness ready in a hurry."

They entered the central drawing-room with windows on both sides. Abu Daud in a magnificent Arab costume was lolling in a chair, blowing smoke rings. He nodded to them casually without troubling to move. A couple of Arab servants were standing near by. Others could be seen in the passage leading to the rear of the car.

Douban said: "Please wait here, gentlemen."

The principal stateroom was just beyond the drawing-room, with a door on the corridor. Douban knocked gently. There was no answer from within. Luke's heart sank slowly and sickeningly. Shihab knocked again, louder, and spoke in Arabic. No answer. He rattled the door. It was locked. A sudden terror seized the servant. The face he turned to the other men was livid.

"I don't understand it!" he stammered. "Always such a light sleeper!"

There was a horrible silence. Only Abu Daud appeared to be undisturbed. Lee Mappin pushed forward. Squatting on his heels in front of the door, he squinted through the keyhole.

"There's no key in it," he said. "See if there isn't a duplicate key on the car."

The negro porter, upon being called for, hastened forward, showing the whites of his rolling eyes. He pulled a ring of keys from his pocket. Time was lost because his hands were trembling so violently. Lee took the keys from him.

"It's the key with an A on it, mister."

The key was found and inserted in the lock, the door thrown open. The elegant little room was empty. Neither of the narrow beds had been slept in. The two windows were closed. There was a strong smell of spirits on the air. Luke recognized it as Scotch whisky. He saw a broad wet spot in the middle of the carpet. Opening off the stateroom was a toilet-room with a shower. Like the larger room it was empty.

CHAPTER SIX

WHAT FOLLOWED WAS LIKE A NIGHTMARE. Shihab al Zuri flung his turban on the floor and, clutching his thin hair, broke into frantic cries. "My master! O my master! Why did he come to this horrible country!" Abu Daud pushed his way into the stateroom with starting eyes. "The jewels! Where are the jewels!" he yelled. He looked around. "They're gone!" he screamed. Luke put this down as a clever piece of acting. Lee Mappin yanked Abu Daud out of the room and got the door closed and locked. "Nothing in there must be touched!" he commanded.

The elegant Mr. Branscombe was at the point of collapse; the negro porter gibbered with fright; a black cook had joined the group; the Arab servants were ashen. All the various detectives came pushing into the car, cursing in their rage and fright. In particular, the faces of the two Secret Service men who had accompanied the car were as white as paper because they foresaw the certain loss of their jobs.

Only Lee Mappin kept his head. "Quiet! Quiet!" he commanded, shepherding everybody into the little drawing-room in the middle of the car. "Have we got telephone connection?" he asked.

The porter nodded, incapable of speaking. He pointed to the little cabinet which contained the instrument.

"Notify the Major and the Superintendent of Police," said Lee to Luke.

Luke obeyed.

Meanwhile Mr. Branscombe was stammering: "The Secretary of State . . . the President's secretary . . . the officers . . . are waiting!"

"Go and tell them they need wait no longer," said Lee, grimly.

Mr. Branscombe wrung his hands together. "But what shall I *say!*"

"We must try to keep this quiet until we have time to turn around," muttered Lee. "Tell them . . . tell them that His Highness was unfortunately taken ill on the journey and the reception must be postponed. Say . . . an attack of gastritis. That sounds convincing."

Mr. Branscombe pushed his way wildly out through the group. Lee muttered:

"That idiot will give everything away in his face!"

Luke had his own private anxiety. "Where are the ladies?" he asked.

A sudden silence fell on the group. The men looked at each other; suspicion was born in every face.

"Well, where are they?" demanded Lee.

"They gone, mister," stammered the porter. "They left the car."

"When?"

His scattered wits couldn't recollect.

Lee applied to Shihab. "Did you see them go?"

"No, Mr. Mappin. I was still asleep."

"I was asleep," said Abu Daud.

Further questioning established the fact that there was no mystery in the departure of Mrs. Morven and Diana. Shortly after nine o'clock they had alighted from the car. The porter had placed their handbags on the platform, and a couple of red-caps had carried them away. Diana had been heard to tell the red-caps that they wanted a taxi. Neither lady had appeared to be agitated.

Lee let it go for the moment. Lining up the six Arab servants, he said to Luke: "Was it one of these men who came to you last night to tell you you were wanted on the telephone?"

Luke studied one walled face after another. The servants were darker than their masters. Arabs, it appeared, were especially adept in concealing their feelings. Each pair of shallow, glittering, black eyes was as expressionless as glass. Only Shihab's little bespec-tacled servant, Cheragh Ali, looked human. He continually mourned and shook his head.

Luke, when he had come to the end, said: "It was not one of these."

"You told me," Lee went on, "that one of the two men who held you prisoner in the hotel room spoke to you. Would you know his voice if you heard it again?"

"I think so," said Luke. "But it could not have been one of these men because the two in the hotel stayed to watch me until some hours after the train had left."

Lee dismissed the servants with a nod. "What were the Sultan's jewels contained in?" he asked Luke.

"A new pigskin case just the same as his other hand luggage," said Luke, "but of a different shape. It was about eighteen inches long and the same in height; perhaps nine inches thick."

Lee turned to the porter. "Was there a case answering to that description among the baggage carried from the car by Mrs. and Miss Morven?" he asked, gravely.

The negro shook his head helplessly. "I just don't recollect, mister. They have five, six bags, new yellow leather like the little boss'."

The question was like a stab to Luke. He hated Lee for putting it. "All the handbags belonging to the ladies were of the same style as the Sultan's," he said, stiffly. "They were a present from the Sultan. They all came from the same maker in London."

"Look for the case," said Lee. "Everybody else stay in this room."

Luke soon established that the case of jewels was not aboard the car.

The Major and Superintendent of Police could now be seen coming along the platform, accompanied by a whole squad of detectives. Press photographers and reporters were trailing after. Evidently Mr. Branscombe's agitated face had aroused their suspicions, and when the Major arrived with his men they were sure they were on the track of a big story. Lee frowned when he saw them.

"They hamper us so!"

He went to meet the party on the front platform of the car. Major Walkley was one of the best police officials in the country; he had need to be in his present job. He was of the army officer-type; handsome, full-blooded, accustomed to command. He and Lee were well acquainted with each other by reputation. Lee offered him snuff, which he declined politely. Lee would have been surprised, indeed, if anybody had ever taken snuff with him. He offered it, he had told Luke, because you learned so much about a man from the manner of his refusal.

"Mr. Imbrie is the Sultan's personal attorney. As soon as he had reason to believe that danger threatened his client, he consulted me, and that's how I happen to be in this case. But of course I shall hold myself entirely at your disposition, Major."

Major Walkley said: "I shall consider myself fortunate to have the benefit of your advice and assistance, Mr. Mappin."

Lee indicated the pressmen with a rueful shrug. "If we could have had one more hour!"

"I know how you feel," said the Major, "but it is impossible to hold back a story of this importance. The press are our masters."

"Luke, you'll have to deal with them," said Lee. "Tell them the facts, but be careful not to direct suspicion against anybody. They're entitled to know who was on the car last night and all that."

"Tell them nobody can enter the car until we have completed our investigation," added Major Walkley.

Luke had managed to preserve a wooden exterior, but inside he was half out of his mind with anxiety. "What am I to do about the Morvens?" he murmured to Lee. "Their name has been kept out of the papers so far."

Lee shook his head. "I'm sorry, but everything will have to come out now. If you try to keep back their names it will only react against them later."

The Major and Lee entered the car, and Luke stepped down to the platform. The photographers had finished shooting the car, and every lens was turned on Luke. The half-hour that followed was the worst he had experienced in his life up to that time. Naturally, the reporters, upon learning that there was a woman in the case, were bent on making the most of her. They did not shrink from asking the most intimate questions. Luke could foresee the unpleasant suggestions their stories were going to convey to the public, but already in his brief career he had learned that a man could never, never afford to lose his temper in dealing with the press.

The reporters hastened away to send in their first stories, and Luke, wiping his face, rejoined Lee and the Major. In the interim, everybody in the car had been finger-printed, Abu Daud under protest. Men had been assigned to trace the Morvens, Luke learned, and a watch arranged to be put on every terminal and every road out of Washington to prevent their leaving town. Major Walkley was keeping in close touch with Inspector Loasby in New York. A search of the entire right-of-way from New York to Washington had been undertaken with the assistance of the railway trackmen. If Ahmed had been thrown out of the train, it seemed strange that his body had not already been found along so well-traveled a way.

"Kidnapped, perhaps," suggested the Major.

"With what object?" said Lee, "when all his available wealth is gone with him?"

"He seems to be an eccentric little person. Could it be possible that he has simply taken his jewels and walked out on the show?"

"Possibly. But I can't see why he should take such a step without consulting Mr. Imbrie, the one man he trusted. If he has walked out of his own accord, he couldn't get far without being noticed and remembered. Such an unusual little figure."

The two Secret Service men swore that Sultan Ahmed could not have left the car of his own will, nor could he have been carried off. Every time the train had stopped during the night, they had been awake and watching. And every moment since it had come to rest in Washington.

Major Walkley looked at Lee. "You believe, then, that he was . . ."

Lee shrugged deprecatingly. "Give me a little more time, Major."

"If he was murdered and thrown off the train," said the Major, "how is it that his body hasn't been found? A half a dozen trains have been over the line in each direction since daylight."

"Maybe it has been found," said Lee. "If not, the train crosses several bodies of water. If no report comes in within an hour, I suggest that you have the rivers dragged."

"Thrown from the train!" exclaimed Luke. "That's not a crime a woman could have committed."

"Not impossible," said Lee. "He was such a little man. Or the woman might have had help."

Luke looked at him, wondering how he could ever have felt that Lee was his friend. "How about Abu Daud?" he asked, holding himself in.

"Possibly," said Lee. "But I can't reconcile it with the disappearance of the jewels."

CHAPTER SEVEN

THE INVESTIGATORS WERE FACED with the problem of what to do with the twelve persons who had made the journey from New York in the private car. It was impossible to undertake a proper examination of such restricted quarters with so many people in the way. Major Walkley solved it by telephoning to the station master for another car. A parlor car was presently backed down the track and coupled to the rear of the private car. The witnesses were then invited to move. A detective was to be placed at either end of the parlor car to prevent anybody from entering or leaving. All obeyed willingly except Prince Abu Daud.

"I will remain in my room in this car," he said, haughtily.

"Sorry," said Major Walkley. "That must be searched along with the rest."

Abu stiffened. "Do you presume to treat me as a suspected person?" he demanded. "If anything has happened to my brother I am the Sultan of Shihkar. I am entitled to the courtesies due to the ruler of a friendly state."

Major Walkley said, dryly, "I trust you will not find me lacking in courtesy, Your Highness. However, my duty is clear."

"I'll stay here," said Abu.

"Please don't make an issue of it," advised the Major. "There is a drawing-room in the next car where you may enjoy full privacy."

Luke could no longer hold himself in. "Why do you waste words on this blackleg, Major? If his brother has been killed *he killed him!*"

Abu Daud smiled contemptuously. "What evidence have you of that?"

"Your brother told me yesterday that you were plotting to kill him."

"That's a lie," said Abu, coolly. "You only say that to distract attention from the woman."

Luke saw red. He started for Abu and the slender young man quailed. Before Luke reached him, he found himself grasped by Lee Mappin on one side, and Major Walkley on the other. With a groan he turned away.

Abu's voice scaled up. "My country is under the protection of the British!" he cried. "The Ambassador shall hear about this!"

"Why don't you telephone him now?" suggested Major Walkley, indicating the instrument.

Abu took him up. Apparently he succeeded in getting the Ambassador on the wire, and gave him a long recital of the indignities that were being put upon him. Just how His Excellency reacted to this the listeners could not judge. Apparently Abu was not satisfied, because he called up the French Embassy also, and made his complaint.

In the end Abu sullenly consented to move into the next car. There was another row over his hand baggage, which he expected to take with him. This was not permitted. All his talk about diplomatic immunity was in vain. He was forced to hand over his keys.

However, to Luke's bitter disappointment, nothing was found in Abu's valises, nor anywhere in his stateroom that could be construed at this stage of the investigation as incriminating.

As a criminologist Amos Lee Mappin was chiefly famous for what he was able to deduce from testimony at the scene of a crime. The mild eyes behind the brightly polished glasses took on a special expression when he was hunting for evidence. They missed nothing. Major Walkley was very willing to let Lee take the lead in the search which followed. None but the cook was allowed to remain in the car. He had started to prepare lunch.

Beginning with the front end there was a narrow cubbyhole with berths for cook and porter. This yielded nothing. Next, the compact little galley, marvelously complete in its appointments, with shelves for food and dishes, a big frigidaire; rows of scoured aluminum pots and skillets hanging from above. So thorough was Lee that he insisted even on emptying the various receptacles for sugar, coffee, rice, flour, etc. He was rewarded by finding in the flour-tin the missing key to Sultan Ahmed's room.

When the colored cook saw the key he turned almost white with terror. "O God! mister; I never see that key before," he stammered. "I been cooking for the Pullman Company twenty years, and my record is clear. It wasn't me! It wasn't me!"

Lee gave him a friendly pat. "I believe you, George. If you had a key to dispose of you wouldn't hide it in your own kitchen."

The negro groaned in relief. "Praise God!" A sudden thought came to him. "Mister, that key wasn't in the flour-tin at eight o'clock this morning. I took flour out of the tin then to make flapjacks for me and Mist' Johnson." (Johnson was the porter.)

"Thanks for the tip, George," said Lee. "It may be important."

He dropped the key in an envelope.

Major Walkley put in a question. "George, after you were up and working in the galley, how could anybody have slipped a key in the flour-tin?"

George scratched his head and considered. "After me and Mist' Johnson eat," he said, "we stood out on the station platform to get a breath of air until it was time to start breakfast for the Ayrabs."

"At this time was anybody guarding the front door of the car?"

"No, sir. Only the detectives on the station platform."

As they moved on, Lee said: "It looks as if the murderer had use for that key after the train arrived in Washington. Otherwise he would have tossed it out of a window."

"If there is a murderer," said Major Walkley. "The key suggests to me that the Sultan, after the train had arrived in Washington, yielded to a sudden impulse, took his bag of jewels, and walked out. Why couldn't he have got off the wrong side of the car, crossed a track or two, and made his way out by another platform? It is true the detectives have asserted they were watching both sides of the car, but they have shown they were careless."

"If there was no plot to murder the Sultan," said Lee, "why should Luke Imbrie have been attacked and imprisoned in New York to prevent him from sharing the Sultan's stateroom?"

"It is possible that we may have to deal with two separate actions here."

"Quite," agreed Lee. "But if your theory is correct, why should the Sultan have troubled himself to stick the key in the flour-tin? Why not carry it away in his pocket?"

"You have me there," said Major Walkley.

Next to the galley came the single stateroom that had been allotted to Shihab al Zuri, the secretary. His servant had slept on the floor. The narrow bed was tumbled and some of Shihab's belongings were scattered about. While Major Walkley and Luke watched from the open doorway, Lee, magnifying-glass in hand, went over everything. He scrutinized the bed, the dressing-table, the floor, the little washroom adjoining. He emptied Shihab's two valises and repacked them. A briefcase filled with papers he saved for later. From the rug he gathered several hairs and stowed them in an envelope; the wastebasket yielded some torn scraps of paper and a little disk of a thin rubbery substance which he put in other envelopes. On each envelope he made a notation of the spot where the contents had been found.

Lee lingered so long over this room that Luke felt impelled to ask, "Do you suspect that the pious Shihab had a hand in it?"

"No," said Lee. "I have no evidence against anybody yet. But I have noticed that Shihab's man, Cheragh Ali, is the most intelligent of the servants. It is possible that he may have been bribed without his master's knowledge."

Next door was the larger single stateroom that had been Prince Abu Daud's. The two rooms shared the washroom between. In each room Lee found the door into the washroom locked. As has already been stated, a search of Abu's belongings yielded nothing that threw any direct light on the situation. He had a brand-new .32 automatic of American make, fully loaded. Lee took it, of course, but he said it had not been fired lately. He gave the same minute attention to the floor, the walls, the furniture in Abu's room. He picked up (a) some nail parings; (b) a soiled handkerchief with a small stain of what appeared to be blood; (c) a tiny glass vial of foreign make, half full of a colorless liquid with a pungent smell that none of them recognized. These things were stowed in envelopes and indorsed.

The middle of the car was occupied by the drawing-room, which was perhaps eighteen feet long. It was also used as a dining-room. There was a sofa at either end which could serve as a bed, but these had not been made up the night before. Lee searched this room with the same care, though so many people had been in and out during the past two hours as to make it scarcely worth while.

On the other side of the drawing-room lay the Sultan's state-room and next to it another double room, slightly smaller, which had been occupied by Diana and her mother. There was a communicating door between these two rooms. They found it locked on both sides. Each of the rooms was furnished with its own wash-room. The rear end of the car formed an attractive observation-room with easy-chairs and settees, and windows to the floor, looking out on the observation platform. Lee called attention to the fact that in the front end of the car the compartments lay to the left as you faced the front, while in the rear of the drawing-room the rooms were on the right side of the car, the passage to the left.

Lee naturally gave the most attention to Ahmed's stateroom. On furniture, woodwork, doors and various objects there were plenty of fingerprints, and Colonel Walkley called in an expert to prepare and photograph them. Lee looked at them through his magnifying glass. He said:

"They all appear to be women's prints. Not a man's finger anywhere."

"Ahmed's own hands were as delicate as a woman's," Luke said. "Also Abu Daud's."

"These prints are not all from the fingers of the same pair of hands," said Lee.

Luke silently gritted his teeth together. Everything that turned up, it seemed, was conspiring to drive him crazy.

"Anyhow," said Lee. "Modern criminals generally wear gloves."

The piece of carpet that showed a wet spot, now almost dry, was cut out and sent away to be analyzed. Judging from the smell, a bottle of whisky had been spilled on the floor, but no whisky-bottle was found anywhere in the car. Ahmed's evening clothes and dress shirt were hanging in a clothes-closet, with his little patent-leather pumps side by side on the floor below. From the pocket of the dress jacket Lee drew a wallet which contained nearly a thousand dollars in American currency. Apparently only one of Ahmed's four valises had been opened. The others were locked; there were no keys to be found.

"If he was murdered," said Major Walkley, "it seems strange that his murderer should not have searched his baggage, and that he should have left that money in his pocket."

"If he got nearly a million dollars in jewels, why bother about chicken feed?" said Lee.

There was a book in a red cover lying on the desk; a national hotel directory. Lee held it thoughtfully for a moment before putting it down. In an ash-tray on the table, mixed up with cigarette ends and ashes, he found some ragged bits of a yellowish gum such as bottles are sealed with. These he carefully separated from the ashes, putting the pieces of gum in one envelope, the cigarette remains in another.

Next, the little toilet-room adjoining. The floor of the shower bath yielded a small, partly-flattened cake of soap which Lee carefully inclosed in an envelope. Let into the wall of the room was a nickel ice-water faucet with drain below. Above the faucet there was a movable wooden panel in the wall, held in place by a nickel catch. After studying it for a moment, Lee unhooked the catch and swung back the hinged panel, revealing the metal water-tank behind. It had a cover that lifted off when water and ice were to be put in.

Lee removed the cover, but he was too short to reach inside. Busy and absorbed in his task, he dragged in one of Ahmed's suitcases while Luke and the Major looked on, stood it on end, and climbed on it. He looked in the tank and a childlike smile overspread his face. Pulling up his sleeve, he thrust his arm into the tank and drew out a dripping paper label. Hopping down from the suitcase, he carried his find into the next room and slapped it on a desk blotter. When he flipped it over, the others saw that it was a label for Glenardrey whisky; the Sultan's private stock.

To the other two it looked as if Lee must have known in advance that he would find valuable evidence in the water-tank. "My God!" murmured the Major.

Lee condescended to explain. "The Sultan was always looking for a hiding-place for his whisky. As soon as I saw that movable panel, the same thought came into my mind that had come into his mind last night: 'There's a good place to put it!' He hid the bottle in the water-tank, and the label soaked off."

"Where's the bottle?" said the Major.

"Tossed out of the window, very likely," said Lee.

He tried the two windows in the room. One stuck fast; the other went up without difficulty. "This one has been opened not so long ago," he said. He examined the sill attentively. "And something was pushed out which has wiped off the dust on the ledge outside. Cloth of some kind; it has wiped the sill clean." Lee paused and took snuff.

This appeared to be conclusive. Luke's skin prickled. So that's that! he thought. The poor little devil!

When they entered the room where the Morvens had slept, Luke could still faintly distinguish the delicious perfume that Diana used. It made him ache. One of those pillows had been pressed by that blonde head. She had told Luke that she was never able to sleep on a railway car, and he wondered what thoughts, happy or despairing, had gone through her head while the wheels rumbled over the rails beneath her. Had her thoughts been of him? Not likely!

The ladies had removed all their belongings and Lee's search revealed only odds and ends discarded or overlooked—a woman's face veil, a tiny pad stained with rouge; a dainty silver hook that Lee could ascribe no use for. After dusting certain fingerprints and examining them through his glass, he announced that some of the same prints were to be found in Ahmed's room next door.

While the search of the car was in progress, reports of the work being done outside were brought in to Major Walkley from time to time. There had been no difficulty in finding the two red-caps who had carried Mrs. and Miss Morven's hand baggage away from the car. These men said they thought the ladies had five bags; one had carried two, the other three. This was bad for Luke because he knew the Morvens had only two handbags apiece. Lee took a hand in the questioning; as he pressed the red-caps they became confused. They were not certain of the number of handbags. They agreed that all were expensive, new, pigskin bags, of the same design but different sizes.

The bags had been put in a taxicab and the older lady asked the driver to recommend the name of a first-class hotel. He had mentioned the Pilgrim, and presumably they had been driven there. The older lady had given one of the red-caps a quarter, saying it was for both of them, whereupon the young lady had slipped the other man another quarter.

At the Hotel Pilgrim their arrival was remembered. All the bell-boys on duty had marked the uncommon beauty of the tall blonde young lady. The two had seated themselves in the lobby with their bags at their feet. When asked if they required accommodations, the older lady had replied that they would know as soon as their friends arrived. Nobody in the Pilgrim could say for sure how many bags they had. They were sitting there about an hour. The old lady had walked around some while the young one stayed with the baggage. Then they had gone away. Presumably they had taken another taxi at the door of the Pilgrim, but so far this cab had not been found.

"These precautions to baffle pursuit have a suspicious look," Major Walkley commented. He stroked his chin. "If it is a murder, and the women did it, they're just ordinary travelers and my course would be clear. But if it is the young Arab Prince, or Sultan as he now calls himself . . . by God! between the State Department and the embassies, British and French, I *will* be in a spot!"

CHAPTER EIGHT

LEE MAPPIN, MAJOR WALKLEY, AND LUKE sat down to lunch in the private car. The porter was sent into the next car to ask Prince Abu Daud and Shihab al Zuri to join them. Shihab came, but was unable to eat anything. Luke could not but feel sorry for him, overcome by such a disaster among strangers whom he looked upon as unbelievers. Abu Daud sent word that he preferred to eat by himself in his drawing-room.

"So much the better," said Lee, applying himself to his food.

When they had finished, Lee suggested that they sit in the principal stateroom where they could talk in private. He and Major Walkley wanted to hear Shihab's story. By this time the pretty little room had been put in order and there was nothing to suggest the tragedy of the night before but the square hole in the carpet. The little beds had become sofas, one extending under the windows, the other along the wall opposite.

Colonel Walkley, Lee, and Luke sat in a row with their backs to the windows, while Shihab faced them from the other sofa. Under stress of feeling, Shihab's deeply lined face had turned clay color and his hands were shaking. There was something piteous in his eagerness to answer Lee's questions intelligently and frankly.

"Let us begin at the beginning," said Lee. "Describe the situation at home in Shihkar."

Shihab repeated the story that Luke had already heard from Diana and from Ahmed. He was bitter on the score of Prince Abu Daud. "In Eastern countries the sons of a Sultan enjoy great latitude," he said; "the people are indulgent towards their follies; but since boyhood Abu Daud's profligacies have exceeded all bounds. What is more, he was continually plotting against his brother's life."

"Have you any proof of this?" asked Lee.

"Not in America. But if there is time, I could get plenty of proof from Shihkar."

"If we require such proof we will see that there is time to get it," said Lee.

Shihab went on to tell how Sultan Ahmed had spent most of his time abroad since the British had extended their protection over his country. He described Ahmed's life in Paris and in London. It was at an Embassy reception in the former city that he had first met Diana Morven, and had become enamored of her. Later he had invited her and her mother to visit him in his palace at Shihkar, and had put on a series of great festivals in their honor, a durbar, Shihab called it. In the royal procession a hundred elephants, a thousand camels, and five thousand horsemen had taken part. Unfortunately, Miss Morven was not popular with the people. They suspected that their Sultan wished to marry the unbeliever.

"Did Sultan Ahmed intend to marry Miss Morven?" asked Lee, quietly. His eyes, masked by the shining glasses, were giving nothing away.

"He never told me so," said Shihab, "but I feared it."

"Why should you fear it?" asked Lee. "If the British were in control, Ahmed really had no further responsibilities toward his people."

Shihab shook his head mournfully. "He was still the ruler. For a ruler of the people to forsake his religion would be a terrible thing."

Lee proceeded with his questioning. Finally he brought Shihab down to the Sultan's arrival in America and to the party the night before. "Did anything happen at this party to excite your suspicion?" Lee asked.

"Suspicion?" said Shihab, frowning. "No."

"Mr. Imbrie has told me that he suspected additional Arab servants had been introduced into the hotel."

Shihab's face cleared. "If Mr. Imbrie had spoken to me about it I would have explained. Additional waiters had been supplied by the hotel and my master ordered that they should be put into Arab costume. He thought it would be more picturesque."

Lee addressed his next question to Luke. "Was the man who led you to the telephone as dark-skinned as the other Arab servants?"

"No," said Luke. "He was as light as an Italian or a Greek."

"Led Mr. Imbrie to the telephone?" put in Shihab. "I don't understand."

"Mr. Imbrie was locked up in a distant room of the suite and detained until after the train had left."

Shihab changed color. "Allah protect us!" he murmured. "A plot! . . . His Highness told me," he went on, agitatedly, "that he had had a message from Mr. Imbrie saying that he had been called away by urgent private business, and would join us in Washington this morning."

"No doubt that message was brought by the same light-skinned man," said Lee. "I suppose that the Arab colony in New York includes men from your country?"

"Oh yes," said Shihab. "Mostly renegades," he added, bitterly.

"Were you in touch with any New York Arabs yesterday?"

"No, sir. I never left the hotel. . . . But Abu Daud was. Men came to his room."

"Have you proof of this?"

"Not at the moment. Let me talk to the servants. . . ."

"All in good time. I would like to question them first."

"Very well, Mr. Mappin."

"To come back to the party," said Lee. "What happened after Mr. Imbrie left it?"

"I didn't see Mr. Imbrie go," Shihab said, unhappily. "I had already retired to my room. I didn't like the party. I thought my master was demeaning himself in associating with such people. They were drunk!"

"Wasn't Sultan Ahmed drinking, too?"

Shihab looked very unhappy. "I didn't see him take anything."

"How long did you stay in your room?" asked Lee.

"Until five minutes to one, Mr. Mappin. I then returned to His Highness' side and told him it was time to go to the train. I brought him his hat and coat and insisted on his leaving. I accompanied him to the station in a cab. My servant was with us and his servant, Douban. The hand baggage had already been sent to the train, except the bag containing the jewels, which was never out of my sight. My servant placed it in His Highness' stateroom. I saw him do it."

"Where was Prince Abu Daud?"

"I don't know how he got to the station. He was on the train. He went to his room and I didn't see him again."

"What happened then?"

"I'm sorry to say that a number of those people followed us to the station. The noise they were making shamed me. I got rid of some of them at the train gate, but three or four succeeded in forcing their way right into our car. A coarse man with a loud voice who boasted of his riches and an old woman in a purple hat who was lost to shame; two of the dancing-girls."

"I suppose the Sultan was encouraging them."

"No, sir; he was tired of them then. He told me to get rid of them. It was always so. They were still on the car when the train began to move. At the first stop I requested them to get off. That was Newark. Then there was quiet on the car."

"Where were Mrs. and Miss Morven at this time?"

"They did not appear, Mr. Mappin. His Highness spoke to them through the door of their stateroom."

"What did he say?"

"He said he wanted to talk to them later."

"And then?"

"When we left Newark His Highness got a notion to take a shower bath. I could not dissuade him from it. It would be his only chance, he said. His two servants were attending him. That's all I can tell you, because I went to bed myself."

"Did you sleep well?"

"No, sir. I hardly slept at all until the train reached Washington. Then I fell into a deep sleep."

"While you were lying awake did you hear anything?"

"Nothing but the usual train noises."

"What about this morning?"

"There is nothing to tell, Mr. Mappin. My servant awoke me at nine-thirty according to instructions. I took a cup of coffee and a roll, and dressed. His Highness had told me not to allow anybody to awaken him." Shihab lowered his head and his voice broke. "You know what happened after that."

Lee said: "Any questions, Major?"

Major Walkley said to Shihab: "Have you any theory to account for the disappearance of the case containing the jewels?"

Shihab shrugged. "I cannot guess what was arranged in Prince Abu Daud's rooms yesterday, gentlemen. Abu is plentifully supplied with money. There was time for him to arrange to have men stationed along the line. I assume that the bag was tossed out of the window at some prearranged spot."

Lee, Major Walkley, and Luke went into the parlor car to question Abu Daud in the drawing-room. The handsome young man received them with an undisguised insolence that made the army officer's neck turn red and put even Lee's equanimity to a strain. The latter removed his glasses, looked through them, blew on them, polished them with care. Thus he composed himself. Abu watched him with a scowl.

"I suppose you're terribly upset about your brother's disappearance," said Lee, mildly.

"Why should I be?" retorted Abu. "He hated me. He never treated me like a brother. He wouldn't give me a cent. On several occasions he has tried to have me murdered and I was only saved by the faithfulness of my servants."

"One moment," interrupted the Major. "You say he gave you no money, but I am informed that you are well supplied. Where did you get it?"

"That's my affair," said Abu.

Continuing, Abu coolly denied having plotted against his brother. The wicked smile in his dusky face seemed to say, Prove it if you can! He denied having received any of the New York Arabs the day before. "You can't believe anything Shihab says about me," he said. "Shihab hates me because he knows that my first act when I succeed will be to kick him out." Abu asserted that he had gone to his room when the train started, and had not left it again until he was called at nine-thirty. With all Lee's skill in questioning, he was unable to entrap the young man into any damaging admission.

When they had left him, Luke said, bitterly: "After that, can either of you gentleman doubt who is the murderer?"

Lee said, grimly: "If you want to call him an unlicked cub I'll shake hands on it. Nothing would give me greater pleasure than to supply the licking. . . . But we've no evidence against him. Not a shred."

"Evidence is all very well," said Luke, "but there is such a thing, too, as an inner conviction."

"Distrust it, my boy," said Lee, wagging his hand. "It's generally just a wish masquerading as a conviction. In this case there's a serious defect in your reasoning."

"What's that?" growled Luke.

"If Abu Daud succeeded in murdering his brother last night, why should he have stolen the jewels? They would have been his, anyhow."

A cold fear struck through Luke. He regretted that he had ever applied to Lee for help.

One by one the servants were examined, starting with Cheragh Ali, Secretary Shihab's man. Cheragh was small and middle-aged, with an air of preternatural solemnity emphasized by his heavy-rimmed glasses. His duties were more those of a scribe than a valet. His English was pretty good; he was intelligent and eager to help, but he could give them nothing new. He corroborated his master's story.

The Sultan's cook was called Abdul. He was a man of forty or so and, like cooks the world over, fat, placid, prone to smile. There was an engaging, disreputable quality in his grin. His English was fluent but scarcely understandable. He claimed that he had slept throughout the noisy party at the Conradi-Windermere. He had come to the train in a taxi with other servants, and as soon as the private car had quieted down had lain down on the floor of the drawing-room and slept there until morning.

Abdul, it appeared, was the custodian of the Sultan's whisky. At Southampton he had carried a case of Glenardrey aboard the ship. It had all been consumed during the voyage, and upon landing in New York Sultan Ahmed had been in a way until Mr. Imbrie went home to his rooms and brought him four more bottles. The Sultan had opened one, and given the other three to Abdul to keep. Abdul had rolled them up in a caftan and put them on a shelf in the clothes-closet of his room. No, there was no key to the closet, but everybody in the party except Shihab al Zuri knew about the Sultan's whisky, and nobody had ever dared to touch it.

The first bottle had lasted Sultan Ahmed all day. Just before dinner he asked the cook for another, and when Abdul went to get it there were only two in the closet. A bottle had been stolen. When the loss was reported to the Sultan he flew into a mighty rage, but he could not publish the news of his loss, for fear that it might reach the ears of Shihab al Zuri. The Sultan ordered Abdul to carry the fourth and last bottle to Mrs. Morven to keep for him until they got on the train. Mr. Imbrie was to have brought a fresh supply of whisky to Washington in his baggage.

Luke perceived with grim amusement that as the purveyor of whisky to His Highness he, too, had become an object of suspicion to Major Walkley.

After Abdul, Douban, the Sultan's principal body-servant, was questioned. Of about the same age as Abdul, Douban had been attached to the Sultan's person since Ahmed was a boy. In every particular Douban looked like an Arab version of the gentleman's gentleman: faithful, efficient, and closemouthed. He described the glee with which Sultan Ahmed had disported himself in the shower bath of the private car, and how his servants had afterwards dressed him in Arab costume and hung his European clothes in the closet.

After his bath, Sultan Ahmed had gone into the room next door to talk to Miss Morven and her mother, and Douban, according to his custom, had lain down to sleep in the corridor outside his master's door. But the corridor was so narrow, nobody could pass without stepping on him, and it was Sultan Ahmed himself who presently kicked him awake and told him to go and lie down in the observation-room at the rear. His Highness and the two ladies had then gone into his room. Douban had lain down in the observation-room. Aziz, his brother, slept beside him. During the night he had awakened whenever the train stopped, but had not seen or heard anything that aroused his suspicions. Most of the time the Secret Service men were also in the observation-room.

Luke thought: If Douban had been allowed to sleep outside his master's door, Sultan Ahmed would be alive at this moment.

Aziz, Douban's brother who was his assistant, appeared to be a well-meaning youth, but stupid. He had no English, and Lee examined him through Cheragh Ali as interpreter. Aziz added nothing to his brother's tale.

Farraj and Haroun, Abu Daud's servants, were of quite a different stamp. Handsome, dandified youths with shameless eyes, they looked to Luke like Arab gigolos, if there is such a thing. They claimed not to be able to speak English, but Luke suspected that they understood every word that was said around them. Lee examined them through two different interpreters, Douban and Cheragh Ali, but in each case the result was the same. On whatever subject Farraj and Haroun were questioned, they knew nothing about it. Their master had received no visitors at the hotel the day before; he had gone out in the afternoon, but they didn't know where he had gone. With unblinking black eyes they separately assured Lee that Abu Daud had always been a good brother to the Sultan Ahmed and had never plotted against him. Farraj and Haroun had slept on the floor of the drawing-room during the journey to Washington. They claimed to have heard, seen nothing in the night.

During the examination of Haroun, a report was brought to Major Walkley from the chemists. The piece of carpet brought to them for analysis, they said, had been saturated with whisky, and the whisky in turn had been loaded with sufficient cyanide of potassium to kill twenty men.

Lee and Major Walkley looked at each other. The latter said, "I'll have to accept the theory that murder has been done."

Since no body had been found by the track-walkers, Major Walkley now issued orders to have the Schuylkill and Susquehanna Rivers dragged in the vicinity of the spot where the Pennsylvania Railroad crossed; also two wide inlets from Chesapeake Bay known as Bush and Middle Rivers. Judging from the testimony given, Sultan Ahmed was still up and around when the train had crossed the Raritan and the Delaware.

"Wouldn't the body float away?" suggested Lee Mappin.

"Not immediately, I think," said Major Walkley. "Have you got a pathologist associated with the force?"

The Major nodded, and reached for the phone. Getting the man he wanted, he said: "Here's a hypothetical question for you, Doctor. If the body of a man twenty-seven years old, scarcely five feet in height, small-boned, but exceedingly obese for his age, weighing a hundred and fifty pounds, say; if the dead body of such a man who had just died were thrown in the water, would it float or sink to the bottom?" The answer came back over the wire. "Thank you, Doctor."

"You are right," the Major said to Lee. "The Doctor says that it would neither sink to the bottom at first nor float on top, but would probably hang suspended in the water, and, of course, drift hither and thither with any current there might be."

"Anyhow," said Lee, "it is necessary to have the streams dragged just to make sure."

By this time the newspapers were out with the first stories of the disappearance of the nation's guest. Regarded as the biggest news story that had broken in Washington in years, it was given the limit of display. Each additional bit of information served as an excuse to bring out an extra edition. By degrees so great a crowd gathered on the concourse to peer through the iron fence at the private car lying down the track, that finally the police had to clear the station in order to give the passengers way to get to and from the trains.

A police detective came into the private car to inform Major Walkley that a man called Solomon Jacobs was waiting outside to see him. He was a Washington pawnbroker of good repute. He had been first to Headquarters and had been directed to the station. He told the detectives he had an important piece of information relative to the disappearance of Sultan Ahmed bin Said, but declined to give it to anybody but the Superintendent himself.

"Show him in," said the Major.

A well-dressed, mild-mannered Jew was brought in. He wasted no time in coming to the point. "Mr. Superintendent, at half-past ten this morning an article was pledged with me. As it is obviously of Oriental workmanship, as soon as I read the afternoon papers it occurred to me that it had something to do with the missing Sultan." From his pocket the pawnbroker drew an elaborately wrought gold ring, set with an immense baguette diamond, oblong in shape, and of the purest water.

Shihab al Zuri was brought from his room. When his eyes fell on the ring, he paled. "My master's!" he murmured.

Major Walkley addressed the pawnbroker. "Who pawned this ring?"

"A young lady," said Mr. Jacobs. "She gave her name as Wilson; her address as the Hotel Pilgrim. She was a tall and beautiful young lady; a blonde; dressed with the greatest elegance. She spoke perfect English, but she looked more European than American. I put her down as belonging to the diplomatic set."

"This is a very valuable ring," said Major Walkley, sternly. "In such a case don't you make further inquiries? Weren't your suspicions aroused?"

"I have been in the loan business for many years," replied Mr. Jacobs, "and in making loans I go by what I have learned about human nature. I am not often fooled. This young lady was obviously accustomed to moving in the highest circles. She was cool and mistress of herself. It was impossible to associate the idea of anything underhand or criminal with such a person."

Major Walkley nodded. "I shall have to retain this ring for the present, Mr. Jacobs. I'll give you a receipt for it. I'm very much obliged to you for your prompt cooperation. It shall not be forgotten."

The pawnbroker glanced sadly at the ring. "I advanced five hundred on it, Major."

"Well," said Major Walkley soothingly, "the young woman and her mother are certain to be found within an hour or two. They can't escape us. And no doubt most, if not all, of your money will be recovered."

Luke Imbrie felt sick.

CHAPTER NINE

IN THE ELEGANT STATEROOM that had been Sultan Ahmed bin Said's, Officer Mahony of the Secret Service was examined by the triumvirate, and afterwards Officer Cutler. The stories of the two dovetailed into each other, and for convenience' sake may be told together. Both men were sore because it seemed certain to them that whatever might have happened, they were going to be blamed for it.

On the day before, the two had been furnished with a room at the Conradi-Windermere. Mahony had remained on duty in the foyer of the Sultan's apartment from ten-thirty until two-thirty, whereupon Cutler had relieved him until six-thirty. By the Sultan's express orders they were confined to the foyer, and they were therefore unable to testify as to anything that had taken place in the rooms of the suite.

All day the telephone was ringing almost continuously. A temporary switchboard was installed in the foyer, and a young woman furnished by the hotel to answer calls. At this point in the story, Lee Mappin made a note to ask Inspector Loasby in New York to get hold of this young woman. What calls she could not answer herself, she switched to somebody inside; the Secret Service men could not say whom. Those callers at the hotel who were approved were fetched upstairs. One or another of the servants would receive them in the foyer and take them in. The Secret Service men didn't know to whom they were taken. Among those callers were several dark-skinned men who might have been Arabs in Western dress. Prince Abu Daud left the apartment about three and was gone until seven.

At six-thirty Mahony had rejoined Cutler in the foyer of the apartment and they remained on duty there together until ten P.M. At that hour the private car was ready, and Cutler went to the Terminal to watch the car until the Sultan and his party joined it. Neither man could testify as to what took place at the party. They didn't get any champagne.

At one-five Mahony accompanied the Sultan to the Terminal and saw him safe aboard the private car. The detective rode outside with the chauffeur. Inside were Sultan Ahmed, his secretary, and two servants. Mahony remembered seeing one of the servants carrying a squarish leather-covered case. He saw the servants put it in the Sultan's stateroom. Several intoxicated guests came aboard the car, but the detectives did not feel justified in ordering them off, since they received no orders to do so. The noisy guests got off at Newark and the Sultan went into his room.

Upon leaving Newark, Mahony and Cutler sat down in the observation-room. Mahony had locked the front door of the private car and had the key in his pocket. In about half an hour, that is to say just after the train had crossed the Raritan River, they heard the Sultan's door open. Mahony glanced into the corridor, saw the Sultan come out and enter the stateroom occupied by Mrs. and Miss Morven. His Highness was then in Arab dress.

In twenty minutes or so—the detectives could fix the time because it was before the train reached Trenton—His Highness came out accompanied by the two ladies, and the three of them went into His Highness' room. As the train was pulling into Trenton they reappeared and, passing through the observation-room, went out on the observation platform and seated themselves there. After a few minutes the old lady came in. She remarked that there was too much wind for her on the platform, and went on into her own room.

Major Walkley asked each man at this point, "Did you look into the corridor to see where she went?"

From each he received the same answer. "No, sir. I couldn't spy on His Highness' guest."

"Then you cannot be certain she didn't go into the Sultan's room instead of her own. The two doors are side by side."

"No, sir, I couldn't be certain."

"It hardly signifies," put in Lee, mildly. "There is a communicating door between the two staterooms. If Mrs. Morven had the intention of returning to the Sultan's room, she could easily have found an opportunity of unlocking the door on his side while they were all in there together."

"Surely, surely," said the Major.

Luke clenched his teeth. Both of these celebrated criminologists, it seemed, were determined to hang the crime on a pair of defenseless women.

According to the stories of both detectives, Sultan Ahmed and Miss Morven had remained sitting on the observation platform for about half an hour longer, or until the train was entering North Philadelphia. Mahony had then gone out on the platform and had respectfully suggested to His Highness that it was not altogether prudent to expose himself while passing through a city. The Sultan laughed at the idea of danger to himself, but Miss Morven agreed with the detective and persuaded the Sultan to come in. The Sultan bade her good-night in the corridor and she went into her room.

"And he?" asked Lee.

"His Highness came back into the observation-room for a moment. He was feeling fine. Said he was sorry for the rough way he had treated us, and said he would make it up to us in the morning. He then said good-night and went into his own room."

Lee said to each man in turn: "This is an important point; think before you answer. When the Sultan came out of his room with the two ladies did he lock the door after him?"

They both said: "No, sir. There was no pause to insert a key in the lock. There was no sound of a key turning or being pulled out."

"Good. After he had said good-night to you and went into his room, did he lock the door after him?"

After thinking, each man replied: "Yes, sir. I could swear that I heard him turn a key in the door."

After the Sultan had gone to bed, the train stopped at North Philadelphia, West Philadelphia, Wilmington, and Baltimore. At Baltimore there was a wait of ten minutes or so while the sleeping-cars for that city were cut out of the train and shunted on a siding. Between stations either one or the other of the detectives took a sleep while his mate sat up and played solitaire. Each time the train stopped, both were on the watch to make sure that nobody tried to enter or leave the private car.

"How did you make sure of that?" asked Lee.

"I went forward to guard the front door of the car," said Mahony, "and Cutler went out on the observation platform, and leaned over the rail to watch the station platform."

"While the train was standing in a station," said Lee, "why couldn't somebody in the car have raised a window on the side opposite to the platform and dropped out? Or have passed something out?"

"Anything is possible," said Mahony, sullenly. "But even in the middle of the night there are plenty of people around a railway station. He would almost certainly have been seen."

"So much depends on that 'almost,'" said Lee, dryly. "When you and Cutler were in the observation-room where were you sitting?"

"Whoever might be sleeping at the time was lying on the sofa. That faces the rear door. The one sitting up was in an easy-chair on the right-hand side of the room as you face the engine. There was a little table between the chair and the sofa."

"Sitting in that chair, you couldn't see into the passage running forward."

"No, sir. The passage is on the left-hand side of the car as you face the engine."

"Somebody might have stolen through that passage to the door of the Sultan's room without your being aware of it."

"I wasn't worrying about that, sir, because I distinctly heard His Highness lock himself in."

"There were two servants sleeping in the observation-room. Where were they lying?"

"Against the right-hand wall behind me when I was sitting in the chair."

"Did they get up at any time?"

"No, sir."

"How about the three servants in the drawing-room. Were they moving about the car at any time?"

"All I can say is that every time I passed through the drawing-room to go to the front door, they were lying in the same places."

"Were the window shades in the observation-room pulled down?"

"Yes, sir."

"I understand that when the train arrived in Washington both you men left the car."

"Yes, sir. We patrolled the station platform alongside."

"You cannot testify, then, as to what was going on inside the car at that time?"

"Mr. Mappin," said Mahony, "we took it that our job was to protect His Highness from danger on the outside. It never occurred to us that there was danger on the inside. We locked the rear door of the car before we left it."

When the examination of the Secret Service men was completed, Lee suggested to Major Walkley that they invite the press men into the car. "They're mad to photograph it and write it up," he said, "and it can't do any harm now to let them. As long as these birds are bound to hinder us, we might as well get what help we can out of them."

"Sure," said the Major, "what have you in mind?"

"If there is anybody who saw the train pass during the night, or who noticed it lying in one of the stations, I want to ask them to come forward and tell us. Also, I think we ought to let it be known that we suspect the body may have been thrown into one of the rivers, so that boatmen and fishermen may be on the watch for it. If there are any funds available, a reward ought to be offered for its recovery. I will myself offer a reward for any evidence that may be picked up along the right-of-way; the whisky bottle, for instance, intact or broken."

"Right," said Major Walkley.

"We must pay particular attention," Lee went on, "to the Susquehanna River. Have you ever noticed the railway bridge at that point?"

"I can't say that I have."

"The rails are laid on top of the spans. There are no side walls nor guard rails of any sort. Anything thrown out of a car while crossing would fall directly into the water."

As preparations were made on the car to receive members of the press, Luke quietly slipped away. He had no desire for a repetition of that ordeal. He got a taxi at the door of the station and had himself carried to the Hotel James Madison, where rooms had been reserved for the Sultan's party, including himself. When he registered, the clerk said:

"A party has called you on the phone several times, Mr. Imbrie. She wouldn't give her name."

Luke went up in the elevator, wondering idly who had called him. Somebody who had read his name in the paper, no doubt; a sob sister in search of a story.

As he entered his room he had a thought that pulled him up all standing. Perhaps . . . perhaps it was . . . ! She knew, of course, that he was going to the James Madison. He paced his room in a fever. Would she call again? He was divided between longing and dread. If she did call, what could he do to help her? The longing was stronger than the dread. Oh, if she would only call once more!

The telephone rang and he sprang at the instrument. "Hello?" Back over the wire came the voice that knocked on his heart. "Luke!" He was so overwhelmed he could only stammer: "Di! . . . Oh, Di!"

"Is there any news?" she asked in a strained voice. "I mean, anything beyond what is in the papers?"

"No. Nobody knows yet what has happened."

"Oh, Luke, how terrible!"

At those simple words his heart went out to her. Of course she didn't know what had happened! "Where are you?" he asked; and then, instantly: "No! Don't tell me! It's not safe over this phone."

"I know," said Diana. "Mother says we must keep out of this."

Inwardly Luke groaned: "You can't! You can't!"

"I'm not telephoning from our rooms," she went on. "I came out to call you from a pay station."

"That was right."

"But I've got to let you know where I am, Luke! I need you!"

Luke's heart swelled big. "Sure, darling," he murmured. "What's the number of the phone you are using? It's on the transmitter in front of you." She gave him the number.

"Wait there until I have time to run out to a pay station. I'll call that number and ask for Miss Johnson."

He hastened downstairs. As he crossed the hotel lobby he glanced anxiously at the telephone girl. She was indifferently plugging in her cords. She had taken no alarm. He ran into a booth in a cigar store at the street level, and presently he had Diana on the wire again.

"Where are you?" he asked.

"Drug store at the corner of Connecticut Avenue and L Street."

"Wait for me in the street outside. Be there in two minutes."

CHAPTER TEN

THEY MET. "Di!" . . . "Luke!" It was all they could say. He drew her arm under his and hustled her down the side street away from the throngs on Connecticut Avenue. Luckily no photograph of the tall and beautiful Diana had been published. Everybody was looking at her, but it would never have occurred to them that this glorious girl could be wanted by the police. On the other hand, Luke's picture was in every newspaper, and his was a figure not easily forgotten.

Diana clung to him, hanging her head. His goddess had become a human breathing woman. "Oh, Luke, I wanted you so!"

"Bless you!" he murmured. "That sounds good in my ears!"

"We mustn't think of ourselves now," she protested. "Mother has gone to pieces completely!"

Luke thought, Damned old fool! He didn't say anything, but only pressed Diana's arm under his own.

"It is too dreadful!" she murmured. "The newspapers make it sound as if we had done something to Meddy!"

"Don't read 'em!" growled Luke.

"How can I help it? I must know what is going on."

"Whatever they may say, I am certain it was Abu Daud," said Luke.

"It would be," she agreed. "But how could he? When Meddy went to bed last night he locked his door. I heard him turn the key."

"I don't know," said Luke. "It's all in a fog."

"Mother and I ought to get out of Washington at once," said Diana, "but I don't know where to go."

"You can't get out," said Luke, bluntly. "Every station, every road is watched."

"Then what are we to do?"

He had no answer to that. "Where are you stopping?" he asked.

"In a quiet little place down this street. It's not a regular hotel, but a sort of lodging-house. It's called the White Door."

"Who told you about it?"

"We got the name out of a hotel directory on the car last night. The advertisement said that the White Door catered especially to ladies traveling alone, and Meddy thought it would be a good place for us. He wanted us to keep out of the news until the official receptions were over. It turned out to be a plain, humble little place. Nobody would think of looking for us there."

"Perhaps I ought not to go in with you," suggested Luke. "I might be recognized."

"I want you to talk to Mother," she said. "I can't do anything with her. She just lies there and cries."

Luke turned grim at the picture this called up.

"It's very quiet," Diana went on. "I didn't meet anybody on the way out. There's no office and no elevator. We walk upstairs and our rooms are at the top of the first flight."

In the unimportant street four little old dwellings in a row had been thrown together to form the hotel. Luke smiled at the contrast between this shabby lodging and the effulgent young woman beside him. Surely Diana had never stayed in such a place before. They went in. There was a harassed-looking woman sitting at a desk in the entry; her attitude towards them was subservient. Diana and her mother had engaged her best rooms.

"She doesn't suspect anything," whispered Diana as they went up the stairs.

On the dark landing above, Luke hung back and reached for her.

"Not here!" she protested.

"Please!" Her soft eyes consented. He drew her to him and kissed her lips. She surrendered. "Anyhow," he whispered, holding her very close. "We've had this!"

"You frighten me," she murmured. "What do you think is before us?"

"It doesn't matter," said Luke. "Together we can see it through."

Diana knocked on a door beside them and went in. It was just such a faded and depressing sitting-room as might have been expected. The furnishings had been new perhaps forty years before. Luke took the commonplace room as a matter of course, but he was shocked by the sight that Mrs. Morven presented. She lay on a sofa without her corsets and wrapped in a kimono; her dyed hair was sticking out in all directions and tears had made havoc of her make-up. Luckily for his peace of mind, Diana was not of the same type as her mother. Diana must resemble her father, Luke decided.

At sight of Luke, Mrs. Morven gave a little scream. "Diana! I thought you were alone! Why didn't you warn me!" Clutching the kimono around her, she struggled to rise. "I mustn't be seen like this! Let me get away!"

"Lie still," said Diana, coolly. "Mr. Imbrie doesn't mind."

Mrs. Morven dropped back on the sofa. "Oh, Mr. Imbrie, what a place for you to find us in!" she mourned. "So common! So sordid! I didn't know that such places existed. The smell fairly makes me ill. I'm sure I should die with shame if any of my friends ever saw me entering or leaving such a place. We got the name of it out of a book, and of course we didn't know what it was going to be like until we got here."

Luke said, "What difference does it make, Mrs. Morven?"

She burst into tears. "You're right!" she wailed. "What difference does it make? We are publicly disgraced! Oh, those newspapers! those newspapers! Why did I ever come to America? It's perfectly disgraceful! I shall sue them for libel. What will my friends think when they read those malicious lying stories? I have many friends in the Diplomatic Corps. Some of them in very high places. . . ."

"Mother!" pleaded Diana.

The old lady was not to be stopped. "Who is responsible for this fix that we find ourselves in?" she demanded, angrily. "I'm sure it's not my fault. I've always been so careful to shield Diana from everything sordid and unpleasant. Where is Sultan Ahmed? He couldn't have vanished into thin air! You were supposed to be taking care of us, weren't you? Where were *you* last night?"

"Bound and gagged and locked in a room in the Conradi-Windermere," said Luke.

Mrs. Morven stared incredulously. "By whom?"

"I wish I knew. It was the same gang, I suppose, who murdered Ahmed last night."

"Murdered?" gasped Mrs. Morven. "Oh, no! no! It can't be!"

"There is no other possible explanation!"

"O my God! We must get out of Washington at once!"

"You can't," said Luke. "Every outlet is guarded."

Mrs. Morven flung herself down in a passion of tears and kicked her heels against the sofa.

Luke looked at her in disgust. "You'll arouse the house," he said. She modified her cries.

"Tell me," said Diana, anxiously, "why are the newspapers hounding us?"

"Well, there are several circumstances that look very suspicious to ordinary minds," said Luke. "Why did you leave the car before anybody else was up this morning?"

Mrs. Morven suddenly came out of her hysterics and sat up. "That was arranged with Sultan Ahmed last night," she said, sharply. "He wanted us to be out of the way before the reporters came around."

"Why did you first drive to the Pilgrim and dismiss your cab. Was that Ahmed's idea?"

"No," said Mrs. Morven. "When we came out through the station, some reporters were already hanging around, and we were afraid they might follow us here. So we changed cabs to throw them off our track."

"Why did you wait so long at the Hotel Pilgrim?"

"Just to make sure nobody was watching us."

"The most incriminating thing in the eyes of these people," said Luke, "is that Diana pawned a ring this morning which has been identified as having belonged to Sultan Ahmed."

"What of it? What of it?" demanded Mrs. Morven. "It was a free gift to Diana."

"Sure. I never doubted that," said Luke, "but . . ."

"Meddy surrounded us with every comfort," explained Diana, "but of course we couldn't take money from him. We were entirely out of money, and so I had to pawn the ring."

"I'm not blaming you," said Luke, gruffly. "Unfortunately, all the Sultan's jewels are missing now and they think . . ."

"Do they dare to say that we stole them?" cried Mrs. Morven. "It's a lie! It's a lie!" The old lady showed symptoms of returning hysteria. "Oh! Oh! To think that I should live to be accused of stealing! I shall never get over this! Never! Never!"

Diana's face had turned stony. "What do you think we ought to do, Luke?"

"You are certain to be found here," he said. "I advise you, while there is still time, to go to the police of yourselves and offer to tell what you know."

A muffled scream escaped from the old woman. "Go to the police! Never! Do you think I'm going to submit to being questioned by a lot of policemen? To be gaped at by crowds in the streets! And newspaper reporters! Think what the reporters would do to us! Never! Never! Never! I'm not going to expose my child to such a disgrace. They might even put us in jail! They'd have to let us out again immediately, but if Diana had been in jail even for an hour who would ever marry her?"

"I would," said Luke, with a grim smile.

Mrs. Morven dismissed it with a contemptuous gesture. "We are perfectly safe here. And as soon as this blows over we can get out of Washington. We'll leave the country."

"This storm hasn't started to blow yet," said Luke.

"I don't care! You'll never persuade me to put myself in the hands of the police!"

Luke turned to Diana. "What do you say?"

She met his eyes squarely. "I shall do whatever you advise."

The old woman, seeing herself outvoted, cried hysterically: "I would die sooner than go to the police! I would kill myself."

"That would be equivalent to a confession of guilt," said Luke.

"I don't care! I swear I'll do it. Go ahead, you and Diana. Leave me here! You will not find me here when you return!"

Diana weakened. After all, the horrible old woman was her mother. The girl hastened to the sofa and dropped to her knees beside it. "I'm not going to leave you," she murmured. They embraced each other. Over Diana's shoulder Mrs. Morven continued to mourn and carry on, but Luke saw a gleam of triumph in her eye. In silence he cursed her heartily. Diana turned her face, wet with tears, towards Luke. "I can't!" she murmured.

"All right," said Luke, gloomily. "I've given you the best advice I could." He looked around for his hat.

Instantly Diana rose and came to him. "Don't go!" she pleaded.

He took her hands. "I must! Lee will be back at the hotel. I'll have to give an account of myself."

"When will I see you again?"

"It increases the risk, dear."

"I don't care. I've got to see you!"

"I'll come back after dark tonight. Whenever I am able to get away."

"Luke, should I try to disguise myself when I go out?"

He smiled at her. "You baby! How could you disguise yourself?"

"Well, I thought I might buy some cheap plain clothes and a common-looking hat. . . ."

He shook his head. "No! Make yourself look as rare and fine as a princess when you go out. And hold your head high. That's your best protection."

She came out into the dark hall with him. They lingered. Luke kissed her repeatedly. "My dear, dear love!" he murmured. "It's a miracle!"

"I love you!" she said, sadly; her arms were around his neck. "I have from the first moment. . . . But how could we live without money?"

WHEN LUKE RETURNED to his room in the hotel he found a penciled note from Lee slipped under the door, asking him to come to room

1117 as soon as he returned. It was just around a corner of the corridor. Luke made his way there with fear in his heart—Lee had such sharp eyes!

Luke knocked, and Lee called to him to come in. The little roly-poly figure was curled up on a sofa, blinking. He had just awakened. Without his glasses Lee had a look of naked helplessness like a baby; when he adjusted the shining circles he was armed with astuteness again.

"Where have you been?" he asked, smiling.

"Nowhere," said Luke. "I came to my room to get a sleep. But I couldn't sleep. So I took a walk to try to tire myself."

Lee made no comment. He was looking at Luke with a half-smile, and Luke immediately became conscious that he had explained too much. In a near panic he asked:

"Any news?"

Lee shook his head. "Very little. We questioned some of the railroad men after you left the car, but the only pertinent fact I got was that the train had been routed all the way from New York on the outermost of the four tracks where there were four tracks." His eyes dwelt on Luke steadily and mildly.

"What did you want of me?" asked Luke.

"Just to keep in touch. We'll have to go to Police Headquarters. All reports will come in there."

Luke discovered that he now had the psychology of a criminal himself; he dreaded Police Headquarters. Yawning elaborately, he said: "I wish I could have a sleep."

Lee said, mildly: "It's no good, old fellow. You haven't the face of a good liar."

"What are you getting at?" demanded Luke, all ready to be angry.

"Your skin has the pale and mottled appearance of a man who is laboring under violent excitement," said Lee. "Your usually steady eyes are a little mad. Within the past few minutes something overwhelming has happened to you. You have been with her."

Luke sullenly flung up his hands.

"Where are they?" asked Lee.

"I'm not going to tell you that," said Luke, harshly.

"But, my dear boy!" said Lee, in mild surprise. "We're in this together, aren't we?"

"You're in with the police," said Luke, violently. "Oh, I know! I know! You're obliged to be," he cried as Lee started to protest. "You have to consider your reputation. You feel a responsibility towards the public. . . . Well, I have no reputation, thank God! And I acknowledge no responsibility except towards her!"

Lee said nothing. He looked away from Luke, thoughtfully stroking his chin.

It was impossible for Luke to remain silent. "Don't think this is easy for me!" he burst out. "I think the world of you, Lee. I value your friendship above that of any man I know. But what can I do? She comes first!"

"Your feelings do you more credit than your sense," said Lee, tartly. "I'm for her, too. But I took it for granted that every man who was honest with himself was for the truth first. Are you afraid of the truth in this case?"

"No!" shouted Luke. "For God's sake, don't anger me, Lee!"

"Pooh! that's childish," said Lee. "Anger or no anger, we've got to get to the bottom of this. If you are for her you must see that the only thing she can do is to come forward and tell all she knows about what happened last night. She must have read the papers. She knows she is wanted for questioning. If she continues to hide, the police, yes, and the public, too, would be justified in believing her guilty." Lee emphasized his words by taking a vigorous pinch of snuff.

"I told them that," said Luke, sullenly. "Diana is willing, but her mother won't. She threatened to kill herself if we made her."

"From what you've told me," said Lee, "I judge it wouldn't be much loss."

"I don't give a damn about the old woman," growled Luke. "But I've got to consider Diana's feelings."

"Mrs. Morven wouldn't kill herself," said Lee, calmly. "That threat is the last card of a hysterical woman. . . . Take me to them, Luke, and I'll persuade them."

"I won't do that," said Luke, stubbornly.

"Why not?"

"In their minds you're associated with the police. It would look like a betrayal. . . . Moreover, if you were unable to persuade them, it would be your duty to tell the police where they are hidden."

Lee strode up and down the room, rubbing his bald pate. "God save us from wrong-headed youth!" he muttered. It was not often he permitted himself to betray so much agitation. He came to a stop in front of Luke. "I suppose you realize what sort of a position you're putting *me* in!"

"Would it do any good to say how sorry I am?" growled Luke.

"No!" said Lee. "This reputation of mine that you speak of has been slowly built up by twenty-five years of hard work. This will damage it beyond repair!"

"Why should it?"

"It is the first time I have retired from a case leaving it unsolved. . . . And such a case!" he added. "Without me they are certain to make a hash of it!"

Luke said nothing. What could he say?

"My getting out will create a sensation," Lee went on. "And it is bound to react against you and your friends."

"Can't help that," growled Luke. "I don't care how bad it looks," he burst out, passionately, "I know that Diana cannot be mixed up in it! . . . And, anyhow, I wouldn't care if she were! I'm for her!"

Lee shook his head. "Perfectly irrelevant!" he said. "How about her mother?"

"I wouldn't put it past her," said Luke. "But I don't see how she could have pulled it off without Diana's knowledge."

"Neither do I," said Lee.

The telephone rang. Lee picked up the instrument and received a message over the wire. "Ask him to come up," he said. "It's Major Walkley," he said to Luke. "This will save me going to Headquarters."

By the Superintendent's pleased smile upon entering the room, they guessed that he brought news. From his pocket he drew a curiously-turned little wooden barrel about five inches high. The top unscrewed. When it was removed they saw that the receptacle was about half full of a white powder.

"I have had it analyzed," he said. "It is cyanide of potassium."

Lee's eyes gleamed. "Where was it picked up?" he asked, eagerly.

"A section hand on the Pennsylvania picked it up between the tracks at a point about midway between Rahway and Metuchen, New Jersey."

Lee thought for a moment while he fitted this piece of information in its proper place. The gleam in his eye faded when he realized that he was out of the case. "I offered a reward of fifty dollars for any evidence picked up alongside the tracks," he said. "Will you see that the man is paid, Major, and I'll settle with you?"

The little wooden barrel bore no marks of any sort. "It's going to be difficult to trace this object," said Major Walkley. "Looks as if it was of foreign manufacture."

"An extremely important piece of evidence," said Lee, gloomily. "It changes the entire aspect of the case."

"Why?" said Luke, irritably. "You already know the Sultan was killed with cyanide of potassium."

Lee merely smiled at him pityingly. He turned to Major Walkley. "Major," he said, "I regret that I have to drop out of this case."

The Major's eyes bulged out. "Drop out of it! What are you saying, Mappin! This is the case of a century!"

"Don't I know it!" said Lee. "Nevertheless, I'm getting out. I came into it as the representative of Mr. Imbrie. Well, Mr. Imbrie and I differ absolutely as to the manner in which the investigation should be conducted, and I have to go."

"Will you accept a retainer from the Commissioners of the District of Columbia?" asked the Major.

Lee spread out his hands. "Under the circumstances, how could I?"

The police officer stared at Luke with an angry flush. "I can only infer from this that Mr. Imbrie doesn't relish the direction that the investigation is taking, and no longer wishes to cooperate with the police!" He shook a military forefinger at Luke. "And let me tell you, young man, it has occurred to me more than once today that you knew more about this affair than appeared on the surface. It was only because Mr. Mappin vouched for you that you were safe!"

Luke was too angry to be frightened by this threat. He stared the Major out.

"What are you going to do?" the latter asked Lee.

Lee consulted his watch. "I have just time, if I hurry, to catch the Congressional to New York."

They exchanged compliments while Lee was gathering up his belongings, and left the room together. Lee nodded coolly to Luke, and the Major ignored him. Luke returned to his own room.

HALF AN HOUR LATER he issued out again. He had no particular objective in view, but his thoughts were driving him crazy. He found a policeman in plain clothes patrolling the hotel corridor, and smiled grimly. Then he was gripped by anxiety. It would be difficult to go to Diana now. However, the man couldn't follow him into a telephone booth. Nor trace a call that had been dialed.

The detective went down in the elevator with Luke. Luke put him out of countenance by staring at his necktie. He followed Luke out into the street. Luke led him around one corner after another, scarcely noting where he went. He finally found himself in front of the building of the — newspaper, and at that moment a bunch of boys burst out screaming an extra. The first sound of their cries was enough. Luke bought a paper. Across the top was spread in letters four inches high: DIANA MORVEN IS FOUND!

According to the story that followed, it was an exclusive beat on the part of the —. One of their reporters, unaided, had found Mrs. and Miss Morven living at the White Door, a small hotel on L Street. Luke knew something about the ways of newspapers. Reading between the lines, he guessed that the landlady of the White Door had stolen upstairs behind him and Diana and had listened at the door. Upon learning that the much-wanted Morvens were lodging in her house, she had sold the information to the newspaper.

Luke stood in the street, staring at the newspaper he had ceased to read. However it had happened, the Morvens would be lodged at Headquarters by this time, and he, Luke, being at odds with the police, would have no chance whatever of reaching them. He felt desperate.

Asking his way to the nearest Western Union office, he wrote out three identical telegrams:

> Amos Lee Mappin
> On board Congressional Limited
> Diana and her mother have been found. Please come back. Abasements.
> Luke.

These he had forwarded respectively to Baltimore, to Wilmington, and to Philadelphia to await the train.

CHAPTER ELEVEN

POLICE HEADQUARTERS IN WASHINGTON is housed in a grimy brick building on Indiana Avenue, which looks as old as the city itself. Luke went there, though he had no expectation of being permitted to see his friends. Upon asking for the Superintendent he was told that Major Walkley was engaged and could not be interrupted. In respect to Mrs. and Miss Morven, the clerk admitted that they were being questioned by the Superintendent at that moment. They were not under arrest and presumably would be free to return to their hotel when the Superintendent had finished his questions. Luke could wait if he wished.

He sat down in the public office, but when reporters came edging up to him, and under the guise of friendly sympathy began putting sly questions, he fled the building. Again he blindly walked the streets. Becoming aware that he had not had a meal in many hours, he went into a place and ate without knowing what he was putting into his mouth.

At eight o'clock he was back at Headquarters. Another clerk received him, but the answer was the same. Mrs. and Miss Morven were still with the Superintendent. "Have they had anything to eat?" asked Luke. "That is always taken care of," said the clerk. Luke wanted to smash his demure face. He ground his teeth helplessly. So damned unfair to subject a couple of gently-bred women to the questioning of a lot of hard-boiled police! Why couldn't he be beside them?

He returned to his hotel to see if there was any word from Lee. Nothing. He went up to his room and flung himself on his bed. After a while there was a knock on the door. "Who's there?" he growled. The answer came, "Lee." Luke sprang up and opened the door. He seized the little man by the shoulders and shook him affectionately.

"Oh, Lee! Thank God you've come! I'm near crazy! Oh, what a good fellow you are!"

Lee took snuff. "I certainly am," he answered, making out to be disgruntled, but his eyes were twinkling behind the polished glasses. "Forced to travel all the way to Philadelphia and back just for a young man's whim!"

"I was a fool!" groaned Luke.

"It kept me from being present while Major Walkley questioned the women. I may have missed an advantage I can never recover."

"They're still at Headquarters," said Luke, snatching up his hat. "Come on!"

Lee hung back. "Wait a minute! We've got to come to an understanding. I can't take up this case and drop it, and take it up and be forced to drop it again. From this moment I must be free to follow it up wherever it may lead."

"Oh, Lee, save Diana for me," groaned Luke.

"I can't promise to do that if she is implicated."

"She couldn't be implicated in a murder. But her mother may be, and if so she will drag down the girl!"

"In that case you will live to thank me for saving you from a fatal step."

Luke flushed red. "The hell with it! I wouldn't give up Diana if she were in it up to the neck!"

"All right," said Lee, calmly. "That's a thing a man's got to decide for himself. But if he's a real man he wants to know what he's doing, doesn't he? And he wants to do it with his eyes open."

Luke considered this, scowling. "You're dead right," he said. "I want to know the truth. So come on."

They found Major Walkley alone in his office with a sour expression, eating a sandwich and drinking a glass of milk. He received them without enthusiasm. "I thought you were in New York," he said to Lee.

"I came back," said Lee, blandly. "Imbrie and I have settled our differences. I now have a free hand."

"As soon as we caught the women he changed his tune, eh?" said Walkley, disagreeably.

Lee shrugged. "I'm prepared to go on working with you on this case if you wish it."

"And if I don't accept the offer?" countered Walkley.

"I'll work independently of you."

The Major didn't relish this suggestion. He stroked his chin. "I would welcome it," he said, "if you weren't mixed up with him. He's in this too deep himself."

"Luke," said Lee, "how about releasing me unconditionally? I never expected to charge you a fee anyhow."

"All right," muttered Luke. "If that's the way you want it."

The Major was mollified. "All right," he said. "But it must be understood that from now on this young man enjoys no privileges in the case."

Luke's heart sank, thinking he was about to be fired out of the room. However, Lee said, cajolingly:

"Have a heart, Major. He's not implicated. His only crime is that he is crazy about the beautiful Miss Morven."

"All right. All right," said the Major, testily. Nothing further was said about banishing Luke.

"What's happened since I saw you?" asked Lee.

"The women won't talk," growled Major Walkley. "I can't get a word out of them. Naturally you can't be rough with women of that sort. I'm stalled."

"Anything else new?" asked Lee.

"A question about their bags has arisen. Only four bags were found in their rooms. Mrs. Morven says that's all they ever had. Yet the porters at the station stated that they had carried five bags to the taxi. The taxi driver is uncertain. The bags were put inside his car and he took no notice of the number. Likewise the bellboys at the Hotel Pilgrim are uncertain of the number. All the bags were alike. The landlady at the White Door says they brought only four to her house. I have not been able to find the taxi-driver who carried them from the Pilgrim to the White Door."

"Where are the ladies?" asked Lee.

Major Walkley jerked his head towards a door at the side of the room. "In there."

"Shall we have them in?"

The Major, with a shrug signifying that it would do no good, rose and opened the door. He said: "Will you please step in, ladies?"

Mrs. Morven and Diana entered, followed by a policewoman. Mrs. Morven was angry and frightened; Diana's beautiful face a composed mask. At sight of Luke she went to him swiftly.

"Why didn't you come to us?" she murmured.

Luke took her hands. "They wouldn't let me."

"I cannot allow any private communications," said Major Walkley, sternly. "Please sit down."

Mrs. Morven dropped in a chair. She looked anxiously from face to face and her lips worked together. Luke and Diana continued to stand with linked arms. Major Walkley glanced at Lee as much as to say the witness was his, and much good might it do him. Lee asked, as smooth as cream:

"Is it necessary for the officer to be present, Major?"

The Major nodded at the policewoman and she retired by the door through which she had entered.

"Mrs. Morven," said Lee, "you are not accused of anything. The only thing Major Walkley has against you is that you won't answer his questions."

"I refuse to talk without advice of counsel," she snapped.

"Surely, if your skirts are clear, you have no need of a lawyer."

"Nobody can make me talk!"

Lee turned to Diana. "Miss Morven, will you tell us what we want to know?"

Diana looked at Luke, her lips shaping the words, "What should I do?"

"Tell everything you know," said Luke.

Mrs. Morven jumped up. "I forbid it!" she cried, angrily. "I'm your mother. What is this man to you?"

Diana faced her out. "I shall answer their questions," she said.

Mrs. Morven began to weep noisily.

Major Walkley said, coldly, "Please step into the next room, madam."

"I won't!" she cried. "I won't leave my child!"

As the Major moved towards the door to call the policewoman, she suddenly changed her mind. "All right, I'll talk," she said, hastily. "I'll tell everything I know. Let me tell you. I don't want my child mixed up in this!"

"Very well," said the Major. "Miss Morven, will you be good enough to step out for a few moments?"

Luke pressed her hand and let her go.

"Start at the beginning of the journey last night," suggested Lee, soothingly.

Mrs. Morven sat squeezing her hands together; her eyes darted from side to side. By degrees she acquired more self-command. "I didn't like the party at the hotel," she said, acidly; "the people were common; there was too much champagne drunk; it was not suitable company for my daughter. You must understand that though my daughter was engaged to His Highness I was not by any means blind to his faults of character, and I had made up my mind that after marriage many things should be changed. . . ."

Lee glanced at Luke with grim amusement lurking behind the bland spectacles.

Mrs. Morven went on: "I had been told that the private car would be ready for us at any time after ten o'clock, so my daughter and I went on to the station and got aboard the car. We went to our room, but we did not go to bed because His Highness had said he wanted to talk to us. Later His Highness came to the car. . . ."

"What time would this be?"

"I can't tell you exactly. It was just before the train started. There were some noisy people with him and my daughter and I stayed in our room. These people got off at the first stop. Ten or fifteen minutes later His Highness knocked on our door and we admitted him. He had changed to his Eastern dress which he found more comfortable. We talked for some minutes and afterwards . . ."

"What did you talk about?" asked Lee.

Mrs. Morven bridled. "What difference does it make? It was a purely private matter."

"It appears to have been almost his last talk on earth," said Lee, softly. "Surely that is important."

"We discussed the final arrangements for my daughter's marriage," said Mrs. Morven, sullenly. "His Highness apologized because it was necessary to keep us under cover, so to speak. He said it was of the utmost importance that the engagement should not be exploited in the newspapers. When the publicity of the official welcome was over, and the newspapers had forgotten him, he and my daughter would then be quietly married in an Episcopal church. As His Highness put it, he wanted to present the British with a *fait accompli* and let them deal with whatever trouble might arise in Shihkar. The British were bound to stand by him, he said, to keep the country from falling into the hands of the French. That's what we were talking about."

"Thank you," said Lee. "One of His Highness' servants, Abdul by name, has told us that he gave you a bottle of the Sultan's whisky to take care of for him. Is that true?"

"Perfectly true," said Mrs. Morven. "After we finished our talk, he asked for it and I gave it to him. The three of us then went into his room, which was next to ours . . ."

"By the communicating door?" put in Lee, casually.

Mrs. Morven bristled. "Certainly not! That would have been most improper. That door was locked on both sides at all times. We went around by the corridor."

"Naturally," said Lee. "What happened in his room?"

"He opened the bottle. He invited my daughter and me to partake. We declined. His Highness took a drink and then hid the bottle in the water-cooler."

"Why did he do that?"

"He always hid his whisky. It was to keep it from the knowledge of his secretary, Shihab al Zuri, who was fanatical on the subject. I thought it very foolish myself, and I told His Highness so."

"And then what happened?" prompted Lee.

"The three of us went out on the observation platform. This was a great novelty to His Highness. I found it too windy and after a few minutes I came in again, leaving them out there. I proceeded to our room and went to bed. In a little while, twenty minutes perhaps, my daughter came in—I can fix the time because she said the train was then entering Philadelphia. She went to bed."

"You heard nothing during the night?"

"Not a thing! . . . I don't see how anything could have happened. The car was full of people servants sleeping everywhere. There were two detectives aboard."

"But something did happen," said Lee. "Because His Highness has vanished!"

Mrs. Morven went on to describe the events of the morning as she had already related them to Luke. She stuck to her story of the four valises; the porters were mistaken, she insisted. Lee questioned her and Major Walkley questioned her, cunning cross-examiners both of them; but neither succeeded in catching her off her guard. She never departed from her original story. When she had retired into the next room Major Walkley said to Lee:

"What do you think of it?"

"Sounds true," said Lee. "It agrees with what the servants and the detectives told us. But if true, why should she have been so reluctant to tell it? And there's another thing that strikes me as odd."

"What's that?"

"That she displays no regret for the loss of the rich son-in-law."

When Diana was questioned she told precisely the same story as her mother.

Major Walkley was shaken. "Obviously," he said to Lee, "we will have to keep the other possibilities in mind. There's what's-his-name, Prince Abu Daud, a villainous-looking youth. He had everything to gain by his brother's death. . . ."

Luke's heart warmed towards the doughty Major. He would have liked to shake his hand then.

"What are you going to do with these ladies?" asked Lee.

"I can't arrest them," said the Major, stroking his chin; "there's no evidence of murder. Neither can I let them go. I'll have to detain them in their own rooms in the hotel."

"It's a horrible joint!" Luke blurted out.

"So you have visited them there," said the Major, dryly.

"Why not detain them in a better hotel?" suggested Lee. "A suite at the James Madison, where the rest of us are, would make their detention easier to bear."

"Who's to pay for it?" grumbled the Major. "I am obliged to retain all their money until the ownership of the diamond they pawned can be established."

"I'll pay," said Lee.

WHILE LEE AND LUKE were still at Headquarters, a telegram was received from the Chief of Police at Bristol, Pennsylvania:

> Major and Superintendent of Police
> Washington, D. C.
> In response your published request for information, Abner Drury, machinist, of Eddington, wife Gertrude, daughter Mary Ann, returning from death-bed relative, three A.M. Monday, stopped car at P.R.R. crossing one mile South this place to allow train sleeping-cars from New York to pass. Last car observation car. All saw three persons sitting on back platform. One was man wearing turban and long gown. Drurys ready come Washington testify if expenses paid. Communicate with me.
> Mitchelson.

"This corroborates the story of the Morvens," Luke pointed out.

"Excellent!" said Lee.

LEE PROCEEDED TO ENGAGE a comfortable suite at the hotel James Madison and the ladies were transported thither with their baggage, accompanied by a policewoman in ordinary dress who had consented to pose as their servant. The Morvens were to be permitted to receive any visitors they chose, and to use the telephone. The only restriction put upon them was that they might not leave their rooms. Major Walkley assured them courteously that this would not be for long, as he was sure of solving the case within twenty-four hours. Lee made his arrangements so discreetly that the hotel management was not aware these guests were under detention by the police.

Later, as Luke was getting ready for bed, Lee came to his room with a message that had just been received on the teletype at Police Headquarters. Early in the day Major Walkley had dispatched one of his men to New York to establish liaison with the police of that city. The message read:

> Through stool pigeons Inspector Loasby has been informed of certain movements yesterday which throw light on the Ahmed bin Said case. On Market Street, New York, there is a saloon and boarding-house kept by one John Hafiz which is a hangout for Turks, Arabs, and Egyptians of doubtful character. Many of these men have assumed American names. One of the frequenters of the place is an Arab who calls himself Yussuf Kelly. He was called to the telephone yesterday (Sunday) about 2:30, where he carried on a conversation in Arabic. Afterwards he went out. He was back at Hafiz' about 4:30. A partner of his, another Arab known as Saul Morton, was waiting for him. After a whispered consultation, Yussuf called up a machine shop in the Red Hook section of Brooklyn and asked for a man called Ben Adam. He was heard to ask Adam to come over to Hafiz' saloon as soon as possible, and told him there was something good in it.

This Adam came. He was a young fellow in his twenties, an Arab, apparently, but he had not previously been seen at Hafiz' place. The three of them went into a huddle over a table in the saloon. They had a map spread before them, but the informer was unable to say what map. Yussuf at that time had a big roll of bills. He passed money to each of the other two, and they separated. Yussuf, drinking at the bar afterwards, got boastful. Said he had a job that would put him in the money for the rest of his life. Said he would shortly be returning to his own country, where he was going to set up a harem. Mentioned the name of Prince Abu Daud as his protector. He went out shortly before six, and has not been seen at Hafiz' place since.

Following up other lines, the police have learned that Ben Adam is a motorboat machinist employed at Riordan's, a small yard in the Erie Basin. Nothing is known there about his private life. He failed to report for work today. It was learned that Saul Morton lived with a girl in Hester Street. From her the police got the information that Saul came home on Sunday afternoon and told how he "was going on a job" that would keep him out all night. Being suspicious that he intended deceiving her with another woman, she followed him when he left the house and saw him meet two men answering to the descriptions of Yussuf Kelly and Ben Adam, at the corner of Attorney and Broome Streets. The three men got into a new Buick convertible sedan, blue in color, and drove away. This was six o'clock Sunday. Subsequently this car was reported to the police as stolen. Saul Morton has not been home since; neither has Yussuf Kelly nor Ben Adam been seen around their usual haunts. But the blue Buick was picked up on West Street, New York, at 3:00 o'clock Monday.

When it was returned to the owner he said it had been driven 350 miles since it was taken Sunday. The license number is 26-VD-l9.

Yussuf is a man in his early thirties, Saul a year or two younger. Both men have police records. Ben Adam is previously unknown to the police. Photographs, fingerprints, descriptions, and records of the first-named two will follow. Around Hafiz' place the story is that Yussuf is a native of Shihkar in Arabia and is wanted in his own country for numerous murders.

When Luke read this a load was lifted from his mind. At last the truth was beginning to appear. "What did I tell you?" he said, handing the message back to Lee. "By God! I can sleep now!"

Lee shrugged good-humoredly and took a pinch of snuff.

CHAPTER TWELVE

THE MOMENT LUKE AWAKENED next morning his hand went out towards the telephone. But he drew it back again. It was only eight o'clock, hardly a decent hour to call a lady. He used up as much time as he could in shaving, bathing, dressing. Afterwards he went out and bought a paper, but there was nothing in it about the missing Sultan that he did not already know. Back in his room on the stroke of nine, he called up the Morven suite. Mrs. Morven answered.

"How are you?" asked Luke, affably. For Diana's sake he could even be polite to her impossible mother.

"All right," she answered, noncommittally.

"And Diana?"

"She's all right."

"Have you breakfasted yet?"

"No."

"Can I come in and eat with you?"

"No. Not this morning."

"Can I talk to Di?"

"No. She'll call you."

There was a strain in the old woman's voice that caused Luke to ask, sharply, "Has anything happened?"

"No," she said, and hung up, leaving him in the grip of an ugly anxiety.

In quarter of an hour he called again, and once more Mrs. Morven answered. "Can I speak to Di?" he asked.

"No," she said. "I told you she'd call you when she was dressed."

Luke was telling her that Di didn't have to be dressed to use the phone when he realized that he was speaking to a dead wire. Mrs. Morven had hung up.

He was at the point of starting for their suite, anyhow, when the phone rang. This was Diana. There was a strain in her voice, too; she spoke very softly, as if her lips were close to the transmitter.

"Luke, can you come to our rooms?"

"Sure!" he cried.

That was all.

They were lodged on the same floor. He hastened through the corridor. The door of the Morven suite was opened for him by the wooden-faced policewoman. There was a little foyer with three closed doors. From behind the middle door came the sound of Mrs. Morven's voice shaken with anger, but he could not distinguish what she was saying. He knocked on the door, and, since he had been sent for, walked in without waiting to be told. It was their sitting-room. Mrs. Morven and Diana were standing there, both fully dressed, and with them Abu Daud. The young Prince was turned out to perfection; he had a smile on his hateful, handsome face that made Luke want to smash it.

Mrs. Morven bit off what she was saying and turned to Luke with fresh anger. "What are you doing here?" she demanded. "I told you we'd call you when we were ready."

"Diana did call me," said Luke.

"Oh," said Mrs. Morven, turning away.

There was a strained silence. Diana's face gave nothing away. Abu Daud, stroking his silky mustache, continued to smile with an insolence so pure that Luke's hands instinctively clenched.

Diana said in a clear voice, "Prince Abu Daud has done me the honor of asking me to marry him."

"What!" cried Luke.

"Indeed," she went on, "he scarcely condescended to ask me. He appears to think that, now that Ahmed is gone, I have no choice but to marry his successor."

"It's a little previous, isn't it?" suggested Luke, grimly. "Ahmed's body has not been found."

"Oh, Ahmed is certainly dead," said Abu, with a cocky air.

"You appear to be tickled about it," said Luke.

"Why not? Hypocrisy is not one of my vices. . . . Under ordinary circumstances I should have waited awhile before saying anything," he went on, "but as things are going, it looks as if Miss Morven and her mother were in a bad spot, and I want to extend my protection to them."

"Your protection?" said Luke. "My God!"

"As the Sultan of Shihkar I am immune from prosecution," said Abu, carelessly; "as my wife, Miss Morven's person would be sacred also."

"I'm not so sure about that."

"Ask your State Department," said Abu.

"You see," put in Diana, "this is a threat. That's why I asked you to come in."

Luke turned to Mrs. Morven. Up until now he was unable to tell whether her anger was directed against Abu or her daughter. "What do you think of this proposal?" he asked.

"No! No! No!" she cried. "I would sooner see her dead!"

"Good!" said Luke.

Abu Daud lost his temper. "Am I not a better man than my little pig of a brother?" he snarled. "I make her the same offer. What has changed your ideas so suddenly? Answer me that!"

"How can you ask?" said Mrs. Morven. "How dare you face us with his blood on your hands!"

"Isn't there a proverb in English," sneered Abu, "about the pot calling the kettle black?"

Luke took a step towards him. "Keep a civil tongue in your head," he warned.

"Or else?" sneered Abu.

"I'll throw you out."

"You wouldn't dare!"

"Don't try me too far," said Luke, smiling. "The Sultan of Shihkar is nothing in my life!"

"Luke, please," murmured Diana.

Luke let his hands fall at his sides. "You are the one most concerned in this," he said to her. "What do you say?"

"I say no," she replied, with a contemptuous glance at Abu.

"There's your answer," said Luke. "Now get out."

Abu sheered away from him, but not in the direction of the door. "They can't get rid of me as easy as that," he snarled. "I know too much. I'll expose them. They're not immune from arrest. They'll go to jail. They'll . . ."

Luke's fist shot out and the elegant Abu Daud suddenly measured his length on the floor. Mrs. Morven screamed softly and the policewoman opened the door. "What's this?" she demanded. Abu picked himself up and backed towards the door. His face was green with rage.

"By God! you'll pay for this!" he muttered. "You'll pay for this!"

The policewoman put her hand on Abu. She was in doubt how to act. "What's going on here?" she demanded, scowling fiercely.

"Oh, let him go," said Luke.

Abu backed out and Luke shut the door. They heard the outer door close. Diana was smiling strangely. "What a blow!" she murmured. "Like the movies." Mrs. Morven was badly shaken. She had forgotten her anger against Luke. "Oh, I'm sorry . . . I'm sorry you did that," she stammered. "He's so dangerous!"

"The heck with him," said Luke. "He was only bluffing. The police have important evidence against him now."

Mrs. Morven took no comfort from that. "Of course he did it," she murmured. "But they won't be able to touch him!"

"We'll see," said Luke. "I don't believe that any damned foreigner can commit a murder in our country and get away with it."

Luke ordered breakfast, and in due course it was brought upstairs. The three of them sat down to it in the sitting-room. Mrs. Morven would take nothing but a cup of coffee.

"I have to think of my figure," she said, simpering.

Her manner towards Luke suddenly had become fulsome. "My! Isn't he a big fellow!" she said to Diana. "What a wonderful protector for two lone women! But I'm afraid he's very hot-tempered!"

Luke found this harder to bear than her previous rudeness.

"Luke," she went on, fawningly . . . "I suppose I may call you Luke, mayn't I, if Diana does?"

"Certainly."

"I am terribly embarrassed, Luke, I hate to speak of it; the police took all our money. Of course we'll get it back eventually, but in the meantime I'm in need of small sums to tip the servants and so on. Could you . . . ?"

"Mother!" remonstrated Diana, blushing red. "We can pawn something until we get our money back."

"How can we get to a pawnshop?" said the old woman, sharply.

"No, please let me," said Luke. "How much?"

"Ten dollars will be enough," said Mrs. Morven.

Luke handed it over.

Mrs. Morven presently got up, saying: "You children eat at your leisure. I've got letters to write." She disappeared into the bedroom on the left.

Luke picked up Diana's hand and conveyed it to his lips. "Isn't this marvelous?" he murmured. "Breakfasting together! It's as if . . . as if . . ."

Diana dropped her mask as soon as they were alone together. She drew away her hand. Her beautiful face was full of pain. "You mustn't, Luke. You mustn't dream dreams. They can't come true."

"Why not? The old lady appears to have given me her blessing now."

"That means nothing," said Diana, wearily. "In ten minutes she will turn against you again. . . . Oh, what a beastly mess, Luke! I wish . . . I wish I were out of it all! I never had any luck."

"You'll soon be cleared!"

"Even if I were cleared a thousand times over, anything between you and me would still be impossible."

"I'll find a way!"

"There is no way! You must put it out of your mind or it will only hurt worse in the end!"

"Don't you love me?" he demanded.

"I have an inclination towards you," she said, with a crooked smile.

"Then I'll never give you up."

"I won't hold you to that," she said, sadly.

When the waiter came to take away the dishes the policewoman glanced into the room. Not seeing Mrs. Morven, she crossed to the door of her bedroom and knocked. There was no answer and she opened the door. By this time the waiter was out of the suite. The policewoman demanded, sharply:

"Where's Mrs. Morven?"

"She went into her room," said Luke.

"She's not here now."

Luke jumped up. Two minutes' search of the suite made it clear that Mrs. Morven was indeed gone. Diana discovered that she had taken her hat. The policewoman was red with anger.

"How could she have got out?" said Luke.

"How could she have got out!" snorted the policewoman. "By the door from her room into the corridor, that's how, and it was you fetched her the key!"

"I did nothing of the sort!" said Luke.

"All right! All right!" stormed the woman. "You can tell that to the Superintendent. I'll trouble you to stay here until he comes!" She called up Major Walkley's office and reported the absence of Mrs. Morven. "I believe it was Mr. Imbrie furnished her with a key. I am detaining him here."

The policewoman remained in the sitting-room to watch Luke. The situation was not without its grim humor, because, after all, she was only a woman and her "prisoner" overtopped her by almost a head. She wasn't armed.

"You needn't be afraid," said Luke. "I'm not going to punch you. I'm staying here."

He paced the room, scowling. The actions of Mrs. Morven put him in a horribly false position. In his secret heart he was wishing that the old woman might get clean away and never come back into their lives. Diana looked out of the window.

In a few minutes Major Walkley arrived, accompanied by Lee Mappin. The policewoman, relieved almost to the point of tears by the arrival of male support, told her story all over again.

"What have you got to say?" the Major demanded of Luke.

"I don't know where Mrs. Morven has gone," said Luke. "I gave her no key."

"I don't believe you," said Major Walkley bluntly. "Right from the beginning you have been interfering to protect these women. I have been too lenient with all of you."

Luke turned white. "Major, in calling me a liar you are taking advantage of your position. I . . . ."

Lee laid a soothing hand on his arm.

"Lee," said Luke, "I had nothing to do with this woman's escape. You know I wouldn't lie to you."

Lee nodded.

Meanwhile Major Walkley had gone to the telephone to ask of the office if Mrs. Morven had been seen downstairs. He received an explanation over the wire, and as he listened his face changed. When he had hung up he said, with a hangdog air:

"Imbrie, I have to ask your pardon. They tell me that half an hour ago Mrs. Morven herself asked for a key to her bedroom."

Luke stiffly acknowledged the apology.

"As they knew of no reason why she shouldn't have it," the Major went on, "it was sent up. She told them to instruct the boy to unlock her door from the corridor and come in."

"Any clue as to where she's gone?" asked Lee.

The Major shook his head. "She just walked out of the door. She didn't take a taxi."

He turned to Diana. "Miss Morven, do you know where your mother has gone?"

"She said nothing to me," answered Diana, indifferently.

"I didn't ask you that. Do you know where she's gone without having been told?"

"We have friends in Washington," said Diana. "Very likely she has gone to one of them for advice or assistance."

"You still have not answered my question."

Diana shrugged. "That's the best answer I can give you."

They heard a sound from Mrs. Morven's bedroom. The door was open, and presently Mrs. Morven herself appeared in the opening in her smart costume and too-youthful French hat. The three men stared. She had an inimitable air of triumph, not unmixed with fear.

"Where have you been?" demanded Major Walkley.

"Just for a stroll," said Mrs. Morven, with a toss of her head. She glanced out of the window. "Such a lovely morning!"

Major Walkley's face grew red. "You have abused my leniency, madam!"

She tried to look innocent—without much success. "Where's the harm?" she said. "I haven't been anywhere in particular or talked to anybody. I just wanted a breath of air."

"Search her," said the Major to the policewoman.

Mrs. Morven, with a glance of plain fear, darted back into her bedroom. The policewoman followed her swiftly, closing the door. In a few minutes she returned, saying:

"Nothing but the room key, Major, and three thirty-five in cash."

"Where did she get the money?"

"I lent it to her," said Luke. "She said she required a small sum for tips." He wondered where the rest of the ten had gone.

Mrs. Morven came in, preening her feathers like a hen.

Major Walkley said to the policewoman: "Hereafter you will be present at all interviews, and you will overhear all conversations that these ladies may carry on over the phone."

"Yes, sir."

As he prepared to leave, he addressed Mrs. Morven sternly: "Last night, out of deference to your feelings, we did not inform the hotel management that you were under detention by the police. They know it now, and if they invite you to leave the hotel I will have no choice but to lock you up at Police Headquarters. You have only yourself to blame. By acting in this suspicious manner you force me to keep you in custody."

Mrs. Morven tossed her head. She was afraid of him, but she was far from being crushed. Some secret assurance upheld her. It was not the picture of an innocent woman that she was making, and Luke's spirits sunk low. She was such a fool! He glanced at Diana. She had her back to them all, but her slumped shoulders suggested disgust or shame.

The telephone rang and Mrs. Morven went to answer it. As she listened to the communication a surprising change came over her face. Under her rouge she blushed like a girl, and her faded eyes sparkled. Her voice fairly purred as she said into the phone:

"I shall be most honored to receive His Excellency. Please ask him to be so good as to come up."

Putting up the phone, she faced Major Walkley and Lee with a new boldness. "Our Ambassador is calling. He will protect our interests. Thank God, British women are always safe, though they may be deprived of their natural protectors."

Lee glanced drolly at Luke. They both knew that she had been born Dolly Wilson of Charles City, Iowa.

Mrs. Morven went to Diana. They could all hear her excited whisper. "Go change your dress, darling. You're too pale; you need a touch of rouge. Let me talk to him for a couple of minutes before you come in."

She bustled back to the three men, spreading out her hands as if to shepherd them out. "If there is nothing further I can do for you gentlemen, I'm sure you will understand that I need to . . . in private, you understand. I shall be at your service at any other time."

"Oh, quite! quite!" said Lee, leading the way.

They left. The Major's face was red, but Lee was bland. Luke went with a burning spot in his breast.

Major Walkley and Lee now wished to question Abu Daud. Further particulars about the men he had lured in New York, including photographs of two of them, had been received at Headquarters. Luke turned his thoughts in that direction with an intense desire. If they could only hang it on Abu Daud! There was now positive evidence against the man, and the crime certainly resembled that of a man rather than a woman.

Prince Abu Daud's suite was on the same floor of the hotel. Major Walkley knocked. There was no answer. Trying the handle of the door, he found it unlocked. A glance showed them that the rooms were empty and that all of Abu Daud's effects had been removed. The Major and Lee looked at each other grimly. The former muttered:

"Every one of them ought to be put behind the bars until we get at the truth "

Downstairs at the desk the Major inquired for Prince Abu Daud. Like most other citizens, the staff of the hotel displayed a silky manner towards the head of the police force. The manager said:

"Prince Abu Daud checked out about half an hour ago. He said if there were any inquiries for him we should say that he had accepted the hospitality of the French Embassy."

There was a silence. The muscles on either side of the Major's jaw stood out. Lee Mappin took snuff noisily. His spectacles glittered.

The manager continued: "About those two ladies, Major, their presence puts the hotel in rather an invidious position. But of course if it's an object with you to have them stay here, and if there's no unfavorable publicity . . ."

"Let them stay for the present," growled the Major. "If you don't say anything to the newspapers, I won't."

CHAPTER THIRTEEN

MAJOR WALKLEY PAUSED in the lobby of the James Madison to consider his next move. From a little distance a group of reporters watched him keenly. Through the window Luke could see a crowd in the street. Police were keeping them moving back and forth in a double file. They had come merely to stare at the hotel where the principals in the sensational case were stopping. One reporter, bolder than the others, stepped up.

"Is there anything to give out, Major?"

The Major frowned portentously. "No! I can't stop in the middle of my work to talk to you boys. There's no use your following me about. Come to the press conference at noon."

"Will Mr. Mappin talk to us then?"

"That's up to him."

The reporter retreated.

"I'll go to the French Embassy," said the Major to Lee. "Though I may be unable to arrest my man there, they can't refuse me admittance. I can question him. Will you come with me?"

"No," said Lee, coolly. "He will defy you, and then what will you do?"

"Hm!" said the Major, rubbing his chin.

"If I might make a suggestion," put in Luke, "why not ask our State Department just where we stand with this so-called Sultan."

"Good!" said Lee.

The Major marched off to a telephone booth. Immediately the reporters moved on Lee in a body. Lee waved his hands.

"Not a word, my lads! I am but a stranger here; Heaven is my home!" Thrusting his arm through Luke's, he led him away into the restaurant, where he made believe to be showing him the mural decorations.

"Lee, what do you really think?" Luke asked, anxiously.

Lee took off his glasses to polish them. His eyes were dancing. "I don't know what to think," he said. "Every new fact we learn seems to cancel out everything we knew before. A marvelous case! I haven't been so stimulated in years!"

"It is more than just another case to me," muttered Luke.

Major Walkley came across the lobby and they rejoined him. His face was glum. "It seems the scoundrel is right. As the ruler of a country with whom we are at peace he is immune from arrest. All we can do is to send him back to his own country."

"That would just suit him," said Luke. "In his own country the Sultan is above the law. He would merely laugh at us."

"Can't be helped," growled the Major. "Seems that under International usage a sovereign is regarded as a piece of his country, so to speak. We can't touch him!"

"That's a rotten situation!"

"I had it direct from the Chief of Protocol. The only hope he could hold out was, that if a coronation oath is required under the constitution of Shihkar, Abu Daud is not legally the ruler until he has taken it."

"Shihkar wouldn't have a constitution!"

"We must ask Shihab al Zuri about that," said Lee.

Once more the three of them went up to the eleventh floor. Major Walkley knocked on the door of Shihab's suite and it was presently opened by the little gray Cheragh Ali with his owlish glasses. He laid a finger on his lips and, opening the door a little wider, indicated the figure of Shihab al Zuri prostrate on a prayer rug with his head bowing towards the East.

"Just one moment, gentlemen, if you would be so kind," lisped Cheragh. "My master is asking for guidance." He closed the door.

Presently it was opened wide again and they went in. Shihab with his deeply harassed face was waiting for them with a clenched hand on his breast, struggling to be calm. "What news, gentlemen?" he stammered. "My master . . . has he been found?"

"No," said the Major.

"His jewels?"

"No."

"Have you no news at all?" asked Shihab, despairingly.

Major Walkley told him of the report that had been received from New York. "Have you ever heard the names of these Arabs that Abu Daud has hired?" he asked.

"How should I know such men?" said Shihab, spreading out his hands. . . . "But wait!" he added. "Several years ago there was a man in Shihkar called Yussuf Ismail. After a career of robbery and murder in the desert, he was said to have fled to America. It may be the same Yussuf. The age would be about right. . . . As to the other two I cannot say. The young men who go to sea from our port find their way all over the world."

"Abu Daud has taken refuge at the French Embassy, where he is immune from arrest," said Lee. "This is what we want to know: Is he now the legal ruler of Shihkar?"

"Traditionally," said Shihab, "the oldest son, or, failing any son, the oldest brother succeeds, but actually in my poor country whoever is able to seize the power becomes Sultan."

"Under your laws is the Sultan required to take an oath upon his accession?"

"There are no written laws in Shihkar. Only custom. The Sultan is supreme. It is true that the British imposed a treaty on Ahmed's father which obligated him and his successors to take an oath to enforce the British code of laws, but it is obvious that Abu Daud intends to denounce this treaty."

"And if we send him back to Shihkar?"

"He will seize the power. All the rabble would follow him. It would be a calamity!"

After considering awhile, Shihab al Zuri continued, "I can see only one chance of stopping Abu Daud."

"What's that?"

"If the Khalif, the supreme head of our religion, could be induced to denounce Abu Daud as a fratricide, the Faithful would be bound to abandon him." Shihab addressed Major Walkley. "Just as soon as His Excellency, the Superintendent, is satisfied that I have done all I can to help him here, I will start for Arabia to lay my petition before the Khalif."

Major Walkley said: "You may start the day that we obtain conclusive evidence that Abu Daud is the murderer."

Lee, sitting with his plump hands clasped across his stomach, asked, in his mild way: "If you succeed in spiking the ambitions of Abu Daud, who would then become Sultan of Shihkar?"

"Hussein el Faiz," said Shihab, "a youth of eighteen, the cousin of Ahmed and Abu Daud. An excellent young man, educated by the priests of Medina. He would make a good ruler."

"Where is he now?"

"I don't know. He has been kept in hiding in order to avoid exciting the jealousy of his cousins. But of course his friends would bring him forward if there was a chance of his succeeding."

"Would he incline to the English or the French?" asked Lee.

"A boy of eighteen," said Shihab. "What does he know about politics? He would be governed by his advisers. Hussein el Faiz has been brought up strictly according to our religion. His strength with the people lies in the fact that he has no foreign ties."

"You would favor the accession of Hussein el Faiz?" said Lee.

Shihab looked at him in surprise. "If it was a choice between Hussein and the profligate Abu Daud, who would hesitate?"

"Nobody," said Lee.

Major Walkley, pursuing his own line of thought, said: "The three men hired in New York could not have entered the private car. Their job must have been to receive the body, either alive or dead, at some point along the line."

"Obviously," said Lee.

"But I am not yet satisfied that the Morvens do not have guilty knowledge of the crime," the Major went on.

"Impossible!" exclaimed Shihab, with a glance of horror. "Two such refined ladies!"

"Mrs. Morven's actions are not those of an innocent person," the Major insisted.

Lee said, quietly, "Have you considered the possibility that Mrs. Morven may have made a deal with Abu Daud in advance?"

This thought had already occurred to Luke's secret mind but he would not acknowledge it. It made him feel sick with apprehension to hear it voiced by Lee.

"But I understand," said the Major, "that they invited Imbrie to throw Abu Daud out of their suite this morning."

"Mrs. Morven may feel strong enough now to repudiate her partner," said Lee. "He has threatened to expose her, but he couldn't do it without incriminating himself."

"When we find the jewels that will tell," said the Major.

"They must be found!" murmured Shihab, squeezing his hands together. "Nearly a million dollars' worth of jewels couldn't just disappear!"

"For our next move," said Lee, thoughtfully, "I suggest that I try to get the British and the French Ambassadors together, to try to find out just how far international intrigues are going to interfere with our work. It would be better, I think, for me to see them alone, as the presence of the Superintendent of Police would lend an official character to the meeting. A mere private person might be able to persuade them to show their cards."

"I agree," said Major Walkley.

"Will you come with me, Luke?" Lee asked. "You can pose as my secretary."

Luke nodded.

"In the meantime, Major," said Lee, "I suggest that you have the French Embassy watched. Let your men keep strictly under cover to avoid wounding the susceptibilities of the Ambassador. And if our princely gentleman should venture out on business or merely to take the air, I suggest that you arrest him and let the legal minds of the State Department thresh out the question while you have him locked up."

"I'll do that," said the Major.

FOUR MEN WERE SEATED IN THE STUDY of the British Ambassador. M. Clément, the French Ambassador, had made no difficulties about joining the conference. The two diplomats made an interesting contrast: Sir Bertram Maunsell, tall, handsome, sanguine, with an open manner and a delightful smile; M. Clément, a smaller man, handsome, too, in his dark fashion, with the traditional reserve of the French public servant, but his own pleasant smile. The two men, having served at the same time in many capitals, were the warmest of friends, but in the endless jockeying of diplomacy, neither abated a jot on account of personal regard.

And seated opposite them, little roly-poly Lee, crossing his short legs with difficulty, and occasionally producing the snuffbox. Luke could not sufficiently admire his friend. Luke himself was a little overawed by this high company, but Lee was perfectly able to meet an Ambassador on his own ground and even go him one better. Lee was known to both Ambassadors through the reputation of his writings; they instinctively recognized in him a member of the elect and unbent accordingly. There were no strings on Lee; consequently he could be really as frank as His Majesty's representative was making believe to be, and that gave Lee an advantage. He was exerting all his charm to win the two diplomats.

After Lee had presented his case, M. Clément said: "You have not yet secured positive evidence against Sultan Abu Daud, Mr. Mappin."

"True, M. Clément, but sufficient evidence, wouldn't you say, to warrant the Superintendent of Police in questioning him?"

"When the man has sought refuge with me I couldn't possibly turn him over to the police."

"If he's innocent, he has nothing to fear."

"Suppose he is not innocent?"

"I can't believe that you would wish to take the part of a murderer."

"I'm afraid it's useless to appeal to M. Clément's feelings as a man," said Sir Bertram, with a good-humored smile. "He has his instructions."

"But yes!" said M. Clément, blandly, "just as you have yours, dear Sir Bertram."

"How about letting Major Walkley question Abu Daud at the Embassy?" asked Lee.

"Impossible, Mr. Mappin! The Embassy is France! To permit one of your police officers to enter would establish a most dangerous precedent. Ask my confrère here. Sir Bertram, would you allow the Superintendent of Police in the British Embassy?"

"There never has been any need of it," said Sir Bertram.

"Not in your time, perhaps; but I could relate occasions in the past. . . ."

Sir Bertram went on with smiling sarcasm: "You see, the French are taking a large view of the situation, Mr. Mappin. They say: What does it matter if a murderer escapes punishment if thereby we get a port on the Persian Gulf."

"Why not let us have it unconditionally?" said M. Clément. "You have a dozen other ports on the Gulf and we have none. There is a great hinterland to the east and the north under French protection which is unable to ship its surplus camels, dates, and wool because of the excessive port duties you have imposed."

"Well, naturally we have to convince the natives of the advantages of British protection."

"What do you purpose doing with Abu Daud?" asked Lee, politely, of M. Clément. "You can't keep him in the Embassy indefinitely."

"I must be guided by circumstances," returned the Frenchman, cautiously. "If you prove him guilty, I suppose I shall return him to his own country for trial."

"Where he would immediately seize power—with your connivance," said Sir Bertram. . . . "But he hasn't got there yet. Just as soon as his guilt is evident, I shall apply to the American government for the custody of his person, and since Shihkar is recognized as being under British influence, my request must be granted."

"I should regretfully decline to give him up," said M. Clément."

"If you tried to ship him to Arabia, I would have the right to seize him en route."

"If you could lay hands on him, dear Sir Bertram."

"Shihkar is ours. We have the best right to try him for his crime."

"I'm afraid that trial would be a hollow mockery, Sir Bertram."

"British trials are always fair, my friend."

"Yes, to the British."

Lee, rubbing his upper lip to hide a grin, was enjoying this. Sir Bertram said to him:

"The French think they have us cornered in this matter of Shihkar. We may surprise them. We stand upon our treaty with the former Sultan. A British Resident is in control, and he will still be in control even if Abu Daud should attempt to seize the power."

"You wouldn't fight for Shihkar," said M. Clément. "It isn't worth it."

"Neither would you," retorted Sir Bertram. "There are much larger considerations which force your country and mine to remain at peace before the world. But that doesn't prevent us, of course, from taking advantage of local conditions where we can."

"If you depose Abu Daud what will you do for a Sultan?" asked M. Clément, quite undisturbed. "Britain would not be permitted to annex the country outright."

"There is a cousin, Hussein el Faiz by name."

"But, my friend, he is the candidate of the Green Turbans, the fanatic Mohammedans, whose aim it is to drive both your country and mine out of Arabia."

"Exactly, but they have a long way to go yet," said Sir Bertram. "Hussein is a gentle youth, amenable. Once we get him in Shihkar it will not be difficult to influence him to rule in the British manner."

"In that case God help him!" said M. Clément dryly.

Sir Bertram laughed pleasantly. "He will be treated with the greatest kindness."

"Surely, surely. Sent to Paris and London to enjoy himself."

"Ah, dear Paris!" murmured Sir Bertram.

"However," said M. Clément, with snapping black eyes and compressed lips, "Abu Daud is still Sultan of Shihkar *de jure*."

"Very questionably *de jure*, my dear fellow," said Sir Bertram, "and not by a long shot, *de facto*."

"We'll see!"

"We'll see!"

"Judging from what I have read in the newspapers, and from what Mr. Mappin has told us here," said M. Clément, "I would suggest that the part the ladies Morven have played in this affair should not be overlooked. No offense, Sir Bertram, because they happen to be your nationals."

"None taken, monsieur," said Sir Bertram. "Britain is proud to claim the girl; as for the Mother, she's yours, Mr. Mappin."

"Thank you for nothing," said Lee.

"Shoving a body through a window! That is not a woman's crime!" said Sir Bertram.

"Women are unpredictable!" said the Frenchman.

Sir Bertram in his enthusiasm jumped up and took a turn. "The girl is one in a million!" he cried. "You should see her, my friend. Tall, slender, blonde, with an exquisite reserve; the finest type of English loveliness; makes you think of a lily, a swan, an angel! It is impossible to think of her in connection with a sordid crime."

"I don't doubt she's beautiful," said M. Clément, "but beautiful women have sinned before this!"

"Not this one," said Sir Bertram, confidently. "I'm banking on her!"

To Luke this was all very well; it was grand to obtain such a powerful advocate for Diana, but there was a little too personal an enthusiasm in Sir Bertram's encomiums. Luke lowered his eyes so that Sir Bertram would not catch him glaring at him.

Lee said: "I assure you that the ladies are not being overlooked, monsieur." He rose. "This has been a pleasant meeting, gentlemen. Now I must get on with my work."

"You can depend on me, Mr. Mappin, for any assistance in my power," said Sir Bertram.

"Thank you. . . . And you, M. Clément?"

"By all means let the truth be brought out," said M. Clément, blandly. "I must be guided by circumstances, naturally."

"And your instructions from the Quai d'Orsay," put in Sir Bertram, wickedly.

"Just so," said M. Clément, smiling.

"I'm in touch with our Resident in Shihkar," said Sir Bertram, "and if any evidence is forthcoming there, it shall immediately be placed in your hands."

"Ask him in your code," suggested Lee, "if he can trace a sale, a gift, or a theft of the drug cyanide of potassium in Shihkar recently."

"I will do so, Mr. Mappin." Sir Bertram went on, "Sultan Ahmed was my country's ward. I wish to offer a reward of one thousand dollars for the recovery of his body."

"Splendid!" said Lee. He turned to the Frenchman. "M. Clément, will you match it—to assist in bringing out the truth?"

To Lee's own surprise, M. Clément answered: "With pleasure. But anonymously, by all means."

Hands were shaken all around, and Lee and Luke departed.

They returned to the hotel for lunch. While there, Lee was called to the telephone by M. Clément. He afterwards repeated the conversation to Luke. M. Clément said that upon his return to the Embassy he had himself questioned Sultan Abu Daud. Abu Daud had vehemently denied having had anything to do with the disappearance or murder of his brother. He had admitted that he would gladly have put Ahmed bin Said out of the way, but said he had been restrained by his fear of the British power. So many people hated Ahmed bin Said, his brother said, that he was sure somebody would do the job for him if he simply waited, and so it had turned out.

Abu Daud had further sworn to M. Clément that he had never seen the men Yussuf, Saul, and Ben Adam; had had no relations with them; had never heard their names before. He charged that Mrs. Morven had poisoned Ahmed in his whisky, and that she had had the assistance of Abdul, Ahmed's cook, in disposing of the body. Her object was to secure Ahmed's jewels and to save Diana from a marriage that the girl detested.

"This is just the lying charge of a guilty man!" said Luke, hotly.

"I hope so," said Lee.

"The bottle of whisky that Mrs. Morven brought to Sultan Ahmed was still sealed. We know that, because you found the bits of gum seal in an ashtray in the Sultan's stateroom."

"Right."

"The Sultan took a drink immediately. Cyanide of potassium kills instantly, yet he was alive for nearly an hour afterwards."

"Right," said Lee again. "But there is another bottle of the Glenardrey whisky to be accounted for. The cook, Abdul, you remember, claimed that it had been stolen from him."

Luke was silenced.

After lunch they proceeded to Police Headquarters. A track-walker of the Pennsylvania Railroad had sent in a number of pieces of glass, evidently the remains of a bottle thrown from a train window. The reason it hadn't been found before, was that the bottle had struck a stone and shattered, and the pieces were hidden in the grass. The track-walker had been able to establish the spot where the bottle had struck because of the smell of whisky which still clung to the earth.

"I wish they were all such good observers," commented Lee.

A man at Headquarters, expert in such matters, was attempting to assemble the pieces in the form of the original bottle. Unfortunately some of it was missing. However, there was enough to show that the bottle had borne no label. Also the neck and the stopper were intact, and by fitting the pieces of the gum seal to the gum that remained clinging to the neck, Lee was able to establish that this was the bottle which Mrs. Morven had brought to Sultan Ahmed and which the Sultan had subsequently hidden in the water-cooler. It had been picked up at a point a furlong south of the station at Bristol, Pa., that is to say, about halfway between Trenton and North Philadelphia.

"Highly interesting," said Lee.

CHAPTER FOURTEEN

AMONG THE MESSAGES RECEIVED that morning at Headquarters from Major Walkley's man in New York was this:

> The net spread by the New York police for Yussuf Kelly, Saul Morton and Ben Adam has so far yielded nothing. Saul has not been home to see his girl, nor has Ben Adam returned to his job in the Brooklyn boatyard. Yussuf has lodged at John Hafiz' for several years, but of course he's keeping away from there now. It is suspected that Hafiz is in communication with him, but they can't establish it. Hafiz is a cool and experienced hand and questioning him is useless. A close watch is being kept on his place inside and out. A stool pigeon is always drinking at the bar. Hafiz' mail is examined before being delivered to him, and his telephone wire is tapped. The police promise results within twenty-four hours.

"Always twenty-four hours," said Lee, dryly.

Major Walkley failed to get the point.

Lee took a small pinch of snuff and inhaled it slowly. "Major," he said, "suppose we set a little trap from this end for our friend Yussuf. If it fails, we'll be no worse off than we are at present."

"What do you suggest?" asked the Major, hopefully.

"I suggest that a letter in Arabic be written to Yussuf as from Abu Daud. I am gambling on the chance that their previous communications were by telephone and that Yussuf is not familiar with Abu Daud's hand. Abu Daud probably doesn't write his own letters, anyhow."

"In Arabic?" queried the Major. "Who could you get to write it?"

"There is one Arab that I can trust—Douban, Sultan Ahmed's valet. Douban loved his master."

"Well, Douban is under detention here at Headquarters," said Major Walkley, reaching for a bell button. "Shall I send for him?"

"Wait a minute," said Lee. "There are certain details to be settled. . . . Have you got a man on your force who looks like a Frenchman? If he can speak French, so much the better."

"I have a real Frenchman."

"Good! Let's use him to carry the note to Hafiz." Lee glanced at his watch. "Two-thirty. If we can get him off on the four-o'clock plane our letter will be in New York by six. . . . May I use your phone?"

"Certainly." The Major pushed over the instrument.

Lee called up the British Embassy. Sir Bertram, true to his promise, came on the wire as soon as he was told who was calling. Lee said: "Sir Bertram, I need a sheet of the official notepaper used at the French Embassy. Could you help me to get it? It is required for a bit of police work that can hurt nobody but the guilty man."

Evidently the Ambassador could and would help, for Lee, smiling, presently said: "Thank you so much. I'll explain when I see you. I'll be waiting for it in Major Walkley's office at Police Headquarters."

"I wish I could command such service from the Embassies!" grumbled the Major.

"Sir Bertram's sending me a couple of French Embassy notes from his files," said Lee. "I'll have to clean the paper with ink eradicator."

"How about an envelope?"

"It must be sent in a plain envelope. We don't want the French insignia to appear on the outside."

While he was waiting for the messenger from the Embassy, Lee sat in the corner, chewing a pencil like a schoolboy and composing the matter of his letter. Major Walkley meanwhile was getting in touch with Detective Grobois, who was to carry it. Lee interrupted his task to ask:

"Give me a suitable rendezvous along the waterfront; an out-of-the-way pier, where you can post your men under cover ready to seize Yussuf if he keeps the appointment."

Major Walkley considered. "On Water Street at the foot of O Street, S.W. there is an open pier that answers to your description."

Lee wrote it down.

He presently brought his completed draft to the Major. "This is to be translated into Arabic," he explained. "Douban will have to supply the proper forms and salutations. He's an intelligent man." Luke read it over their shoulders.

> Yussuf:
> You did a good job night before last, and I shall ful-fill my obligations towards you. Unluckily, things have not gone so well at this end. The police were hot after me, and I was forced to seek refuge in the French Embassy, where I am writing this. His Ex-cellency the Ambassador has promised to put me aboard a vessel in the Potomac River tonight, which will carry me to the French island of Martinique in the West Indies. From there a French dispatch boat will carry me to Marseille in France, and another ship to French Syria. I will reach Shihkar through the French mandated territories to the north. In Shihkar all is prepared for my return. I will have the full support of the French, and the British are not prepared to fight.
>
> I am told that somebody in Hafiz' saloon has betrayed you to the New York police, and that they are close on your trail. I am very unwilling to leave one who has served me so well in danger, and I have

persuaded the Ambassador to allow you to accompany me to Shihkar under the protection of the French, provided you can get to Washington before dawn. In Shihkar you shall be my right-hand man. From midnight until dawn tonight a boat manned by French sailors will be waiting for you at the open pier on Water Street, foot of O Street, Washington, Southwest district. One of the sailors will be waiting at the shore end of the pier to guide you to the boat.

This will be carried to New York by M. Grobois, a secret service man in the employ of the Embassy. His instructions are to place it in John Hafiz' hands unseen, and immediately disappear. We are told that Hafiz' place is closely watched. Use any means that may be available to get here in time, as, after I leave the country, I shall not be able to help you.

Sultan Abu Daud.

"Wherever he may be, Yussuf has access to the newspapers," Lee pointed out. "Notice that everything in my letter is borne out by what he would read in the papers."

"Isn't it unnecessarily elaborate?" suggested the Major.

Lee regarded his composition with the pride of authorship. "It is just those little unnecessary touches that carry conviction."

The Major smiled broadly. "Certainly this ought to fetch him!"

Lee said: "Send a message to New York that Grobois is coming to Hafiz' and for the police to keep hands off."

The notepaper presently arrived by an Embassy messenger. Lee cleaned it for the reception of a new communication, and afterward went into consultation in the adjoining room with Douban, the Arab valet. Douban was delighted to undertake this task. He wrote a beautiful Arabic script. In the meantime Detective Grobois reported to the Superintendent. French from his pompadour haircut to his pointed shoes, Lee was well satisfied with his appearance. After being coached by Lee in the part he was to play, Grobois departed with the letter in time to catch the four-o'clock plane for New York.

"And now for Havre de Grace," said Lee. "Can you furnish me with a car, Major? I'll take Imbrie with me."

"Certainly. You are sure that Havre de Grace is the place?"

"Everything bears it out; the long bridge across the Susquehanna which has no guard rail; the fact that Yussuf was particular to get a motorboat engineer to help him, and the distance they traveled that night. It is almost precisely 350 miles from New York to Havre de Grace and return."

Major Walkley ordered the car.

Lee said: "Please inform the press that donors who wish to remain anonymous have offered two thousand dollars' reward for the recovery of Sultan Ahmed's body, and that I have gone to Havre de Grace to direct the search personally. Let this be telephoned to Havre de Grace ahead of me. And perhaps you'd better swear me in. I need a badge."

"You can have the badge without being sworn," said the Major.

"I'll be back in your office at eleven-thirty," said Lee smiling. "Don't want to miss the fun here tonight."

DRIVEN BY A SKILLFUL POLICE CHAUFFEUR, they were in Havre de Grace within two hours. The news of Lee's coming had preceded him. He had been well publicized during the past two days, and people were standing along the shady main street of the little town, watching for him as if he had been the circus. He was driven first to the police station, where he introduced himself to the chief. After the amenities had been exchanged, Lee said:

"Is there a barroom that is frequented by boatmen and others who work alongshore?"

"Sure, Conley's," said the Chief. "But you won't find any boatmen there now." He led Lee to a back window overlooking the wide mouth of the Susquehanna and the misty Chesapeake beyond. The expanse was dotted with small boats. "All out looking for the two thousand," he said.

"I doubt if they'll find it floating," said Lee. "I'll hang out at Conley's until darkness begins to drive them in. . . . Look," he went on. "I have reason to believe that three bad men from New York spent Sunday night here in your pretty town. They were driving a new Buick convertible sedan, painted blue. The license number was 26-VD-19, but it is possible they put on other plates for the journey. If I am right, the blue convertible, top down, was standing somewhere in the street here from eleven Sunday night to seven or eight Monday morning. This is what the three men looked like." He read the descriptions furnished by New York

The Chief promised to investigate, and Lee and Luke went on to Conley's, a small, ancient hotel near the approach to the highway bridge. Upstream near by, and much higher than the other, the railway bridge crossed, the tracks laid on top of the long spans, which were without guard rails of any sort.

The barroom at Conley's smelled as if beer had been spilled on the floor for a century past, but it was a true, old-time American bar, and Lee sniffed it with approval. The place was almost empty when they entered. Ten minutes later it was crowded. Lee was the center of attraction. Perched on a high stool, nursing one of the white-spatted ankles, he conversed affably with all comers—or rather, he got them talking and arguing about the case, while he listened with flashing glasses, and occasionally dropped in a question.

There was a telephone booth in the bar, and after the talk had been going on for a while, without, apparently, getting anywhere, the bell rang. The man who happened to be nearest, answered it, and emerged saying: "Call for Mr. Mappin."

Lee murmured to Luke: "Stand by!" Luke followed him to the booth. Lee said: "If you see me pull my ear, I want you to trace the call, and hang on to the caller if possible until I come. The car is at the door if you need it."

Lee closed the door of the booth after him. Almost immediately Luke through the glass saw his hand go to his ear. Luke slipped out of the bar and, running across the street to a drug store, went to the telephone there. To the operator who answered, he said:

"This is Amos Lee Mappin's assistant. Somebody just called up Mr. Mappin at Conley's and is talking to him now. Will you give me the source of that call?"

In a moment came the answer: "Havre de Grace fifty-six is connected with Conley's. That's the Hotel Susquehanna, half a block south of where you are."

Thirty seconds later Luke was entering the Susquehanna. This was a slightly more up-to-date hotel with dusty artificial palms and mission furniture in the lobby. The booth was in the lobby and to Luke's satisfaction he saw that it was still occupied. It was a tall, pretty young woman dressed in clothes of cheap material. She looked worried. Luke sat down facing the booth, and lit a cigarette in order to appear at his ease.

When she emerged, he rose, raising his hat. "How do you do; my name is Imbrie."

She shrank back. "I don't know you."

"I'm Mr. Mappin's assistant. He wants you to wait here for him."

She paled, and put a hand on the back of a chair for support. Suddenly she started for the door. Luke clapped a hand on her shoulder.

"Let me go!" she cried.

Instantly the hotel clerk and a couple of other men ran up. "This lady just called up Mr. Mappin," explained Luke. "He told me to trace the call and keep her here until he came."

"Let me go! Let me go!" wailed the girl. "I ain't done nothing."

The three men appeared uncertain how to act. The clerk said: "Better wait, sister. If you're on the level, nobody's going to harm you."

"Do you know who she is?" asked Luke.

He shook his head.

At that moment Lee's fat little legs twinkled past the windows and he ran in, panting. Above the convex white waistcoat his face was as red as a beet. He made reassuring sounds to the frightened girl. By this time a couple of servants had run in from the kitchen, and in order to escape all the curious eyes, Lee led the girl out on the sidewalk. He signaled to their car below, and the chauffeur, making a double turn, drew up alongside them.

"Let's sit in the car where we can talk without being heard," said Lee.

"I won't get in!" she cried. "You can't make me!"

Lee said to the chauffeur: "Take the ignition key and go for a walk. Go get your supper." The man obeyed. "Now the car can't move," said Lee to the girl. "You are perfectly safe."

She was persuaded to get in. The three of them sat on the back seat of the sedan, and Lee applied himself to calming the girl. "If what you told me over the phone is true, you have nothing to be afraid of, my dear. Have a cigarette to quiet your nerves."

She accepted a cigarette and Lee lighted it tenderly. He went on, for Luke's benefit: "She called me up to put a hypothetical question. If a man hired out his boat to another man and a crime was committed in the boat, would the owner be held responsible? And I answered: Certainly not, if the owner didn't know that his boat was required for a criminal purpose."

"They said they was going to fish," whimpered the girl.

"Certainly! Perfectly natural! Where is the boat now, dear?"

"My husband and his brother have gone to search for the body."

"And I hope they find it!" said Lee. "I reckon a little nest egg of two thousand wouldn't be unwelcome, eh?"

"You're sure they won't do anything to them?"

"Absolutely, darling. Not if they didn't know anything was wrong."

Lee's cajolery was having its effect; she quieted down. "Well, of course it looked kinda funny," she admitted, "so late at night and all, but there's so many funny people in the world, how can you tell?"

"Sure," said Lee, patting her hand. "What's your name, dear?"

"Duggan."

"Where do you live?"

"On the river at the foot of Mitchell Street."

"Tell us the whole story."

"Well, Sunday night these three men come to the door. Musta been after eleven and we was all in bed. I didn't see them; I only heard them talking. But I seen them in the morning. They was dark men, but not like negroes. My husband went down. They wanted to hire a motorboat to go fishing, they said. My husband thought it was funny, but they paid what he asked without any kick. They said they didn't want anybody to go with the boat, because one of them knew engines, and my husband didn't like that. But when they offered to put up a cash deposit for the safe return of the boat, what more could he say? So they started out and my husband come back to bed. He said the young fellow in the party knew engines all right. He didn't see any fishing tackle.

"We could hear the engine popping as we lay in bed. Seemed to be heading straight across for Perryville, which was funny. No fish over there. By and by she stopped and my husband laughed. 'Damned if I'm going over to them,' he said. 'I'm protected by the deposit.' But the engine never started again, and he couldn't go to sleep for thinking about it. After awhile he got up and looked out the window, and he could see a faint light on the water where they lay. Couldn't make nothing of it. So he got dressed and took a skiff and went over there. He rowed up near them real soft, and they never heard him. They wasn't having engine trouble. They had anchored the skiff on the flat. They had the lantern in the bottom of the boat and they was sitting there, playing cards. Paid twenty dollars for a boat to take it out and play cards in it! What do you know about that?"

"Sounds screwy," suggested Lee.

"Screwy is right, mister. My husband he rested on his oars for a long time, watching them. Towards morning they pulled up anchor, started the engine, and headed upstream. My husband followed them, but before he got to the railroad bridge he heard them coming back and he pulled out of their way."

"Did a train pass over the bridge about that time?"

"Yes, sir. Just before that, he said, there was a long train of sleeping-cars went over the bridge. They passed him coming back and headed straight out in the Bay. It was getting light, then, and he could follow them with his eyes for a long way. Straight across the Bay they was headed. He come back home. They brought the motorboat back about seven o'clock okay, and collected their deposit. My husband didn't say nothing to them. They had no fish. My husband couldn't make nothing of it at all until the newspapers gave him an inkling. As soon as he heard of the reward that was offered, him and his brother started out to look for the body. They have a notion of where it was taken."

"Fine!" said Lee. "I hope they bring home the bacon."

Mrs. Duggan giggled and put a hand over her mouth. She had now made up her mind that Mr. Mappin was a pleasant gentleman and a great card. Having got all they could out of her, they took her home in the car when the chauffeur returned. Lee said, in parting:

"Mr. Imbrie and I will have supper at Conley's, and will be hanging out in the bar until nine o'clock. If the men get home before that tell them where we are. After eleven o'clock they can get me by phone at Police Headquarters in Washington. I'll pay all expenses."

Lee and Luke loitered in Conley's after supper, but nothing material developed out of the talk there. Nine o'clock was their deadline.

BACK AT HEADQUARTERS IN WASHINGTON, shortly after eleven, they were getting ready for the night's expedition, when Havre de Grace called Lee. Young Mrs. Duggan's voice came over the wire, so excited she could scarcely articulate.

"Is this you, Mr. Mappin? They got him, Mr. Mappin! They got him!"

"Good!" said Lee.

"He was buried on the beach at Gum Island just about where they expected. All in his Ayrab dress and all. He wasn't spoiled at all, Mr. Mappin; looked just as natural! My husband didn't tell nobody what he found. He borrowed a truck and him and his brother started right for Washington with him. They'll be there one, two o'clock."

"Quick work!" said Lee. "I don't know what local laws and regu-
lations they may be breaking, but it will save time in the end."

"That's what I said, Mr. Mappin."

"I may not be here when they arrive, but I will leave full instructions for them."

"There won't be no trouble about the reward, Mr. Mappin?"

"None whatever, Mrs. Duggan. I promise you your husband
shall carry it home with him."

"I can scarcely believe it!"

CHAPTER FIFTEEN

A FEW MINUTES LATER Lee and the others set out for Southwest Washington in a big seven-passenger car. Major Walkley considered it *infra dig* to take part in the arrest of a mere accessory to murder, but Lee and Luke wanted to see the fun. A sergeant and three men were detailed, all in plain clothes except one, who was dressed as a French sailor under a concealing overcoat. Lee said, consulting his watch:

"If he comes by railroad we won't have to wait long. The only train he could get arrives at Union Station shortly before midnight. If he's not on it, I shall take a little nap, because it will take him two hours longer by car."

Concealing their automobile in an alley, they covered the last two blocks on foot. Water Street was completely deserted at this hour. There was a smell of river water and produce on the air. The designated pier was an open one, cluttered with trucks parked for the night. Several of the market boats that bring watermelons or soft crabs or fish were tied alongside. There was no light nor sign of life about them. On the other side of this arm of the river the lights of a park were reflected in the oily water.

There was a small shed near the shore end of the pier and three of the detectives took cover behind it. Lee and Luke sat down on the running-board of a truck opposite. Looking back over the floor of the truck, they commanded a view of the entrance to the pier. The fourth detective, having removed his overcoat and produced a sailor's cap from his pocket, was standing there with a cigarette.

They had been waiting less than half an hour when Luke saw a solitary figure approaching under the lights of empty Water Street. "By God! it worked!" he whispered, excitedly. The man crossed the street unhesitatingly, and spoke to the pretended sailor. The latter threw away his cigarette and led the way on to the pier. As they passed the shed the three detectives stepped out and the sergeant said, not loud, "Put up your hands!" At the same moment the seeming sailor turned around with a gun. The man's hands went up very promptly. When Lee and Luke joined the group he was saying, hoarsely:

"What's this mean? What's this mean?"

"You're under arrest," said the sergeant, crisply.

His hands were pulled down and handcuffs snapped around his wrists. The linked hands dropped against his thighs with a thud; his head hung down. Luke could imagine the hell of disappointment that filled him. The dream of a ship in the river, home, riches, power, women!—and the awakening to find himself caught in a police trap!

He was a hardy one; not another word escaped him until they were all in the car again. The prisoner rode on the back seat with a detective on either side; Lee and Luke on the two folding seats, and the other two men in front. Lee turned on the interior light to have a look at the prisoner. An unprepossessing specimen with a dark, brutalized face, looking older than his years. He spoke in the coarse voice of the New York tough, with only a trace of foreign accent.

"This is all a mistake, men. What do you think you want me for, anyhow?"

"Accessory to the murder of Sultan Ahmed bin Said," said Lee.

"I never saw the man, so help me. I don't know nothing about him."

"We know all about you," said Lee. "I wrote the letter which brought you down here. You took money from Prince Abu Daud to pick up the Sultan's body as it was thrown from a train on the Susquehanna bridge. You buried it on the beach at Gum Island. It has been recovered."

"You got me wrong, mister," he protested. "I don't know nothing about all this."

As they drove into the alley at Headquarters, Luke saw a small covered truck standing in front of them, and guessed that their man from Havre de Grace had that moment arrived. The driver of the truck was in the act of opening the rear doors. The lights of their car shone inside, and they saw a significant form lying on the floor, covered with a piece of sailcloth.

Lee, who was first out, said: "Bring the prisoner up here."

The fisherman was a stalwart young fellow, deeply bronzed by the sun. Lee said to him, indicating the prisoner, "Do you know this man?"

"Sure," said Duggan, coolly. "That's the chief guy that hired my boat Sunday night."

In obedience to a sign from Lee, Duggan climbed into his truck and threw back the sailcloth. There lay the remains of Ahmed bin Said, Sultan of Shihkar, with the damp robe of fine camel's wool clinging to his fat little body. Notwithstanding Mrs. Duggan's description, he was not a pretty sight. He was very dead. The hand-cuffed man took a look at him, caught his breath between clenched teeth, and quickly turned away.

"You win," he muttered. "I had no hand in croaking the guy, but I buried him for a price."

He was led into the building.

Lee took the young fisherman to the Superintendent's office, where he gave him a check and a few words of advice. "This happens to have turned out all right for you," he said; "but if you want to keep out of trouble, I suggest that you never hire out your boat again unless you or your brother go with it."

"You're right, Mister," said Duggan. "I learned my lesson."

Lee and Luke returned to the hotel for a much-needed sleep.

At nine o'clock next morning they were back in the Superintendent's office. Shihab al Zuri was there also. A certain peace had come into the secretary's harassed face since the police had told him the mystery was cleared up. An autopsy had already been performed, and the chemists reported that Sultan Ahmed had died from a dose of cyanide. Major Walkley was highly elated by the night's work.

"We now have a perfect case against Prince Abu Daud," he said. "It is supported at every point."

Lee took a pinch of snuff.

"In that case," said Shihab, "I ought to start my journey at once to lay a petition before the Khalif."

"There is one thing that remains to be done," said Lee. "Yussuf must identify Prince Abu Daud as the man who employed him to dispose of the body."

"Hm!" said the Major, stroking his chin. "That won't be too easy! . . . You're clever about such things, Mappin. What do you suggest?"

Lee said: "We might think up a scheme to decoy Abu Daud to a window of the French Embassy and have Yussuf outside. . . . First we must find out if Yussuf is prepared to come clean."

The swarthy Yussuf was presently led into the Superintendent's office. Unkempt, savage, a little bloated after his sleepless night, he looked the perfect desperado. His glittering black eyes furtively searched the faces of the men who confronted him.

"Yussuf," said Major Walkley, "who hired you to dispose of the body?"

"Prince Abu Daud," was the muttered reply.

"How much did he give you?"

"A grand. . . . I was promised another if he wasn't found in a week's time. Major," asked the man, hoarsely, "what do they give you for putting away a stiff?"

"That depends on the judge. You can make things easier for yourself by coming clean."

"I already told you the truth."

"If we confront you with Prince Abu Daud, are you willing to identify him as the man who hired you?"

"I never seen him, Major."

Everybody in the room was astonished by this reply—except, possibly, Lee. The Major's face turned red. "What do you mean?" he demanded.

"When I left Shihkar Abu Daud was only a child. I wouldn't know what he looks like now."

"Whom did you see in New York?"

"Nobody but a servant in the hotel."

"Explain the circumstances."

"Well, Prince Abu Daud got in touch with me at Hafiz' by telephone. He told me to come up to the Conradi-Windermere Hotel and send up the name of Tafas. So I went. . . ."

"At what time?" asked Lee.

"Shortly after three Sunday afternoon."

"Go on."

"In the lobby of the Sultan's apartment there was a telephone girl. I give her my name and she phoned it in. A servant came out . . ."

"Would you know him again?"

"Maybe. He was an Arab boy. He took me inside . . ."

"One minute," interrupted Lee. With a pencil he hastily sketched a floor plan on a sheet of paper. "This is the Sultan's apartment in the Conradi-Windermere. Can you follow the plan?"

"Sure."

"Then show me where the servant led you."

Yussuf took the pencil. "Through this door on the right of the lobby, Captain, down this inside corridor, and into the fourth door on the left."

"Good! That was Abu Daud's suite. Go on."

"It was an elegant parlor," said Yussuf. "The servant left me there alone. After a minute I heard a voice saying: 'Come over here.' It come from behind a door at the side that was open a couple inches. I went over there and sort of stumble against the door to get a look at him, but it was held on the other side. I think he was sitting against it. He said: 'Pull up a chair and sit down.' So I did, and he made his proposition. How I was to motor down to Havre de Grace, Maryland, and hire a motorboat and be waiting near the bridge to pick up the body when the train passed over. He told me to bury it because a body in the water always come to the surface, however you may weight it."

"Were you surprised at his proposition?"

"No," said Yussuf, coolly. "Naturally, Prince Abu Daud wanted to be Sultan. That's how it is in Eastern countries."

"Go on."

"He put his hand around the edge of the door to give me the first installment of the money. . . ." Lee said: "Describe the hand."

"A slim hand. It was covered with a black glove, Captain."

"Go on."

"I knew where to put my hands on a good car, and we was out of town before six-thirty. I had a couple of fellows to help me, but I won't tell you who they are."

"That's all right. We know them."

"You know what happened down at Havre de Grace. We was back in New York by one o'clock Monday, and we scattered. That's all."

Lee asked: "Would you recognize the voice of the man who made you the proposition if you heard it again?"

"I sure would, Captain. I mind it well."

Lee whispered to Major Walkley and the latter said to the warder who had brought Yussuf in, "Take him out into the corridor. I'll call you back directly."

Picking up the telephone, Lee called the French Embassy. After a moment or two he got M. Clément on the wire. "Good morning," said Lee. "So sorry to trouble you with my business again. Do you think that Prince Abu Daud would consent to answer a few harmless questions over the wire?" Lee waited. Putting a hand over the transmitter, he said to the others: "He said he'd find out." Presently Lee smiled broadly. "Good morning, Prince. It is very kind of Your Highness to consent to answer my questions." Lee winked at Major Walkley, and the swarthy Yussuf was quickly fetched back into the room. Lee was saying into the phone: "Prince, would you mind telling me in detail, how you spent last Sunday when you were staying at the Conradi-Windermere?"

As Abu Daud commenced a lengthy and no doubt lying recital over the wire, Lee silently handed the instrument to Yussuf, who applied the receiver to his ear. After listening for a moment, Yussuf shook his head. The Major's face fell.

"You're sure? You're sure?" he whispered, urgently.

Yussuf continued to shake his head. Lee took the instrument from him and hung up, leaving Abu Daud at the other end of the wire to make what he could of it.

"You are sure that is not the voice of the man who hired you?" demanded the Major.

"Not the same voice at all," said Yussuf, doggedly. "This voice," he pointed to the telephone, "was like a college boy's, womanish, putting on style." (They all recognized his description of young Abu Daud's finicky accents.) "The voice in the Conradi-Windermere was more like a man's."

Yussuf was taken away.

"Then our case against Abu Daud falls to the ground!" said the Major, bitterly disappointed.

"I feared there would be a catch in it somewhere," said Lee. "Abu Daud would never be so simple as to put himself in the power of this man."

Shihab al Zuri was terribly cast down. "Abu Daud is the guilty one just the same!" he insisted.

"I'm certain of it," said the Major. "He put up somebody else to talk to Yussuf in the hotel. But we can't hang it on him!"

"Well, we have other lines to follow up, gentlemen," said Lee, cheerfully.

CHAPTER SIXTEEN

WHILE THE SCENE WITH WAS GOING ON, Mrs. Morven again succeeded in escaping from her room at the Hotel James Madison, through bribing a bell boy. On this occasion the hotel management, anxious to stand well with the Superintendent of Police, intercepted her in the lobby and she was escorted back to her room. Major Walkley was furious when the incident was reported to him. He gave orders to have the two women brought to Police Headquarters and confined in separate detention rooms.

Later, Lee Mappin and Luke were with the Major when his phone rang. His face turned grim as he listened. Hanging up, he said, sternly, to Luke:

"Miss Morven has asked if she may be permitted to see you."

Luke turned hot and then cold again. "I am in your hands, sir," he said, meeting the Major's glance squarely.

"Hm!" grunted the Major, boring him through and through. "Answer me one question: Do you know anything about the activities of these ladies that I don't know?"

"Not a thing, sir."

"You believe them innocent?"

"As to the girl I would stake my life, sir."

"And the old woman?"

Luke shrugged.

"Well, you're honest about it," said the Major. "Go and talk to the girl, and see if you can't persuade her, and through her her mother, to act in such a manner that I won't be forced to treat them as criminals."

A wardress admitted Luke to the room where Diana was confined. It was not like the ordinary prison cell; there was a neat bed, a bureau, washbasin; but the heavy bars outside the window stood as a perpetual reminder that it was a cell. The wardress followed Luke in and remained standing close to the door. She was a humane woman; she did not watch them too closely, nor try to hear all they said.

Luke, forgetting everything, took Diana in his arms. For a moment or two her guarded face softened and her eyes looked piteously into his. "Luke, my dear!"

"O God! this is driving me crazy!" he whispered.

She braced herself, smiling remotely. "If I can stand it, you can."

"Oh, Di! I love you so!"

"You must cure yourself of me!"

All his doubts of her recurred to him. He held her away from him, searching her face. She turned aside her eyes, still smiling painfully. At that moment he could not have told whether he most loved or hated her. "Di, what are you hiding from me?" he groaned.

"Nothing guilty, Luke."

"Why hide anything?"

She didn't answer. They sat down on the edge of her cot. Luke heard a dull pounding on the wall behind him. Diana said, with an embarrassed laugh:

"That's mother trying to establish communications."

Luke flung an arm around her, but she slipped out of it. "Not before this woman," she whispered. And, after a moment, "Do you think I'm a murderess, Luke?"

"No!"

"Do you think my mother is?"

"I don't know."

"She is not," Diana whispered, earnestly. "She has done nothing wrong. Oh, you must believe that! That's why I sent for you. We must have one friend who believes in us."

"She may be deceiving you," said Luke.

"No. She couldn't. I know her too well. She's a foolish woman, but not wicked. I can't always prevent her from acting foolishly. Do you blame me for standing by her?"

"Yes, if she's acting foolishly."

"Maybe a man can feel that way, but I can't."

"To the rest of us her actions appear worse than foolish," Luke said, sullenly.

Diana looked down at her hands. "If you feel like that you'd better go. I stand by my mother."

"Oh, Di, you have me on the rack," he groaned. "You mustn't hold me to account for all I say."

"Do you think this is easy for me?" she whispered.

"I can't believe in your mother while she acts in such a shifty manner."

"Go," said Diana, hopelessly. "What difference does it make? You and I were fated from the start. However this may turn out, it will leave ugly scars. Go away and forget me. I'm spoiled for you."

"I don't admit that," said Luke, scowling.

"Please go," she begged. "We're only torturing each other."

"Kiss me before I go."

She shrank away. "Not before this woman! Besides, what's the use? Kisses can't change our fate. Only make it harder."

He got possession of one of her hands. "Let me kiss you," he insisted. "It doesn't bind you to anything. It's my pledge that whatever may happen I shall always think of you as fine and true!"

"Oh, well," she said, with misty eyes, "for that I'll kiss you."

They kissed and Luke made his way out.

In the corridor he heard Mrs. Morven beating frantically on her door. "Why don't you see what she wants?" he said to the wardress.

When the door was open Luke kept out of sight. Mrs. Morven said, breathlessly: "Mr. Imbrie? Mr. Imbrie? Has he gone? Oh, please call him back, dearie, and I'll pray for you. I *must* see him! You can watch us and listen to us."

Luke, as the associate of the famous Amos Lee Mappin, who was working hand in glove with the Major of Police, enjoyed great consideration around Headquarters, and the wardress wasn't sure how to act. She looked at Luke.

Luke's lips shaped the words, "Why not?"

The wardress saw no reason why, if he was permitted to see one prisoner, he shouldn't see the other. "Mr. Imbrie's here," she said to Mrs. Morven, and Luke stepped forward.

"Thank God!" said Mrs. Morven. Seizing Luke's hand, she drew him into the room. As before, the wardress followed, and remained standing with her back against the door. She watched them, but when they lowered their voices she couldn't hear what was said.

The room was just like that next door. Mrs. Morven with her hair touched up and waved, her cheeks rouged, wearing a smart dress and hat from Paris, was an incongruous object there. Her made-up eyes were harassed and bloodshot. She drew Luke to her bed at the other end of the room, and made him sit beside her.

"Luke, my dear!" she murmured, fondling his hand, "how good you are to look at! So big and strong and wholesome!"

Luke disliked her most when she took this fawning tone. He submitted with an ill grace to having his hand held.

"Tell me," she said, "how much do you love my Diana?"

Luke scowled. "I can't make vows and protestations. You'll have to take it on faith."

"Surely! Surely!" she murmured. "How like a manly man! Hates to speak of his feelings! . . . Do you want to marry her?"

"I do."

"At first I was against it. But circumstances alter cases. I think she cares for you, too. She's so reserved! I wanted to tell you that after we get out of this hideous mess I won't put any further obstacles in the way. My child's happiness comes first!"

Luke looked at her in astonishment. It was impossible to hate her so much when she talked like this, but he was still suspicious. What is she getting at? was the question in his mind.

"You are our only friend!" she murmured.

"I thought you had many friends in Washington."

"Not at a time like this!"

"Well, people are like that when you get in a jam."

"You'll stand by Diana, Luke?"

"Is it necessary to ask it?"

"Through thick and thin?"

"Sure!"

Her expression changed. She darted a swift glance through her lashes at the wardress, and sat a little back so that she was partly hidden behind Luke. "Listen," she said, sinking her voice to a whisper. "I'm going to say to you: 'Luke, do you think I'm guilty?' You are to say: 'No!' loudly, and I'll say, 'Give me your hand on it!' When we clasp hands I'm going to pass something to you. Mind you don't drop it!"

Before Luke could collect his wits, she was putting it into effect. "Luke, do you think I'm guilty?" "No!" "Give me your hand on it!" He felt a small hard object pressed against his palm and closed on it.

"What's this?" he whispered.

"Key to the lock-box." She giggled nervously. "Every time they searched me I had to hide it in my mouth."

Luke turned cold. "What lock-box?"

"You know; one of those places where you drop a dime in the slot when you want to check anything. While Diana waited for me in the Hotel Pilgrim Monday morning, I went to the bus terminal and put it in a lock-box. It's only good for twenty-four hours. After that they open the boxes. That's what I went out for yesterday, to change it to a box somewhere else and pay again. This morning they stopped me from going out. You must find another hiding-place immediately, or it will be found."

"What will be found?" he asked, woodenly.

"The bag with the jewels, of course."

Luke was appalled. All was confusion in his mind.

For the moment the power to act was paralyzed. "The number of the box is on the key," she was whispering. "The box is in . . ."

"Don't tell me where it is!" he whispered, swiftly.

She stared at him. "What's the matter with you?"

"I can't help you out in this."

Mrs. Morven turned pale under her rouge. "You must! You must! There is nobody else I can ask. If the police find it, all the agony I have suffered these last two days will be for nothing!"

"Does Diana know about it?"

"She knows where the bag was put the first day."

"Does she know that you are asking me to get it?"

"No," said Mrs. Morven sullenly.

Luke felt a little better. He was beginning to get his grip. "I can't do it," he said.

"Why not?"

"Don't let's go into that. You wouldn't understand."

"You've *got* to do it! This is Diana's wedding portion! If it's lost you have nothing. It's your only hope of getting married."

Pain like a stab wound struck through Luke, but his mind was made up now. "Good God! Diana and I couldn't start that way!"

"You don't love her then!"

"Don't take that line!" he warned her. "Besides," he went on, doggedly, "we couldn't get away with it. And how foolish we would look when we were caught with the goods!"

"We could! We could!" she insisted. "I've got away with it for two days, locked up and watched as I was. You're free; nobody suspects you. You could get the bag and put it where it would never be found!"

"I'll have nothing to do with it," said Luke.

"You're afraid!" she sneered. "A real man would dare more than that for the woman he loved!"

Luke looked at her with purest hatred. "I wish you were a man," he muttered.

"You wouldn't be running any risk at all," she urged. "You're not supposed to know what the bag contains . . ."

"Cut it out," said Luke, harshly. . . . "Look! I'm dropping the key on the bed between us. You'd better put your hand over it if you don't want the woman to see."

Mrs. Morven covered it. Luke left her abruptly. She broke into a hard, dry sobbing, more rage than grief. The wardress was startled. She looked questioningly from one to another, wondering if she'd done wrong to admit Luke.

"What's the matter with her?" she asked, outside.

Luke did not answer. He strode through the corridors with a blackness in his mind. Topping all, was the hideous suspicion that Diana had sent for him for the purpose of working on him to prepare him for her mother's proposition. His impulse was to march out of the building and wash his hands of the case forever. However, that would instantly have aroused suspicion, and he knew that Lee would be able to worm it out of him. He was obliged to return to the Superintendent's office to see it through.

He found Lee Mappin and the Major excitedly discussing a new development in the situation—that is, the Major was excited. They were so intent upon it, neither thought to ask Luke if he had learned anything, and so for the moment he was spared a direct lie. After listening for a moment or two he made out that Sir Bertram Maunsell, as a countermove to the French Embassy, had made a demand on Major Walkley for the release of Mrs. and Miss Morven, who, he said, were being deprived of their liberty without due process of law. Major Walkley was angry.

"These women are not privileged characters. British or not, they are subject to our laws!"

"Surely," said Lee, soothingly.

"I won't let them go! I can procure warrants for their arrest."

"In that case," Lee pointed out, "the Ambassador will instruct his attorney to apply for writs of habeas corpus."

"He means to take them into the Embassy where I can't touch them! The whole case will crumble!"

"It is very intriguing," said Lee. "I have never been up against this situation."

"That's all very well for you," grumbled the Major. "You have no responsibility. It's my job to solve this case. The eyes of the world are upon me

"Surely!" said Lee. "Let's consider where we stand. What concrete evidence have we against these women?"

"They were the last to see the Sultan."

"That sounds bad, but it's not evidence."

"Mrs. Morven brought him the whisky."

"The original seal was on the bottle when she handed it to him."

"Two negro red-caps have testified that they removed five valises from the private car. They have only four of their own. The fifth one contained Sultan Ahmed's jewels."

"Presumably," amended Lee.

Luke listened, tormented by his guilty secret. He did not particularly mind lying to the Major, but it hurt him to deceive his friend. On the other hand, it was impossible for him to speak out and condemn the women. I'm no policeman, he told himself; let them find it out. He moved his chair a little to the rear of Lee's so that Lee could not see his face without turning squarely around.

"Major, such evidence wouldn't stand up at a habeas corpus hearing, nor anywhere else," Lee went on. "The taxicab driver doesn't bear out the redcaps, and neither do the boys at the Hotel Pilgrim. The woman at the White Door Hotel says that the Morvens had only four valises when they arrived there."

"What would you advise me to do, then?" growled the Major.

"Since it seems likely that you'll be forced to release them in the end, I suggest that you do it at once with a gesture of magnanimity. Thus we'll keep in the good graces of the Ambassador."

"I'll never be able to lay hands on them again."

"Oh, I don't know. Their case is not the same as that of Abu Daud. The possession of a port on the Persian Gulf does not depend on the Morvens."

"It goes against the grain!" muttered the Major.

"Look," said Lee. "Your job, as you said, is to solve the crime. If you do that and are prevented from apprehending the criminals, nobody could blame you."

"You wish to see these women escape, then?"

"Not at all," said Lee, coolly. "I dislike to see the ends of justice defeated." He took a small pinch of snuff. "Whether it's poetic justice or the human sort."

They were still discussing the question when an aide entered to report that the taxicab driver who had driven the Morvens from the Hotel Pilgrim to the White Door Hotel on Monday morning had been found and was waiting outside.

"Ha!" cried the Major. "Maybe he can supply confirmation of the women's guilt. Bring him in!"

It was a youthful chauffeur, shabbily dressed, but with an incorrigible grin and a bright eye. Evidently he had a good conscience because he was not in the least abashed at facing the Superintendent of Police. His name, address, license number, and so on were taken down, and a question or two established that he was the man wanted. Two more questions disposed of him.

"How many valises did these ladies carry from the Hotel Pilgrim to the White Door Hotel?"

"Four, sir. There was no doorman at the White Door and I carried them in myself. Two trips."

"Did you stop anywhere between the Pilgrim and the White Door?"

"No, sir. The lady she give me the address when she got in, and I took them straight there."

"All right. That's all, then."

"Wait a minute," said Lee. "How much time has this cost you from your work?"

"About an hour, sir."

Lee handed him a dollar. "Take this to make up for it."

The chauffeur beamed. "Thank you, sir. There's not many would think of that."

When he had gone, Major Walkley reached for the phone. "I'll do what you recommend," he said, heavily.

Lee said: "Exact a promise from His Excellency to give the ladies up if additional evidence against them is forthcoming."

The Major presently got Sir Bertram on the wire. He said: "Since you make a point of it, Sir Bertram, it will give me pleasure to release the two ladies in your custody."

Luke could hear Sir Bertram's voice ringing over the wire: "Splendid! I can't tell you how much obliged I am to you for raising no difficulties, Major Walkley."

"May I make a condition?"

"What's that?"

"That you will agree to surrender them, should a real case develop against them."

"Certainly, Major. I have no wish to obstruct your laws. . . . I'll come myself to fetch them."

"They will be waiting in my office for you, Sir Bertram."

As he hung up, Luke thought, bitterly: So the old woman gets away with her loot! There's no justice! He felt as guilty as hell, but he could not speak out. He could not put Diana behind the bars.

The two ladies were presently conducted into the Superintendent's office. Diana bowed gravely to Luke and did not look at him again. Mrs. Morven was in a great state of excitement. To Luke she was as transparent as window glass. She was simmering with triumph, but dared not make too great a show of it for fear of angering Luke. After all, she was in his power.

Almost immediately afterwards Sir Bertram came; tall, handsome and fit, the pattern of a high-born Englishman. Notwithstanding his self-possession, his eyes dwelt on Diana with a kind of stricken look. He was hard hit. All the old woman's dreams are coming true, thought Luke. An Ambassador is an improvement on a kept Sultan. Diana smiled at Sir Bertram and the cup of Luke's bitterness slopped over. Well, what could you expect? he asked himself.

There was some polite conversation signifying nothing. Lee, in particular, was exerting himself to be agreeable. Luke took no part in it. Once he caught Lee glancing at him curiously and thought: I'll have to submit to a cross-examination later. He hardened. Well, he'll get nothing out of me. I'll have to quarrel with him.

Before Sir Bertram left with the two ladies, Luke contrived to speak once with Diana. "You can smile at an Ambassador," he murmured.

She answered, low-voiced, without looking at him, "I can play a part with all men . . . but you."

CHAPTER SEVENTEEN

LEE WISHED TO CONSULT with Shihab al Zuri, and Luke accompanied him back to the James Madison. Lee was thoughtful during the ride, and made no reference to what had happened. Luke thought, He's waiting until he gets me alone in his room. I won't go there.

They found Shihab al Zuri in his room with little Cheragh Ali in attendance. Neither took the slightest interest in their surroundings. They had scarcely been out of the hotel. When his master's visitors settled themselves, Cheragh Ali tip-toed out of the room.

Lee told Shihab what had happened and the secretary expressed satisfaction. He said: "It would be most unjust that those ladies should suffer while the real criminal goes free."

"Shihab," said Lee, "one of the reports from New York speaks of a secret organization called the Scimitars, which meets in John Hafiz' place. Their meetings are carefully guarded and the stool pigeons could learn nothing. Do you know anything about them?"

"Surely," said Shihab. "The Scimitars are a political organization with branches wherever there are enough Arabs to make a unit."

"What is the object of the organization?"

Shihab shrugged deprecatingly. "Arabia for the Arabs!"

"Not unreasonable," said Lee, dryly. "Are you in sympathy?"

"In my heart, yes," said Shihab. "How should I not be? But politically I am unalterably opposed to them. Arab independence is an empty dream. And any action the Scimitars may take can only end in useless bloodshed."

153

"Very sensible of you," said Lee. "I asked you about the Scimitars because it has occurred to me that the extra servants at the Conradi-Windermere who were supposed to have been furnished by the hotel may in fact have come from this organization. It was two of these supposed servants, you remember, who attacked Mr. Imbrie."

Shihab considered. "It is possible," he said. "Abu Daud courts this element. He may have won them over by lying promises. Of course, if he came to power he would repudiate them. He's in the pay of the French."

"In that case, wouldn't he stand a good chance of being assassinated?"

"The Sultan is always in danger of assassination," said Shihab. "Abu Daud would go to Paris or London to live, and leave his masters to rule in Shihkar."

Luke no longer had any interest in Shihkar. Such was the urgency of his own thoughts that it was intolerable to sit there and listen to them talking politics. He excused himself and left the room. He went down in the elevator and drifted out of the hotel. He plodded along one street and another with his head down, oblivious to his surroundings.

Luke was dragged two ways. Prudence urged him to go back to his job in New York and forget the whole sorry business. Better take the next train without seeing Lee again. He could write to Lee. Lee wouldn't believe his excuses, but in that way he could avoid an ugly face-to-face quarrel.

Such was the plain course of wisdom, but Luke was unable to take it. He believed that all was over between him and Diana, but he could not leave the place where she was. Within a day or two it was certain to be discovered that Mrs. Morven had the Sultan's jewels, and they would both be arrested. Sir Bertram's infatuation for Diana would hardly be proof against a disclosure of that sort. An Ambassador had to think of his career. Diana would need a friend, and Luke had to be there.

He found himself in a park alongside the Potomac, and dropped on a bench facing the wide, sunny river. It was a perfect summer's day with a cool breeze from the south; the scene was one of great beauty. Many people were strolling up and down in their best clothes, with comfortable relaxed smiles on their faces. In Washington every day has the effect of a holiday because of the number of sightseers in town. Luke had eyes for none of it. His painful thoughts were going round and round in a circle without arriving anywhere.

He was brought to himself by the sound of a pitiful little sniff beside him. He looked and saw that a pretty young girl was sharing his bench. He had not noticed her coming. The tears kept welling up in her eyes and she was dabbing at them with a wisp of a handkerchief, in the absurd manner of a woman who is trying to preserve her make-up. Another soul in trouble. Luke's sympathy went out to her with a rush. Besides, she was *very* pretty.

"What's the matter?" he asked, involuntarily.

She started, and drew away from him with an affronted air.

"I wasn't trying to be fresh," said Luke. "I'm up against it myself. We're in the same boat."

She studied him dubiously through her long, curled lashes. Her face was piquant rather than regularly beautiful; full, dark eyes, tip-tilted nose and most kissable lips. "Do you spik Franch?" she asked.

"Not so you could notice it."

"My Angleys, she is no good."

"I get it all right."

There was a silence. Luke looked at her with pleasure. Her clothes were not expensive but they were put on in a manner that distinguished her from every other woman in the park. That was the French of it. A comical little hat at a jaunty angle with a silly veil to the end of her nose. Exactly right. "It's too pretty a day to be crying," said Luke.

The tears welled up afresh. She caught her breath. "I am unhappy," she said like a child.

"Well, spill it."

"Spill it? I don't know that."

Luke grinned. "I mean let it come out; tell me about it. Did your boy friend wash out on you?"

"Wash out?"

"Did he leave you in the lurch? Damn poor taste, if you ask me."

"He isn't a boy," she said; "he's forty-two."

"Too old for you."

"He didn't leave me. I left him. He's no good."

"Same here," said Luke. "I knew a girl who was as beautiful as an angel and she's a crook—or as good as. Shake!"

He extended his hand and she laid her hand within it, with an appealing glance in his face as if to beg him not to take advantage of her. Luke thought her adorable. He didn't realize what a dangerous emotional state he was in; longing for comfort and forgetfulness. He retained her hand. She pulled at it timidly. He released it.

"Tell me about it," he said.

The handkerchief came into play again. It all came out in cascades of broken English. The gist of it was: "I met him in Paris last year. He was a steady, earnest man. He said he had a good business in Washington, epicerie, what you say? grocery. He ask me to marry, and I trust him, I say yes. So he come back to America and I stay in Paris to make ready. I must wait for the quota. At last I come and I find out he has no grocery. He stand behind the counter. He has no home for me. He has nothing. So I leave him."

"You didn't marry him?"

She wrinkled her fetching nose. "Mon Dieu, no! He is old! he is *fou!* I hate him!"

"You're well out of it," said Luke.

The tears welled up. "I don't know what to do. I haven't sufficient money to pay passage back to France. I have no friend in Washington."

Luke patted her hand. "Don't worry," he said; "we'll talk it over. Meanwhile it's lovely weather. I need a friend, too."

She showed him her passport from which he learned that her name was Clèlie de Lisser. Clèlie! a cute name; it rippled pleasantly on the tongue. They laughed together at the libelous photograph of her pasted in the passport. Once the first strangeness was past, she was as confiding as a nice child. She told him all about her father, who was an estate agent in a small way in the suburb of Passy, and about her own work as a cashier in one of the establishments Duval. In spite of her rather gay appearance, it seemed that she had led a quiet and discreet life in Paris.

"Have you been to the French consul?" asked Luke.

"But no! He would cable to my father. And my father is so poor! I want to find work here."

"Well, we'll see what we can do," said Luke.

She was very sympathetic in her turn, and he found himself telling her about his troubles. He named no names and gave no precise particulars; it was a relief to unburden himself a little.

"I know her type," murmured Clèlie. "English. Beautiful and so cold!" This was accompanied by a speaking glance which assured him that she was not cold.

The time passed quickly, and he was astonished to discover presently that it was one o'clock. "Let's eat," he said.

They taxied to a restaurant on Pennsylvania Avenue. The business of eating together is a great aid to intimacy. Under the table Luke embraced Clèlie's little feet between his own, and that seemed to be all right with her. Occasionally she gave his hand a fleeting caress and he was filled with a kind of deceitful happiness. Her English seemed to improve as time passed. She had a talent for mimicry, and kept him laughing with her imitations of the grocer's clerk.

Afterwards they went to a picture theater. In the dark, Luke drew Clèlie's arm through his, and held her hand just like the surrounding couples. When they tired of the show they sauntered out into the street and walked along now frankly arm-in-arm, looking in the shop windows with much foolish talk and laughter. Dance music coming through open windows drew them like a magnet into the cocktail lounge of a big hotel. Clèlie danced divinely, yielding herself without reserve, and Luke for the moment forgot the ache inside him.

"You have cured my pain!" he whispered.

Between dances they sat at a little table and drank absinthes frappée, and grew even more light-hearted and expansive; leaning towards each other until their noses all but touched, losing themselves in each other's eyes. They hardly required to talk any more, but only to look. Enchanting forgetfulness!

"Your eyes are gray," murmured Clèlie; "your nose is big; your teeth are strong and white. Like a wolf! Brrh! I shiver!"

"I could eat you up," said Luke. "But you'd like it."

"*Mais oui!*" she murmured, with a provoking grin. He pressed her feet together under the table.

"Life is so strange!" she said at another time. "If I had not sat down on that particular bench we would never have had this!"

"The sweetest things always come by accident," said Luke.

"And must not be pushed too far," she added. "Today we meet; tomorrow we part."

"Don't speak of tomorrow!" he protested. "Tomorrow is hell! Let tonight be heaven!"

"Shall we dance?"

Dinner without leaving the hotel; another show, and back to the hotel for more dancing. The cocktail lounge was now called the supper-room. By this time they felt as if their identities had merged. They danced like a single body. Talk had become entirely superfluous.

It was two o'clock when the orchestra put up their instruments. Clèlie's face fell like a little girl's. Out in the cool air of the street she appeared suddenly to come to herself.

"*Mon Dieu!*" she murmured, horror-stricken. "I forget I live so far! It is called Lincoln Heights. I go on the tramway. Maybe the cars don't run so late."

"How did you get out so far!" asked Luke.

"It is a French family. They give me a room."

"I'll get a taxi," said Luke.

Clèlie's eyes widened. "In a taxi . . . alone . . . so late. . . . I am afraid!" she faltered.

"I'm going with you, baby."

"No! It is too far."

"The farther the better!" said the enamored Luke.

She gave the driver an address which meant nothing to Luke, and it didn't register on his mind. When they started he took her in his arms; she lifted the kissable lips and he asked for nothing more. Away back in his mind he knew there was going to be an unpleasant awakening by-and-by, but he only kissed her the more. Blessed, blessed forgetfulness!

Of course he took no notice of the passage of time. Occasionally, stirred by curiosity, he turned his head to look out of the window, but Clèlie always drew his face around to kiss him again, and he forgot. She was a past mistress in the art of kissing, but he was too far gone to put two and two together.

Finally he did notice that the street lights were now much further apart. The cab turned out of the concrete into a rough and bumpy road; presently stopped. The driver said:

"This is your number, miss."

They got out. It was a road, as yet unpaved, in a brand-new subdivision. On each side were little wooden houses in various stages of construction. The one in front of them seemed scarcely out of the hands of the builder.

"Is this the right place?" asked the surprised Luke.

"Yes," said Clèlie, "the family have just move' in."

Luke had a warning of danger then, as if his guardian angel's wings had brushed him. But Clèlie leaned against him and he disregarded it. He hesitated about paying the taxi driver; was she going to ask him in? She whispered:

"You come in, Luke?"

"Is it all right?" he asked, breathless with pleasure.

"Yes. We make no noise. Nobody know."

He felt certain compunctions, but, like a man, thought: Well, that's up to her, and banished them. He paid the driver and the cab turned around and went back to town. The girl led him up the walk to the little house. All the windows were dark. They tip-toed up the steps. Clèlie pulled down his head and whispered, "Quiet as two little mouses!" She kissed his neck and opened the door with a key. She drew him in, and closed the door without a sound. As she drew him on, Luke stumbled loudly on the bottom step of the stairs. A cold fear struck through him—but Clèlie laughed. Women have their own kind of courage, he thought.

The interior was as black as black velvet. There was a strong smell of plaster and varnish on the air. Clèlie drew him on up. Once Luke got his hand on the stair rail he could follow without stumbling. At the top she whispered again, "It's the front room." They passed along the landing. She opened a door and, drawing him into a dark room, closed it softly. "Let go my hand while I find the light," she whispered.

He released her and presently the lights flared on. Luke found himself in a perfectly bare room, a floor and four walls. Clèlie, as swift as a snake, darted through a door at the back and pulled it after her. Luke was stunned with astonishment. Before he could collect himself, before he could make a move, something thick and soft and all-enveloping was thrown over his head from behind and pulled tight. Several men flung themselves on him, bearing him to the floor.

Luke, maddened with rage, put forth every ounce of his strength. Half suffocated by the quilt that obstructed his mouth and his nostrils, he could distinguish three assailants; one sitting on his legs; another lying across his middle whose hands were feeling for his throat; a third trying to hold his hands. Luke could throw them off one at a time, but there were always two others. The struggle was too violent for the human frame to endure very long. Suddenly they all fell still, Luke lying under the three men, all panting hoarsely.

During this momentary lull Luke heard a door close downstairs, and guessed that Clèlie had left the house. Her work was done. Filled with the inexpressible bitterness of betrayal, he heaved and threw all the men off him at once. He clawed at the thing over his head, and pulled it partly off before they seized him again. The empty room was brightly lighted. He recognized the two young Arabs, Farraj and Haroun, Abu Daud's servants. There was some satisfaction in learning who his real enemy was. The third man was a hired American thug, a human gorilla, with a face distorted by savagery. This one had a gun.

They pulled the quilt over his head again. Luckily for Luke, there was a lack of team-work amongst them; the Arabs were jabbering in their own tongue, while the American shouted: "Hold his arms! Hold his legs! And I'll let him have it in the belly!" He had drawn away a little, and Luke knew what to expect. With a heartbreaking effort he got to his feet, the two Arabs hanging on him. The quilt fell away from his eyes, and he saw the hired thug a couple of yards away, holding his gun ready.

"Let go of him!" the man yelled. "I'll get him!"

The instant the two released him, Luke dropped, and the bullet passed harmlessly over him. He had spotted the light switch; he leaped and pressed it as the man fired again. The bullet thudded into the plaster alongside Luke's head. Turning, he sprang for the door into the hall. The two Arabs immediately fastened on his back, but Luke succeeded in getting the door open, and the three of them fell out on the landing.

The American thug, cursing horribly, switched on the room lights again, and flung himself on the struggling mass outside the door. Clubbing his gun, he struck viciously at the spot where he thought Luke's head was, but in the mêlée most of his blows went wild. More than once Luke was struck, but not in a vital place. Judging from their yelps of pain, the American hit his partners as often as Luke. Meanwhile Luke was dragging himself inch by inch towards, the head of the stairs.

"Get off him! Get off him!" yelled the American voice. "He can't escape me!"

As the Arabs rose up, Luke clung to them as desperately as they had at first fastened on him. The American charged in to separate them. All four men fell against the light rail along the landing. It cracked and gave and they tottered over the edge, falling three or four feet to the stairs below. Cursing and clutching at each other, they slipped and bumped down to the bottom.

Luke fell free of the others. A faint light came in from the street. Scrambling to his feet, he ran through an archway, into the front room; through another archway to the back. He fell against a swing door which let him into the kitchen. They were close at his heels.

There was a stepladder in the kitchen. He slung it behind him, and made back for the front of the house through the hall. Charging through the swing door, his pursuers crashed over the ladder and he gained a precious five seconds.

He got the front door open. As he went through it a shot crashed behind him, and a red-hot pain seared his thigh. He fell to the porch floor and rolled down the steps. He did not stop there, but scrambled around the corner of the house and ran to the rear, thinking they would not expect him to go that way. He heard them come out and pause as if uncertain. Darting across a narrow open space, he got cover behind the house next door, which was still under construction. Warm blood was trickling down his leg and filling his shoe.

Taking a slant around the corner of the house, he saw the flash of an electric torch. They were coming. It was useless to try to run. He dropped through an open cellar window of the unfinished house and watched. The light appeared; they were flashing it around the piles of building materials. He dropped, crouching against the cellar wall. Presently they cast the light through the window and he gave himself up for lost. The white circle of light searched the cellar, but the rays did not quite reach down to where he lay pressed against the wall. They moved away and he breathed again.

He took the time to undress partly and tie his handkerchief as tightly as he could around his thigh. As far as he could judge in the dark, it was only a flesh wound; the blood was not spurting. He drew himself painfully back through the window. He saw the reflection of the light a couple of houses beyond, in the direction of the main highway. Apparently no other house on this new road was occupied. No light showed anywhere, and there was no sound to suggest that anybody had been awakened by the shots.

As the light was still moving from him, he followed it. A few hundred yards away on the highway, the lights of passing cars still occasionally flashed by. He saw the electric torch pass between the houses in the direction of the street, and he followed to see where they went. The beam of light crossed the street and searched, like something alive, around the unfinished houses over there. Luke crawled back to the rear of the houses on his side, and made his way as quickly as he could towards the highway.

In the shadow of one of the little houses he almost fell over one of the Arabs before he saw him. The man raised a cry, "Here he is!" and made a grab at Luke. Luke hauled off and struck him in the face. That blow was nerved by all a young man's love of life, and the Arab went down without a sound. Luke ran for his life then, clenching his teeth to master the pain. The other two men ran for the spot where the cry was raised, and Luke cut through between two houses for the sidewalk where he could run faster. Under the violent exertion, his wound started bleeding fast.

He reached the corner of the highway. A car was approaching at a high rate of speed, heading for Washington. With a thankful heart Luke recognized it for a taxi by the lights on the roof. He ran out in the street, signaling it. No great matter if he were run down, for he was a dead man anyhow unless it picked him up. The brakes screamed and the taxi slid to a stop. As Luke opened the door he saw two of his assailants coming at a run, the third following. The American thug shouted:

"Stop, driver! You've got a robber there!"

"Step on it, fellow!" said Luke grimly, "or we're both dead men

The driver lost no time in making up his mind. The car jerked into motion, and the three men were left standing on the corner. Above the noise of the engine Luke could hear the American's wild cursing, but he did not shoot. When Luke realized that he was safe, his head spun around. He clung desperately to consciousness. Can't pass out here, he told himself.

"Take me to the Hotel James Madison," he muttered to the driver.

"Okay," was the cheerful answer. "How did you get into a jam way out here, mister?"

"A woman brought me," said Luke, grimly. "It's the kind of a story a man doesn't like to tell on himself."

"I get you," said the driver, sympathetically.

"They fool the best of us, mister. . . . Did they roll you?"

"No," said Luke, "I've got my money."

"You were lucky."

"What was the name of that street where you picked me up?"

"I couldn't tell you, mister. I don't come out as far as this twice in a year."

When they drew up in front of the hotel, Luke gave the driver a five-dollar bill in addition to his fare. "You've earned it," he said, grimly. "Better give me your number in case I need a witness. Write it down for me. Don't say anything about this unless you hear from me."

"Okay, mister."

"You'll have to have your cushions cleaned before you take another fare. . . . I seem to have left . . . considerable blood behind me."

"For God's sake, mister! Why'n't you tell me they got you?" He started to scramble out of his seat. "I'll help you in."

"No!" said Luke. "I don't want to make a sensational entrance. I can navigate all right."

The lobby of the hotel was deserted and dark. To Luke the lighted desk seemed half a mile away. His left foot squelched in his shoe with every step and he realized that he must be leaving a bloody trail behind him. The lofty hall was rocking from side to side like a ship at sea. Reaching the desk at last, he clutched at the counter.

"Key to 1103, please," he muttered.

"My God, mister, what's the matter?" gasped the night clerk.

Luke's knees gave under him. "Notify Mr. Mappin," he faltered. The floor came up slowly to meet him and that was all he knew.

CHAPTER EIGHTEEN

WHEN LUKE CAME TO HIMSELF he was lying on the bed in his own room. A young doctor was bending over him, dressing his wound. It hurt like Sam Hill and Luke let out a yelp of pain.

"It's nothing at all," said the doctor, in the cool way that doctors have; "a mere flesh wound."

"Is that so," said Luke. "I wish you had a flesh wound so I could pour iodine into it."

The doctor laughed and started bandaging.

Behind him Luke saw Lee Mappin with his rotund little figure wrapped in a gay blue dressing-gown. "Feel all right now?" he asked.

"Sure," growled Luke.

"What did you do to the man who shot you?" asked Lee, blandly.

"Nothing."

"Dear me, how disappointing! . . . I ask because the doctor is entitled to know if this is a case which ought to be reported to the police."

"It was an entirely unprovoked attack," said Luke. "I didn't retaliate."

"Are you satisfied, Doctor?" asked Lee.

"I feel that I am safe in your hands, Mr. Mappin," said the doctor. "You know best what ought to be done."

"Let me have a talk with my young friend first."

"You know where to find me if you want me."

Lee ushered him to the door. "Can I give the patient a drink?" he asked.

"Certainly. Unless there is an infection he'll be up and around in a day or two."

Returning to the bed, Lee poured Luke a shot of whisky which the young man thankfully swallowed. Lee gripped Luke's shoulder. Behind the polished glasses his eyes were shining with affection. "Bless my soul! it gave me a nasty turn when I found you weltering in your blood down in the lobby. Do you feel able to tell me about it now?"

"Sure," growled Luke. "You've got to know." However, he hesitated; it was hard to begin.

"Who shot you?" asked Lee.

"I was shot at the order of Abu Daud."

"How do you know?"

"Three men attacked me. The gun was held by a local bad man. The other two were Haroun and Farraj, Abu Daud's servants."

"So!" said Lee. "Then there's no mistake about it this time."

"I told you from the first that Abu Daud was a murderer."

"So you did, but what is the connection between this attack on you and the murder of Sultan Ahmed?"

"It's all part of the same thing," said Luke, angrily. "Why are you so reluctant to believe that Abu Daud killed his brother? It's as plain as a pike staff."

"Don't excite yourself!" said Lee. "I wish you took snuff; it's so soothing! . . . Maybe Abu Daud did, but there's no evidence."

"No evidence! You have Yussuf's story that Abu Daud hired him to retrieve the body."

"But Yussuf can't identify Abu Daud. There is a possibility that the man who hired Yussuf was masquerading as Abu Daud."

"Who else could it have been?"

"Well, Abdul the cook, say, or anybody." Lee took a pinch of snuff. "You have evidently forgotten, but the Secret Service men told us that Abu Daud was out of the hotel at the hour that Yussuf said he went there."

"Well, I'll be damned!" said Luke, disappointed. "That's so."

"Abu Daud attacked you," Lee went on, "because you knocked him down yesterday and because he could see that Diana was favoring you. A simple case of jealousy."

"Can't I have him arrested for it?"

"I'm afraid not, as long as he stays in the Embassy."

"Well, by God! I'll show him up!" cried Luke. "I'll write to the Ambassador and tell him what kind of a guest he's harboring!"

"Certainly you can do that. Or you could give it to the newspapers. But I hope you won't."

"Why?"

"It would only confuse the real issue. Give me a day or two longer, and then you can do what you like."

"Oh, well," growled Luke, "I'm not too anxious to publish the story. Let it drop."

"Where did the attack take place?" asked Lee. This was the question Luke dreaded. "In an empty house away to hell and gone out in the suburbs."

Lee was surprised. "How did they get you to such a place?"

Luke's reply was to break into a low, furious cursing. The gist of it was: "To think that a woman could take me in like that! By God! I'm done with women from this time forward. They're all alike! Hereafter I swear I'll live like a monk!"

"How old are you?" asked Lee.

"Twenty-seven. What's that got to do with it?"

"You'll be up in a day or two."

"Don't razz me, Lee! I can't take it now."

"That wasn't a razz, my boy. When I was your age I would have fallen for her, too."

"This was no vulgar charmer, Lee. A girl in a thousand. She was fond of me, too—at least for the moment. A man can't be mistaken about that. And then coolly to hand me over to be murdered! It's incredible!"

"It has happened before," said Lee. . . . "However, they are not all alike."

Lee was listening to Luke's story with a slightly quizzical expression suggesting that he was well aware something was being held back. However, he was disposed to be merciful tonight; he made no attempt to probe Luke. When he had come to the end Luke said, bitterly:

"It must sound comic to you."

"Not comic," said Lee. "It was too near a thing. Thank God, you were man enough to save yourself."

Luke's heart sank when Lee got up to return to his own room. He dreaded having to face his own thoughts in the dark.

"Sleepy?" asked Lee.

"I wish to God I was," muttered Luke.

"The doctor left some dope for you in case of need," said Lee.

Luke gratefully accepted the tablet that was offered to him.

"See you in the morning," said Lee, with a final affectionate squeeze of Luke's shoulder. "If you should want anything during the night, phone me."

As soon as he was left alone, Luke's thoughts resumed the same old weary round. He firmly believed that Abu Daud had murdered Sultan Ahmed. But if Abu Daud was the murderer, how did it come that Mrs. Morven had secured the Sultan's jewels? There must have been some kind of deal beforehand between Abu Daud and Mrs. Morven, with Diana as the *quid pro quo*. Mrs. Morven had repudiated the deal after the murder. But now if Abu Daud was safe from arrest in the French Embassy, what kept him from denouncing her? How could Diana have been a party to such a crime? Yet she must have known of it. . . . And so on. And so on.

Finally a merciful numbness began to steal over his brain. He slept.

In the morning no complications had developed; no fever; no infection in the wound as yet. Lee breakfasted with Luke in his room, and announced his intention of going up the railway line to direct a search.

"If my calculations are correct," he said, "something was thrown out of Sultan Ahmed's private car that has not yet been picked up."

"Lee, what *are* your calculations?" asked Luke, knowing in advance what kind of answer he would get.

Lee wagged his hand. "I never divulge them in advance."

"Why not?"

"I must think of my public," said Lee, grinning. "They would be so disappointed if I ever turned out to be wrong."

Luke stayed in bed all day and read the papers. The public interest in the case was unabated. This morning the press had no first-rate disclosures to offer, and Luke marveled at their ingenuity in filling so much space with so little new matter. The gossip of Headquarters; a facetious interview with Lee Mappin; a story of his, Luke's, days at Oxford, with photographs. Where did they rake up the stuff? One story noted that Luke had not been seen since early morning.

The account of how the British Ambassador had descended in person on Police Headquarters and rescued Mrs. and Miss Morven from durance had been run on the previous day. Today there was a rehash of it, illustrated by photographs of the Embassy with a star marking the windows of the suite where the ladies were lodged. In the space allotted to a famous purveyor of gossip, whose column was syndicated throughout the country, Luke read this:

> Washington is all agog over the report that a famous personage, a dignitary so exalted that even your irreverent reporter dare not mention his name, has fallen flat before the charms of a young lady prominently concerned in the *cause célèbre* of the day. Dame Rumor hath it that His Excellency, in order to marry the girl, is prepared to go to the length of giving up his career and retiring to his estates.

This provided Luke with a bitter cud to chew. He told himself that it was no news to him, but it hurt just as much. The fact that it was published seemed to clinch the matter. Like many a man before him, Luke thought; Why do I have to go on loving her after I've found out she's no good?

Lee had left instructions that no calls were to be switched to Luke's room, and that anybody who might ask for him was to be told that Luke was spending the day out of town. Just before lunch there was a knock at the door, and expecting to see one of the hotel servants, Luke sang out: "Come in!" The door had been left unlocked because he was unable to get out of bed to open it. A young man with an insinuating smile entered.

He said, affably: "Good morning, Luke." (The younger principals in the Sultan Ahmed case were always referred to in the press by their first names.)

"Good morning," said Luke. "Who are you?"

"Representative from the — newspaper."

"Glad to see you," said Luke. "I'm not receiving today, so please get the hell out."

The young man made no move to obey. "Sorry you're laid up," he said. "What's the trouble?"

"A touch of malaria," said Luke, dryly. "A souvenir of my travels on the Amazon."

The young man produced a little notebook. "Amazon? That's new. Give us the story, Luke."

Luke gave him a tall story, made up on the spot. The young man made believe to take notes of it, though he was aware that his leg was being pulled. Meanwhile his bright eyes were traveling around. He sniffed, and interrupted Luke to ask:

"Do they treat malaria with iodoform nowadays?" He pointed to the medicaments on a side table. "And iodine? And bandages?"

"Sure," said Luke. "They bind you up to control the shaking."

"On the level, Luke," said the young man, cajolingly, "we got a tip that you returned to the hotel at three-thirty this morning with your shoes full of blood. Who shot you?"

"Somebody is full of hop," said Luke. "There's nothing in it."

"I wasn't born yesterday," said the reporter, "or I wouldn't be occupying my present distinguished position on the —. Come clean, Luke. Give me the dope. You can't suppress such a story at a time like this. The public is mad for it."

"Let 'em gnash their teeth," said Luke. "Or throw 'em any bone you like. I don't know what you're talking about."

They sparred back and forth. Luke was not to be cajoled into talking, and the young reporter went away in unperturbed good humor without his story. It was all one to him. In a couple of hours the — came out with the usual four inch headlines across the front page:

LUKE IMBRIE MYSTERIOUSLY SHOT

In a box at the top of the page Luke read:

QUESTIONS FOR THE AUTHORITIES
TO ANSWER

Who shot Luke Imbrie?
Where did the attack take place?
Why was he shot?
Why is he now trying to protect his assailant?

The story followed in the —'s usual style. "Employees of the James Madison neither affirm nor deny the story. . . . Rugs in the lobby were sent to the cleaner's this morning for the removal of bloodstains. . . . Luke found in bed. . . . He denies the story. . . . Surrounded by bandages and medicines for the treatment of wounds. . . ."

Thus the public appetite for sensation was whetted and the — scored a beat over its competitors.

Lee Mappin merely shrugged when he got home and read the story. "I had told the Major," he said, "so he was prepared for this."

Lee's day in the country, it transpired, had produced no concrete results. He was cheerful about it. "I have organized the search in such a way," he said, "that what I am looking for must be found if it's there."

CHAPTER NINETEEN

ON THE FOLLOWING MORNING Luke insisted on getting up. When he appeared downstairs in the lobby, the reporters were lying in wait for him. He parried their questions with as much good humor as he could muster. While he was breakfasting with Lee, a bell boy passed through the dining-room, paging him. He offered Luke a slip of paper on which was written, "Miss Morven calling on the phone." Luke jumped up so quickly that his chair all but fell over backwards. "Where's the nearest booth?" he demanded of the boy.

A minute later he heard the slow, low-pitched voice over the wire: "Luke! Thank God!"

All his bitterness, all his suspicions vanished away. His own voice deepened and softened. "I didn't expect to hear from you . . . dear!"

"I have called you up four times since I read that terrible story in the paper, but they wouldn't put me through to you."

"I didn't think you gave a damn."

"That's unkind. Are you all right?"

"Right as rain. It was only a scratch."

"What happened to you?"

"I can't tell you over the phone."

"Was it A. D.?"

"Yes."

"That man is like a poison in our lives!" murmured Diana. "You're sure you're all right?"

172

Luke yielded to an overwhelming impulse. "If you don't believe me, I'll come and show myself to you."

"All right."

"What! Do you mean I can come?" he cried, delightedly.

"It's foolish, but I must satisfy myself about you."

"Let's be foolish! What is the earliest decent hour at which one may call at an Embassy?"

"Come when you like. We have our own suite. You won't be disturbing anybody."

"In an hour!"

As soon as the spell of her voice was broken, Luke's doubts came winging back. Common sense reminded him that nothing had been explained or cleared up by this conversation. I'm as changeable as a weather vane, he thought. O God! I love her!

"That was Diana," he said as he reseated himself at the table.

"I suspected it," said Lee.

"She has called me up four times since she heard of my accident. She must have a good heart."

"I never doubted it."

"I'm going to see her this morning," said Luke, defiantly.

"Why not?" said Lee.

DIANA, TALL, COOL, AND LOVELY, was waiting for him in the delightful sitting-room that had been placed at the Morvens' disposal. She looked at him with the unfathomable sadness he had seen in her eyes before. He made to take her in his arms but she evaded him.

"No kisses!" she murmured.

"You let me day before yesterday."

"It was a weakness."

"Why?"

"You said kisses are pledges. I couldn't redeem mine."

"Are you going to marry the Ambassador?" he asked.

"Ah, don't quarrel with me so soon!" she protested. "He hasn't asked me."

"When he does, what will you say?"

She turned to him with a kind of recklessness. "As a friend, what would you advise me to say?"

"Oh, take him, of course," said Luke, harshly. "What a chance!"

Diana turned her back. There was a silence.

"I was a fool to come here," muttered Luke.

"I was hoping we could be friends," she murmured.

"Friends!"

She faced him again. "Suppose," she said with a deep look, "that it turned out Ahmed bin Said had bequeathed me a part of his wealth. Would you be willing to take it with me, as a means of supporting me and my mother?"

Luke could scarcely believe his ears. So that's what she calls it, he thought; a bequest! His voice sounded strange in his own ears. "Did you think I would take his money?"

She lowered her glance. "No. I was only asking."

"No will has been found," said Luke, harshly. "If there is a will, it's important evidence. It ought to be turned over to the police."

"I know of no will," she said.

Another silence. "I'm going," said Luke.

Involuntarily her hand went out. "Tell me what happened last night. That's what you came for."

He told her the story grimly. He wanted to hurt her by describing how he had been tempted by another woman. Diana ignored that, but paled upon learning how narrowly he had escaped with his life.

"Three of them!" she murmured.

In the middle of Luke's story there was a knock at the door. A servant handed in a letter and went away again. Diana, struck by the handwriting, tore open the envelope, and her eyes flew along the lines of writing. It was evidently a disconcerting communication. Her breast rose; she frowned and her hand stole to her lips.

Excusing herself to Luke, she went into the adjoining room. Mrs. Morven was in there. Luke could hear the murmur of two voices. Once Mrs. Morven raised her voice and Luke heard her say:

"He can't know anything. I forbid you to go!"

Diana presently came back, still holding the letter. Her face was a pale mask. She crumpled the letter in a ball and put out her hand to drop it in the waste-basket. But the wad of paper struck on the edge of the basket and rolled a little way on the floor. Diana let it go.

"Go on with your story," she said.

Luke averted his eyes from the paper and obeyed. Half beside himself with jealous curiosity, he could mask his face, too. Presently Mrs. Morven called, and Diana excused herself again. Luke pounced on the wad of paper and opened it up. This was no time for high-mindedness. He felt that he would go crazy if he didn't learn the truth about Diana once and for all. It was a letter in an unformed male hand on the notepaper of the Hotel Bradford. He read:

> Dear Diana:
> My nights and my days are a torment since I am prevented from seeing you. I can't bear it any longer. I am mad to see you. The Embassy is watched by the police day and night, but I have succeeded in getting past them. I am writing this in the Hotel Bradford. I'll wait here for you for an hour. I'll be in the writing-room to the left of the main entrance. I am a little disguised, but you will know me. There are things I've got to tell you. Don't fail me, Di. Don't drive me to desperation. You and your mother are in my power but I'm not going to tell on you unless you force me to it. I kiss the hem of your garment!
> Abu Daud.

It was the first time that Luke had read another man's love letter. Crumpling it, he dropped it, as if it was red hot, on the same spot where he had found it. His face was hard with contempt.

Diana returned. "Go on with your story," she said.

The balance was soon told, and Luke looked around for his hat.

"Do we part friends?" murmured Diana.

"No," he said, bluntly. "That's a silly pretense. You and I have got to be either more or less than friends."

A low cry broke from her and her hands went out to him. "Kiss me once," she said, "and hold me close to you. It's the last time!"

He seized her roughly and forgot everything. So after all, the cold Diana had passion. It was she who finally thrust him away, murmuring:

"Go! Go! Go!"

He was never clear as to how he got out of the building.

In the street he quieted down. Revenge was sweet. He glanced at his watch. Not much time to spare. He climbed in a taxi, telling the driver to let him out on Pennsylvania Avenue, a block short of the Bradford.

There was a policeman on fixed post at the hotel corner. Luke went up to him and said: "I'm Luke Imbrie. Do you know who I am?"

"I reckon," said the grinning policeman. "You would have a hard time to find man, woman, or child in Washington today who didn't know about you, Luke."

"Well, if you read the papers," said Luke, "you know who Prince Abu Daud is."

"Sure."

"I've been tipped off that Abu Daud is waiting in the writing-room of the Bradford for a girl. If you arrest him it will mean promotion."

"Lead me to him," said the policeman.

Luke saw Abu Daud as soon as he looked into the writing-room. His disguise consisted of a baggy suit several sizes too big for him and a pair of heavy-rimmed glasses. He saw Luke at the same moment and jumped up, snarling. But there was only the one door in the room and he was trapped.

"There's your man," said Luke.

"You're under arrest, Prince," said the policeman. "Better come along with me quietly."

The young Arab's face was green, and he was forced to support himself with a hand on the desk. He could conceive of no worse hell than to be betrayed by Diana to Luke, and rage was strangling him. Luke, reading his thoughts, said:

"There's one thing I want to tell you; Miss Morven knows nothing about this. I read the letter you wrote her while she was out of the room, and acted for myself."

"Damned spy!" whispered Abu Daud, hoarsely.

"Why, sure!" said Luke, grinning. "A man needs to be a spy in order to keep up with you."

"Now, gentlemen," said the policeman, soothingly, "we don't want no trouble here. It will all be smoothed out at Headquarters."

"Sure," said Luke. "This brave lad set on three men to murder me night before last, that's all I have against him, Officer. A mere trifle."

When they reached Headquarters Abu Daud had recovered his usual nonchalance. It was only Luke who could enrage him. He was not intimidated by the police department. Lee was with the Major when they entered the latter's office. The faces of the two men presented a study. The Major was overjoyed; Lee took snuff.

"This is an outrage," said Abu Daud, haughtily. "My person is immune from arrest. I shall lodge a protest with your State Department."

"By all means, Prince," said the Major, ironically. "I'll furnish you with stationery. But while the State Department has your case under advisement, you must allow me to have the pleasure of entertaining you."

Abu Daud's eyes glittered.

"Oh, we have very comfortable rooms," said the Major, "though perhaps not the equal of those at the Embassy."

"Send for my servants," commanded Abu Daud, scowling.

"My servants will wait on you," said the Major. Becoming serious, he asked the young man if he cared to make a statement.

"I have nothing to add to what I have already told you," said Abu Daud. "My hands are clean. I have nothing to fear. There can be no evidence."

"Time will tell," said the Major.

Abu Daud sent a venomous glance in Luke's direction. "But I have a piece of information," he drawled, "that may be of interest to you."

"What's that?"

Abu Daud gave attention to his fingernails. "My brother's jewels are in the possession of Mrs. Morven."

There was a moment's silence. The Major's eyes bugged out; he rubbed his chin fiercely. Lee did not appear surprised. Luke thought fatalistically: Well, it's out! He was aware that Lee was looking at him, but he would not meet his eyes. Abu Daud was enjoying the sensation he had created.

"How do you know this?" demanded the Major.

"I was sure from the first that she had them, and I set my servants to watch her. When she left the Hotel Pilgrim Tuesday morning one of my men followed her to the Greyhound Bus terminal. She removed the case containing the jewels from a lock-box there and put it in a box in another terminal, depositing ten cents. On Wednesday morning when the British Embassy car took her away from Headquarters, she got out at the store of Woodward and Lothrop and the car went on without her. She went back to the lock-box, got the bag with the jewels, and took it with her in a taxi to the Embassy."

"The jewels are actually in the Embassy!" exclaimed the Major. "Good God!"

When Abu Daud had been removed, Major Walkley said: "It seems that I can't go to the British Embassy without creating international complications."

"I'll go for you," said Lee. "Will you accompany me, Luke?"

"O God, no!" muttered Luke.

"If you find the jewels," said the Major, "remind the Ambassador of his promise, and bring the women back here with you."

Lee described later how, when he was shown to the Morvens' suite, he charged Mrs. Morven with having the jewels and she broke into a storm of denials. Whereupon Lee coolly entered her room, opened the door of the clothes-closet, and hauled out the bag from behind her dresses. Mrs. Morven had hysterics then. She claimed that Sultan Ahmed had presented the jewels to her daughter the night before he died. Throughout this scene Diana sat like a beautiful ghost, looking at the floor and saying not a word.

Lee then went in search of the Ambassador, taking the evidence with him. His Excellency was terribly upset. Lee said to him: "She says the Sultan gave them to her daughter. There is no proof of it. It would be easier to believe her if she had said so in the beginning."

Sir Bertram threw up his hands. "Take them away," he said. "I don't want to see them again. This is a blow to me, Mappin. I would have staked my life on that girl's honesty!"

When Lee returned to Mrs. Morven, that lady refused to leave the Embassy without seeing Sir Bertram. So he had to come, and the scene that followed was a painful one for everybody. Diana said nothing. Lee brought them both back to Headquarters—and the jewels.

Mrs. Morven and Diana were left sitting in the outer office while Lee carried the elegant pigskin case in to the Major. It was laid upon his desk and the cover thrown back. With eager eyes the three men looked inside. They saw a number of leather-covered boxes such as jewelers use, and many little twists of tissue paper. The boxes contained the manufactured jewelry: necklaces, bracelets, brooches, rings; the paper parcels, when untwisted, revealed unset gems: rubies, sapphires, diamonds, emeralds, pearls, gleaming with the devilish beauty peculiar to precious stones. To look at them, to handle them, made the heart beat faster.

"There's no inventory to this stuff," said the Major, agitatedly. "My God! it's as dangerous as hell! We may be accused of stealing from it!"

"Well, there are three of us," said Lee, dryly. "Presumably we're watching each other."

"Shut it up!" said the Major. "It makes me nervous. The bag must be sealed in the presence of all of us, and deposited in a bank vault."

The ladies were brought into the Major's office separately, Diana first. She was perfectly composed, seemingly indifferent; it was as if the real Diana were somewhere else. Luke avoided looking at her as much as possible. He never caught her looking at him. Prompted by the Major, she told the story of the happenings on the private car precisely as she had told it before. Neither the Major nor Lee could shake her.

"You have told us," said the former, "that when you entered your stateroom your mother was in bed."

"Yes."

"Was she asleep?"

"No. We talked a while."

"What did you talk about?"

"I can't remember. It couldn't have been of any importance."

"Then you went to bed?"

"I did."

"You slept?"

"Not right away. I slept very little on the train, if at all."

"Did you get up at any time?"

"Did your mother leave her bed?"

"Can you swear to that?"

"I can."

"Couldn't she have got up while you were sleeping?"

"No. My sleep was so broken I would certainly have been aroused if she had moved."

"Under what circumstances did you first see this bag containing the jewels?"

"May I go back a little way to explain?"

"Certainly."

"The Sultan had deposited the larger part of his jewels with the Midland Bank in London. The rest of them, he had said from the beginning, were to be mine. He gave them to me on the train on Sunday night. That was what he had asked us to wait up for."

"Why did he choose that particular moment for presenting them to you?"

"Because the arrangements for our marriage were concluded then."

"You mean you had only then given him your promise?"

"Yes, if you prefer it that way."

"Why had you held off until then?"

"That concerns only myself," said Diana, quietly. "I decline to answer."

"Please describe the circumstances under which he made the presentation."

"When he had changed into Arab dress he came to our room. A little later the three of us went to his room."

"It was then that he opened the whisky and poured himself a drink, and afterwards hid the bottle?"

"Yes. And after that he presented me with this bag and its contents. His wedding gift, he called it. I had better keep it, he said, because my life was a better risk than his. I should explain that he was always joking about the possibility of being assassinated."

"Not without reason," said the Major, dryly.

Diana was silent.

"Please continue."

"We put the bag in my room, and went on out to the observation platform."

"Did anybody see you passing from his room to yours with the bag?"

"Have you any proof that he gave it to you—a letter, or a deed of gift?"

"Why, no," said Diana. "How could any of us have foreseen what would happen?"

"Why didn't you tell us this in the beginning?"

"I wished to do so, but my mother thought the jewels would be taken from us—since we had no proof."

Following Diana, Mrs. Morven was brought in. With a great deal of circumlocution and repetition she told the same tale. She made a bad witness for herself; she talked too much; one instinctively felt that she was lying—yet her story was the same as Diana's, and she could not be shaken in any important particular.

The two were removed to the rooms where they had been confined before.

Major Walkley was in high feather. "It is now perfectly clear what happened!" he said, rubbing his hands.

Lee took snuff.

"When Mrs. Morven went to her room, leaving the other two on the observation platform," the Major continued, "she had already unlocked the communicating door on the Sultan's side. She now went in there from her room and doctored the whisky—nobody but she and her daughter knew where the bottle was hidden. She knew the Sultan would take another drink before going to bed. Then she lay in her bed, waiting. She would hear the body fall. Then she and her daughter went in and pushed the body out of the window."

Luke, who had been sitting quietly by the window, taking no part in the talk, cried out, "Impossible!"

"Hey?" said the Major, staring.

"I'm sorry," muttered Luke, "but it is incredible that that sort of women could have done such a thing!"

"I've known well-born women to do worse," said the Major, dryly. "Money is the be-all and end-all of Mrs. Morven's existence. For years she'd had a cruel struggle to get along without any. Nearly a million dollars would be an irresistible temptation."

"But the Sultan wanted to marry her daughter," put in Lee. "That would have brought the money into the family."

"Sure. Sure. But naturally she didn't want to hand her daughter over to an Arab even if he was a king, if she could get his wealth without it. . . . I won't say, though, that she didn't have a man's help in disposing of the body. Abu Daud says Abdul helped her. Maybe it was Abu Daud himself. I haven't by any means given up the theory that there was an understanding between Mrs. Morven and Abu Daud. Some man helped her, because it was a man who engaged Yussuf to retrieve the body and bury it. . . . We have a devilishly clever woman to deal with. Note that after having done her work and put the jewels in her room, she remembered to lock the communicating door on the Sultan's side, and come around by the corridor, locking the door of the Sultan's room after her. We will discover who were her accomplices all in good time. We have the principal, that's the main thing. The District Attorney can now go ahead and ask for indictments. Nobody can say I haven't done my job."

Lee said nothing.

CHAPTER TWENTY

AFTER THE ARREST of Mrs. Morven and Diana, events moved swiftly. A grand jury was sitting, and the District-Attorney prepared to ask for indictments. Crowds surged around Police Headquarters and afterwards went way out to the district jail overlooking Anacostia Creek, hoping to get a glimpse of the famous prisoners. Public opinion was running strongly against them, but there were many sentimentalists who were romantically impressed by Diana's beauty and aloofness. Boxes of flowers were sent to her hourly, with or without the cards of the donors. Diana was displeased. It was not an occasion for flowers, she said, and requested that they be sent on to a local hospital without being brought to her.

The French Ambassador's demand for the release of Abu Daud— Sultan Abu Daud as he was termed by his friends—put the State Department in somewhat of a spot. To release him, it was held, would be tantamount to recognizing him as the sovereign *de jure* of Shihkar, and that might very well be a cause of offense to the British. The visit of the delegation from Shihkar which had been subtly designed to exhibit the solidarity of the British and American governments to the world, had turned out to have quite the opposite effect.

Nevertheless, the State Department did, on strictly legalistic grounds, order the release of Abu Daud, coupling it with a polite intimation to the French Ambassador that public order would best be served by his immediate departure from our shores. It was generally believed that before coming to this decision, the Secretary

of State had consulted the British Ambassador, and that the Briton
had said, in effect, "Turn him loose and we'll take care of him." Sir
Bertram Maunsell was extraordinarily bitter against Abu Daud, and
with calculated indiscretion went so far as to make some scathing
remarks about him to the press.

Abu Daud departed from Headquarters in triumph. The crowd
in the street howled at him, and only the presence of numerous
police saved him from worse treatment. His complexion turned
noticeably greenish. Nevertheless, being free now to move about
Washington as he pleased, he returned to Headquarters within
an hour, bearing an immense box of roses, and demanded to be
allowed to see Miss Morven. Permission was refused, and he
departed, breathing threats.

Luke was amazed when this came to his ears. "The man must
be out of his senses," he said to Lee. "It's only a few hours since he
betrayed the women to the police!"

"It's a madness that men are liable to in the East or in the West,"
said Lee. "It plays strange tricks with a man's sense."

On the same afternoon the British light cruiser, *Banbury*, detached from the West Indies squadron, dropped anchor in the
Potomac. She had come to convey the remains of Sultan Ahmed
bin Said back to his native land. Shihab al Zuri, his secretary, prepared to accompany the body on its last sad journey. The servants
Cheragh Ali, Douban, Aziz, and Abdul were to go also. Lee Mappin
pointed out to Sir Bertram that this would remove many of the
witnesses from the jurisdiction of the court, and that against Abdul,
in particular, an actual accusation had been made. Sir Bertram,
on his own responsibility, ordered the cruiser to wait for forty-
eight hours.

The commander of the *Banbury* sent a polite invitation to Sultan Abu Daud to take advantage of this means of returning to
Shihkar, and Abu Daud with equal politeness declined. This was
the joke of Washington for twenty-four hours.

At evening, as Lee Mappin and Luke returned to their hotel for
dinner, among the crowd that was still milling in front of the door,
Luke picked out the sharp black eyes of Abu Daud's servant, Farraj,

neat and inconspicuous in his American clothes. Luke gave no sign of having recognized him. When they got inside the hotel he told Lee.

"There is no ground on which the master's immunity could be claimed for the servants," said Luke. "If these two rats were arrested it would draw Abu Daud's fangs, because he's not the sort of man to do his own dirty work."

"Right," said Lee.

He phoned Headquarters and Farraj, still watching the hotel door, was arrested. Half an hour later Haroun, Abu Daud's remaining servant, was taken into custody as he was about to enter the French Embassy. The two Arabs, confident of the power of their master, appeared entirely unconcerned.

On the fatal journey from New York to Washington that Sunday night, those two men had slept in the drawing-room of the private car along with Abdul, the Sultan's cook. When Major Walkley examined them, Farraj and Haroun now swore that they had seen Abdul get up during the night and disappear into the corridor leading to the rear of the car. They said they did not see him come back.

Abdul, who was still under detention at Headquarters, upon being confronted with the two, wept and swore that they were lying, and there it rested.

After dinner Lee Mappin and Luke returned to Headquarters. Luke identified Farraj and Haroun as two of the men who had attacked him. Later Abu Daud turned up with a haughty demand for the release of his servants. Major Walkley had a bit of fun at his expense that, anyhow, was no crime against international law—and Abu Daud departed cursing. The police were on sure ground with the servants. The State Department declined to interfere.

"We'll indict this pretty pair for assault with intent to kill," said the Major. "It will be a long time before they see Shihkar again."

Later that night Lee Mappin and Luke were drinking whisky and sodas in the former's room before going to bed. It was impossible for them to patronize a bar during these exciting days because of the number of people who followed them about, gaping. Luke's face was lined with fatigue. He needed a drink. He said:

"Lee, I've been thinking."

"You astonish me," said Lee.

"Don't razz me," said Luke, with a grim smile. "I can't play up to you tonight."

"What's on your mind, son?"

"This story that the Morvens told today, I know it sounds incredible, but excepting for the one suppressed fact, it is the same story that they have told from the beginning, and though mother and daughter were examined separately, they bore each other out in every particular."

"Well?"

"Has it occurred to you that they may be speaking the truth?"

"Surely," said Lee; "I have that possibility in mind."

"Well, thanks for so much," said Luke. "To my mind it strengthens the case against Abu Daud."

"How do you figure that?"

"You've been saying all along that Abu Daud would not have killed his brother and made away with the jewels because the jewels would have come to him anyhow upon his brother's death. Now we know that he didn't make away with the jewels. Suppose he knew that his brother, the Sultan, was about to present the jewels to Miss Morven, and killed him to prevent it, only to find that he was just too late, that the transfer had already been made?"

"That is plausible," said Lee.

"Why should Mrs. Morven have hid the key in the flour tin?" said Luke.

"Well, the tin on its shelf was just inside the door and the door was open as she went by when leaving the car."

"But if she was so clever, why didn't she hang on to the key a minute or two longer and drop it out of the window of the taxi?"

"I have asked that of myself," said Lee.

"Here's another thing in their favor," Luke went on. "Everybody is agreed that the crime must have been the result of long and careful plotting."

"That's right."

"Supposing Mrs. Morven to have been the prime mover in it, how could she have informed herself so quickly of everything she needed to know? I mean, the exact location of the Susquehanna bridge, the time the train would pass over it, the fact that it had no guard rail, and so on?"

"The point is well taken. But remember she was in New York for a week before the Sultan arrived."

"I was in their company almost continually during that time, and I swear to you Mrs. Morven gave no evidence of being anything more than a silly, light-minded woman without a thought beyond dresses and restaurants and shows."

"Maybe she was fooling you."

"But how could she have made any plans until the Sultan arrived and she found out exactly what his plans were? I remember only a few hours before they set out for Washington how surprised and gratified she was to learn that the party was to travel in a private car."

"That's well argued."

"And if the crime was the result of weeks or days of planning, according to the theory advanced by Major Walkley, it was only an accident in the end that enabled her to carry it out. I mean, how could she have known in advance that she would get an opportunity to slip into the Sultan's room and fix his whisky, while he and Diana were sitting out on the observation platform?"

"There your reasoning is not so sound," said Lee. "Because if Diana was in the plot—as she must have been if her mother is guilty—it was a simple matter for her to detain the Sultan long enough for her mother to do her work."

Luke struck his fist violently against his thigh. "I won't believe it!" he cried. "I will never believe that Diana had any foreknowledge of murder!"

"Unfortunately, your heart is concerned in it," said Lee. "As for me, I must go by the evidence."

Luke jumped up. "That girl has had a rotten bringing up," he cried. "She's never had a chance. It is perfectly possible that she might have been drawn into some scheme to trick Ahmed out of his jewels, but murder, no! You have only to look at her!"

"She is awfully good to look at," murmured Lee.

"Honestly, Lee, do you believe that such a girl is capable of planning a cowardly murder, a poisoning?"

"I'm not prepared to say yet."

"O God! what an answer!" cried Luke, flinging away. "Have you no blood in your veins?"

Lee took off his glasses and polished them. "What's my blood got to do with it?" he asked, blinking. "Have a little patience," he went on. "We have two days before the British cruiser sails away with the witnesses. Much can happen in two days."

Luke came back to him. "Lee, what are you holding back?" he demanded. "For God's sake, if you have any hope, let me hear it. I'm pretty near the end of my string."

"You have been informed of all the evidence we have gathered. Think it over for yourself."

"I have thought it over until my brain is addled. What do *you* think?"

"I am sure of nothing yet," said Lee, cautiously. "I don't want to raise any false hopes. I will only say this: In spite of the worthy Major, we have not yet got to the bottom of this case. Not by a damn sight!"

NEXT MORNING Mrs. Morven sent Luke a message, asking him to come to her. He didn't go. He knew he couldn't keep his temper in the presence of the woman. If it had been from Diana, how differently he would have felt! At Headquarters he learned that Mrs. Morven had been telephoning to everybody she had ever known or heard of. Lee Mappin took it upon himself to see that she was provided with a first-class lawyer. Half the lawyers in town were clamoring for the case on account of the publicity involved.

In the middle of the morning that enterprising newspaper, the —, came out with an extra that gave the public excitement a new flick. Sultan Abu Daud had been spirited out of town, the story said. On the previous night in the company of the French Ambassador he had attended a dinner at the Chronos Club given by a visiting French industrialist. All evening the reporters had waited outside the clubhouse, hoping to get an interview, only to learn, when the affair broke up, that Sultan Abu Daud had not been present. Instead, he had merely passed through the clubhouse and out by a rear door where a big car had picked him up and whisked him away to parts unknown.

At noon another extra solved the mystery. Sultan Abu Daud had arrived at Hoboken, New Jersey, in the early morning hours, whence he had been secretly conveyed by launch and put aboard the steamship *Richelieu* of the French line. The *Richelieu* had sailed at ten o'clock and Abu Daud was safe on the high seas.

Lee Mappin, who had occasion to speak to Sir Bertram Maunsell during the afternoon, found that the Ambassador was not at all disturbed by Abu Daud's "escape." "Oddly enough, some friends of mine sailed on the *Richelieu* also," he said, slyly. "I am in receipt of hourly bulletins concerning the doings of His Highness on board."

The jail prisoners were allowed to have newspapers, and when Abu Daud's servants, Farraj and Haroun, read this story and discovered that their master had abandoned them to American justice, they went to pieces. Like the childish savages they were, they flung themselves on the floor of their cells, tearing their hair, and their shrieks rang through the jail, setting the whole place in an uproar. When Major Walkley was informed of it, it occurred to him that this provided a good opportunity of learning the truth. He therefore notified Lee Mappin, and proceeded to the jail. Lee and Luke joined him in the warden's office.

Farraj and Haroun were an abject pair, weeping and shaken, yet snarling still. They had plenty of English now, and were eager to testify against the master who had forsaken them. Farraj was questioned first. There was little trace in him of the former greasy dandy with glittering black eyes who copied all his master's affectations. He wanted to know if he would be set free if he told everything.

"I can't make any promises," said the Major. "Naturally the court will be easier on you if you tell the whole truth."

"I was only the servant," whined Farraj. "I had to obey my master." He went on to describe the plot that had been laid to get Luke Imbrie; how Clèlie de Lisser, a typist employed at the French Embassy who had fallen for Abu Daud's velvety eyes, had first been sent to secure the new house by the payment of a small deposit, and later had followed Luke to Potomac River Park. Meanwhile Farraj, through underworld channels, had hired the human gorilla, who was known to them simply as Hairy (Harry?), and the three men had proceeded to the new house to which they had a key. During the day and evening Clèlie, while dancing and dining with Luke, had called up Abu Daud to report progress whenever she retired to powder her nose. The men in the new house had had a long wait.

All this was very well, but it was not what Major Walkley most wanted to hear. "Let us go back to the journey down from New York on the private car," he suggested. "Were you telling me the truth when you said you saw Abdul get up in the night and go through the passage towards the rear of the car?"

"I lied," said Farraj. "My master told me to say that. It was Abu Daud who went down the passage. It was Abu Daud who killed the Sultan."

"So you say," said the Major, "but all you know is, that you saw him disappear in the passage."

"No," said Farraj, "I peek around the corner; I see Abu Daud go into the Sultan's room."

"How did he get in?"

"He had a key to the door."

"Where did he get it?"

"I don't know that."

"What time was this?"

"I don't know. Very late."

"After the train had left Philadelphia?"

"I don't know Philadelphia. I guess so."

"How long did he stay in there?"

"I don't know. Maybe half an hour. When he come out he see I was awake; he say he kill me if I tell he went in there."

Lee put in a question. "When he came out he must have had two keys, because the key that belonged in the door was missing next morning. What did he do with them?"

"I don't know."

"If the Sultan was asleep when Abu Daud went in there," said Lee, with deceitful mildness, "how do you suppose Abu Daud could poison him? And if he woke up, whatever induced him to swallow the poison?"

Farraj squirmed, but he proved to be equal to the question. "Abu Daud tell me next day how he kill the Sultan. When he go in, Sultan start up, say: 'Who's that?' Abu Daud say: 'It's me, brother.' Go down on knees beside bed; say: 'I come to ask your pardon because I was a bad brother. I wish to be friends.'"

The Major interrupted. "Didn't the Sultan ask him where the hell he got the key?"

"No," said Farraj. "The Sultan say: 'Rise, brother; let us drink to our friendship.' So he get out the whisky-bottle, and Abu Daud put the poison in his drink when he not looking, and he fall down, and Abu Daud push him out the window."

Lee looked at the Major drolly, and the latter burst out laughing. For Luke it was no laughing matter.

"That will be about enough from you," said the Major.

Haroun was a healthier looking specimen than Farraj and less sharp. He was badly frightened and took refuge in a kind of peasant stupidity. He corroborated Farraj's story about the attack on Luke. That was easy, because it was no doubt true. He said he had seen Abu Daud go to the Sultan's room, but professed ignorance as to what had taken place inside. In one respect his story was better than Farraj's because he said Abu Daud knocked on the Sultan's door, spoke softly to him, and was admitted.

The Major wearied of them both and had them returned to their cells.

"So that lets out His Highness Abu Daud," said Lee. "It is clear that these two know nothing of what happened. It is further clear that Abu Daud could not have acted without their knowing about it. In their anxiety to convict their master they have succeeded in exonerating him!"

"Well, thank God we have the women safe!" said the Major.

At that moment Luke's spirits registered an all-time low. He had banked heavily on Abu Daud's guilt. If Abu Daud were innocent . . . what?

CHAPTER TWENTY-ONE

THE NEXT DAY WAS SUNDAY, and H.M.S. *Banbury* was to set sail at evening. An inventory of the jewels that Ahmed bin Said had brought to America had been found among the late Sultan's papers by his secretary, Shihab al Zuri, and the first task in the morning was to check the jewels in the presence of a representative of the police and officials of the bank where they were lodged for safekeeping. Lee Mappin and Luke accompanied Shihab al Zuri to Headquarters. The gaunt secretary apologized for appearing in Arab dress.

"I dislike to appear in the streets this way," he said, "the people stare so! But when my servant got out my American clothes this morning, the shoes were missing."

"Do you mean that somebody has taken them from your room?" asked Lee.

"Apparently so."

"You should complain to the management."

"It is hardly worth while," said Shihab. "The shoes hurt me very much, and I should have to get a new pair in any case."

In the taxicab he spoke apprehensively of his forthcoming voyage on H.M.S. *Banbury*. "I have visited the ship. The quarters allotted to me are very pleasant. But she is so small. And the voyage to Shihkar is so long! I know I shall be sick the whole way."

"You're not obliged to travel on the *Banbury*," suggested Lee. "You could sail on the *Queen Mary* or the *Normandie* from New York, take the Simplon-Orient from Paris, and join the Banbury at Port Said."

"No, no!" said Shihab, "I must accompany the body of my be-
loved master. I owe him that last, sad duty!"

From Headquarters Major Walkley and Shihab set off for the
bank. Lee did not see any necessity for him to be present when the
seal on the jewels was broken; he wanted to go to Havre de Grace
to spur on the search for the missing evidence. The usually imper-
turbable Lee was getting anxious now; the time was so short. It
may be mentioned here that the jewels in the pigskin case were
found to be intact, according to the inventory, with the exception
of the diamond ring pawned by Diana Morven on her first day in
Washington.

Luke accompanied Lee. As they set out in a police car he asked:
"What are we looking for?"

"The second whisky bottle," said Lee.

Two hours later they were in Conley's Hotel at Havre de Grace,
and Lee was listening to a report from Duggan, the young fisherman, whom he had put in charge of the boats engaged in the search.
Duggan told him that they had dragged the river bottom from shore
to shore, above the railway bridge, below the bridge, and under
the bridge. All kinds of junk had been fished up, including bottles,
but no bottle such as Scotch whisky comes in.

"Did you make a test to see if an empty bottle would break if
dropped into the water from that height?" asked Lee.

"Yes, sir. I gave two empty bottles to a trackman, who carried
them out on the bridge and dropped them. One broke on striking
the water; the other sank, came to the top, and floated awhile before finally sinking."

"Then we know no more than we did before," said Lee.

"How do you know the bottle was empty?" asked Luke.

"Because the whisky had been spilled on the stateroom floor.
. . . If the bottle was dropped in the river, the chances are against
us," Lee went on. "It may have smashed; or, if the murderer put in
the stopper, it may float all the way to Spain without being discovered."

Duggan was told to keep up the search until nightfall and then
wait for further instructions.

Lee said to Luke: "It is not certain, of course, that the bottle was thrown out of the window immediately after the body. In his excitement, the murderer may have overlooked it for the moment. When he saw it, the train may have been approaching the end of the bridge. In that case he would not have thrown it out until after passing through the town."

They proceeded to the railway station. The railway authorities had placed every facility at Lee's service, and a little gasoline track car was waiting for them. This quaint vehicle was lifted on the track, and they set off southward with more noise than speed.

"I hope no train is due," said Lee, nervously. "These electric locomotives slide along at a hundred miles an hour with no more noise than a sewing-machine."

The track foreman glanced at his watch. "None due until one-fifteen, sir."

"Suppose there should be a special today."

"We would be told of it. They're not taking any chances when you're on the track, sir."

"Very gratifying, I'm sure," said Lee.

When they came out into open country, Lee had them stop the car. It was lifted off the track, and they made their way slowly on foot along the right side of the right-of-way, heading South. Lee said:

"Of course, I'm having the whole stretch of track searched, but if I have figured right, it should be found along here."

They met a couple of men searching on the other side of the right-of-way. Lee called out to them: "You're wasting your time, boys. If it's anywhere at all, it's on this side of the tracks."

Lee searched with his head as well as his eyes. He would stop, survey a stretch of the way and consider, before he covered it. He passed over open, unobstructed places without troubling to look; they had been searched many times before. But at every piece of cover or of broken ground he stopped and could be seen thinking it out—suppose a bottle had been thrown from a moving train here, what would happen to it?

His eyes brightened when they fell on a dense growth of black-berry bushes below the track. "Look at it!" he said at once to Luke.

"It has never been disturbed. All the canes are growing in the inimitable disarray that nature intended. A man instinctively avoids a brier patch, and the searchers have passed around it without thinking."

There were two bush-hooks among the tools on the track car and Lee set men to work with them. "Watch those hooks!" he warned them. "Look before you swing!"

The canes began to fall. To the men of the track crew it was like a piece of magic when the whisky-bottle was actually found lying in the middle of the brier patch. They stopped in their tracks, goggling; then raised shouts of astonishment. Lee stood aside with a careless air, and took a pinch of snuff.

He was excited, though. He wouldn't let anybody touch the bottle. He gazed down at it as if he had laid bare a treasure beyond price. He wouldn't touch it himself until he'd had his fill of looking at it. "Observe, son," he said to Luke, with a fond air, "the bushes broke its fall. It lies there as softly as a bird in its nest! It is intact even to the Glenardrey label and the stopper is in it! It has a couple of gills of whisky remaining in the bottom, enough to permit of an analysis. We are in luck."

His excitement was infectious. "Who threw it out of the train?" cried Luke.

"Give me time! Give me time!" said Lee, waving his hands. "This requires hard application!"

Lee finally picked up the bottle and put it under his coat as if it were too precious to be exposed to the air. They made their way back to the track car and returned to the Havre de Grace station. Lee shook hands with the track crew and presented each man with a handsome tip.

Then down to Conley's, where he called up Major Walkley in Washington. "Major," he said, "I have found an important piece of evidence—just how important I'll be able to say when I get to you. I'll be in your office at four. Please ask the district attorney to meet me there. I suggest that he'd better hold up his application for indictments until he gets this new evidence. I'll need a little quick work from the toxicologist also. I further suggest that you ask Sir

Bertram Maunsell and Shihab al Zuri to be present, since they both
have a close interest in the case. And if you think proper, have Mrs.
and Miss Morven brought to your office. They have the closest interest of any of us. One thing more, Major, have the prisoner,
Yussuf Kelly, brought to Headquarters, so that we can have him in
if necessary."

Lee sent word to Duggan to call off the search on the river, and
they set off for Washington at terrific speed. Lee was sunk in a
deep study. Luke only asked him one question:

"Lee, for God's sake, what does the bottle signify?"

Lee answered, equably: "Dope it out for yourself, son. That's
what I'm trying to do at this minute. Two heads are better than
one."

Arriving in Washington, Lee had the driver take them first to
the James Madison. He left Luke sitting in the car, and in a couple
of minutes came out carrying a small satchel.

At Police Headquarters Lee went direct to the toxicologist's
laboratory and handed the chemist the all-important bottle. "How
long will it take you to establish whether there is cyanide of potassium in this whisky?" he asked.

"Only a few minutes, Mr. Mappin, as long as I know what I have
to look for."

CHAPTER TWENTY-TWO

IN MAJOR WALKLEY'S OFFICE all the principals were waiting. Sir Bertram Maunsell was talking to the pale Diana with a softened look in his handsome face. Mrs. Morven, with her finery a little disarrayed, sat alternately flushed and pale, biting her lip and twisting a rag of a handkerchief. The mournful Shihab al Zuri sat surveying them all patiently through his glasses; the district attorney, Bassett by name, was clean-cut and business-like; the portly Major like a human interrogation point, fairly bouncing with impatience to hear the news.

Lee put his little satchel on the desk and asked for the exhibits in the Sultan Ahmed bin Said case. They were put before him, including the first whisky-bottle which had been carefully glued together, though some of the pieces were missing. Everybody sat facing Lee in a semicircle, with Major Walkley seated at the desk, nearest to Lee on his right.

"Ladies and gentlemen," said Lee, "you are all familiar with the evidence in this case, and I will recapitulate the story very briefly. It has been established that as soon as the train left Newark, New Jersey, Sultan Ahmed took a shower bath and changed into Arab dress. He then knocked at the door of the ladies' room next to his. This would be about twenty minutes later, while the train was still crossing the state of New Jersey.

"The three of them spent some minutes in talk and then went into the Sultan's room, where the Sultan opened the bottle of whisky Mrs. Morven had been keeping for him, and took a drink.

Afterwards he hid the bottle in the water-cooler. The three of them then went out on the observation platform. It has been testified that the train was coming into Trenton at the time.

"It has been considered as a suspicious circumstance that Mrs. Morven presented a bottle of whisky to the Sultan." Lee pointed to the mended bottle on the table. "This is it. We know it, because the pieces of the gum cap were found in an ash-tray in the Sultan's room. When placed together with what remains clinging to the neck of the bottle, they form a complete cap. Notice that the label is missing. It was found in the water-cooler. It is unfortunate that the bottle was smashed to pieces. We may infer, however, that it was full or nearly full when thrown out, because the earth was still strongly impregnated with whisky at the spot where it struck.

"This bottle never had any poison in it. How do I know that? Because it was picked up a furlong south of the town of Bristol, Pennsylvania. When the train passed that point, Sultan Ahmed, Mrs. Morven, and Miss Morven were sitting out on the observation platform. The bottle was thrown out less than one minute before the train passed the Drury family in their car beside the track. The Drurys, you remember, have testified that they saw three persons sitting on the rear platform."

At this point in the story Major Walkley ruffled up his hair. Already his theory of the case was beginning to come apart.

Lee brought forward the little barrel-shaped wooden container. "Here's the cyanide of potassium," he went on. "So far we have not succeeded in establishing the origin nor the ownership of this box. It is apparently of foreign manufacture. All I want to call your attention to now is the fact that it was picked up *between the tracks*. One of the railroad officials has testified that this train was routed the whole way on the outside track on the right, hence it follows that this box must have been tossed out of one of the windows on the left-hand side of the car, facing front. There is unanimous testimony to the effect that at the moment when the train was passing the spot near Metuchen, where this object was picked up, Mrs. Morven and Miss Morven were in their stateroom on the right-hand side of the car."

Luke Imbrie glanced at Diana, but her eyes were lowered. Luke felt as if tight iron bands around his chest were giving way and he could once more breathe with blessed freedom. He thought confusedly: Good old Lee! . . . His heart's in the right place. I can trust him! He's going to save her! . . . What a fool I was not to have doped this out for myself. Never in God's world would I make a detective!

There was a knock on the door. It was the young pathologist bringing the second bottle. He placed it on the desk in front of Lee with a slip of paper.

"Thank you, Doctor," said Lee, glancing at the paper; "that is what I expected."

The young man looked around. He would dearly have liked to remain in the room, but since nobody invited him, he had to go.

When the door closed Lee pushed forward the bottle, saying: "This is the second bottle of whisky in the case." He read what was written on the paper: "The chemist says this whisky contains cyanide of potassium in more than lethal quantity. . . . This bottle was picked up in a brier patch on the right-hand side of the tracks about a mile and a half south of the station of Havre de Grace. It has not rained since Sunday night, and judging from the way the ink on the revenue stamp has run, I should say that this bottle had been in the water-cooler also, but in this case the label did not soak off altogether. It is partly loosened. This bottle was absolutely essential to prove my case. Notice that it has been opened by a neater hand than the Sultan's! In this case the top of the revenue stamp has been torn off, and the point of a penknife passed through the gum cap that held the stopper. The top of the cap has fallen off the stopper.

"It is Glenardrey whisky, you see. As none of this brand has ever been imported into this country, this can be no other than the bottle which was stolen from the Sultan's private store some time on Sunday. We need not stop at this moment to inquire who stole it. All the members of the Sultan's party passed freely in and out of the different rooms of the suite. The closet where it was put was not locked.

"It must be evident to all of you now, that there was somebody in the Sultan's room while the Sultan and these two ladies were sitting on the observation platform. . . ."

"How did he get in there?" interrupted Major Walkley.

"At that time the door was not locked, Major. . . . This was the murderer, I take it. He couldn't have known in advance how much time he would have, so he brought with him the second bottle of whisky, which he had doctored at his leisure. . . ."

"Wait a minute," said the Major. "How could he have known where the Sultan's whisky was hidden? That was an ingenious hiding-place. It would take time to find it."

"He knew where it was hidden," said Lee.

"How?"

"He saw the Sultan hide it."

"What!"

"When the bottle was dropped in the tank the murderer was not three feet away."

"In the little washroom! Impossible! Where?"

"Behind the curtain of the shower."

"My God! How do you know that?"

Lee searched among the envelopes containing the exhibits. "When the Sultan took his shower he dropped the soap, and it lay on the floor of the bath, unnoticed. You were with me when I picked it up. When the murderer went behind the curtain he stepped on the soap." Lee produced the little partly-flattened cake of soap and exhibited it around. "See, there's the print of his heel."

Everybody stared at the soap with parted lips. A great silence filled the room.

"He was watching his chance," Lee resumed, "and he entered the Sultan's room while His Highness was talking to the ladies in the adjoining room. When they all came back to the Sultan's room, he hid himself behind the curtain of the shower. It was a piece of luck for the murderer that the Sultan happened to choose a hiding-place in the washroom. Otherwise he would have had to search the stateroom.

"As it was, when the Sultan left the room with the ladies, all he had to do was to replace the bottle of good whisky with the bottle of poisoned whisky. Having both bottles in his hand, he could pour precisely the same amount of the poisoned whisky as had been taken from the other bottle down the drain. He then threw the bottle of good whisky out of the window. Being almost full, it was heavy, and it was smashed to pieces when it struck the ground.

"The murderer then retired behind the curtain and waited for the Sultan to come back. Anybody who was familiar with Sultan Ahmed's habits could count on the fact that he would take another drink before retiring. It was his custom to drink his whisky straight and to swallow it in one gulp. The murderer would know that, too. In this instance we know that the Sultan put the bottle to his lips, because there was no glass found in the stateroom, and none was missing from the washroom.

"He fell dead with the bottle in his hand, and most of the whisky ran out on the carpet. If the victim attempted to cry out, the murderer was right there to stifle his cries. When he was satisfied that the Sultan was dead, he threw up the window and stood there watching, until the train slowed down and ran out on the Susquehanna bridge. He then pushed the body out of the window. Perhaps for a moment he forgot the bottle; perhaps he hadn't time; at any rate, he waited until the train had run through the town of Havre de Grace before he threw the bottle out."

"It was Abdul!" cried Major Walkley, striking the desk. "He was the custodian of the Sultan's whisky."

Lee shook his head. "The fat, easy-going, timid Abdul is never the man to have stood hidden behind the shower curtain waiting for his master to return."

"It has been charged that he was Mrs. Morven's accomplice!"

"There is nothing to sustain that but Abu Daud's unsupported statement. Abu Daud's servants have confessed that they were lying by their master's orders when they corroborated it. . . . Take a look at the soap again, Major. Abdul possesses no shoes that would leave such an imprint."

"Then who was it?"

Lee opened the little satchel on the desk. "Here are the murderer's shoes. A new pair of American shoes; rubber heels. Notice that the heel precisely matches the imprint on the soap. I happen to know that these shoes have not been worn since Sunday night. With my magnifying glass you can still see particles of soap adhering to the heel of the shoe for the right foot."

Everybody in the semicircle leaned forward breathlessly. "Whose shoes are they?" demanded the Major.

Lee spoke in a curiously regretful voice. "Shihab al Zuri's."

Every head turned with a common movement towards the gaunt secretary in his turban and robes. Shihab made no move nor sound, but all the color of life drained out of his face, leaving it like soiled wax. His lips parted. He intended it for a smile, but it was the awful grimace of a man stretched on the rack.

Lee was going over the envelopes containing the exhibits. He opened one, saying: "Here is the neatly-cut circle of gum that fell from the stopper of the second bottle—that is, the poisoned whisky—when it was opened." He glanced at the envelope. "According to the notation I made at the time in Major Walkley's presence, I picked it up on the floor of Shihab al Zuri's stateroom."

Mrs. Morven suddenly pitched forward from her chair. Sir Bertram caught her before she fell to the floor. Diana ran to the water-cooler. Drawing a glass of water, she dipped her handkerchief in it and bathed her mother's temples while Sir Bertram fanned the old lady. Mrs. Morven opened her eyes, and, as Diana flung an arm around her, hid her face on her daughter's shoulder and wept in relief.

Luke had eyes only for Diana. His breast swelled as if it would burst with gladness. There is no stain on her! he thought. I knew it! Then he caught Sir Bertram looking at her in a way that expressed the same feeling, and his soaring spirits dropped like a shot bird. Of course she'll take the Ambassador, he thought. I haven't a chance in the world!

Major Walkley addressed Shihab wonderingly, "What did you do it for?"

Shihab was sitting like a waxwork figure with glass eyes. His lips moved stiffly before any sound came out. Finally he said in an inhuman croak, "I loved my master . . . like a son!"

Lee said to the others: "Strangely enough, I believe that is true. But his religion came first. He knew that Sultan Ahmed was preparing to forsake his religion and marry an unbeliever. Such an act in the ruler would have given a blow to the old faith that would have been felt throughout Islam. And in order to prevent the disgrace, Shihab killed him."

There was a silence in the room.

"If required, another piece of evidence is available," said Lee.

The Major said, "Better tell us all you know."

"Let them fetch in the man who calls himself Yussuf Kelly," Lee said to him in an undertone, "and have him stand by the door."

It was done. The glittering beady eyes of the Arab bad man traveled from face to face as he tried to figure out what this meeting portended for him. Shihab al Zuri's back was turned to him.

Lee said to Shihab: "Do you wish to make a statement?"

By now Shihab had partly recovered himself. Some color had returned to his face; his eyes were shining with pure fanaticism. "May I be excused from speaking until I have had time to think things over?" he said.

Yussuf, hearing that voice, started, stared at Shihab's back, cried out: "That is the man who hired me to pick up the body. I know his voice!"

"That's all that is necessary," said Lee.

Major Walkley made a sign to the warder who had brought in Yussuf, and he was led out again. Lee said:

"So you see it was not Abu Daud, but Shihab al Zuri posing as Abu Daud, who, upon landing, got in touch with the Arabs in New York. Very likely he had established contact before he sailed for America. Yussuf is only an Arab outlaw; but there is also in New York a branch of a world-wide organization known as the Scimitars. Shihab described it to us as a political organization; to an Arab there is no division between politics and religion. The acknowledged slogan of the Scimitars is 'Arabia for the Arabs!'

Their secret aim is to make Islam the religion of the world. Shihab undoubtedly obtained what help and information he required from the Scimitars. Now that we have established the case, there will be little difficulty in obtaining additional evidence. Shihab is at the head of another organization called 'The Green Turbans.' They have educated and trained a candidate for the throne of Shihkar according to their own ideas. His name is Hussein el Faiz."

Shihab al Zuri stood up. He had become calm. "May I be permitted to retire?" he asked, deferentially. "I must consider how to defend myself."

"To a cell," said Major Walkley, sternly.

"Naturally," said Shihab, bowing.

He was taken away. When the door closed after him, the restraint was broken, and it seemed as if everybody started talking at once. They crowded around Lee Mappin, congratulating him, trying to shake his hand or clap him on the back. Only Diana hung back, suddenly as diffident as a child, with misty, grateful eyes. The astute Lee was genuinely embarrassed. The little man loved praise as well as any, but he couldn't take it to his face. Behind the polished glasses his distressed eyes darted sideways, seeking escape.

"I did nothing," he said, "but follow my nose. It's the Major's case, really."

In the encouraging atmosphere of congratulations, the deflated Mrs. Morven quickly took air again. The French hat was awry and tears had smeared her make-up; unconscious of that, she assumed all her social graces. "You, Mr. Mappin!" she said, shaking a roguish forefinger at Lee, "I'm not going to forgive you all at once for your terrible suspicions of me. You'll have to sue for it, sir!"

Lee looked at her a little wildly.

"Seriously," she went on, "Diana and I are going to establish our little nest here in Washington. After the Continent there is no other place in America I could endure. It will be a very *petite maison*, of course, but the amenities will be provided. Every time you are in Washington I insist that you shall put up with us, and perhaps, in time, I shall forgive you."

She offered Lee her hand like a duchess. He took it, blinking behind his glasses.

"Thanks," he said.

Luke thought grimly, Nothing will ever down that woman. He got the opportunity to say, low-voiced, to Diana: "I'm so glad it's cleaned up clean. I never doubted you."

She smiled crookedly. "You think so now. But you *did* doubt me. However, I'm not holding it against you."

Sir Bertram, in the general expansiveness, invited Lee, Luke, Major Walkley, and District-Attorney Bassett to dine at the Embassy that same night. "Entirely informal," he said. "There will be nobody but ourselves. We have so much to talk over

He then carried away the ladies in one of the ineffable Embassy cars, leaving Luke with a sore heart. He commanded no fleet of Rolls-Royces. Lee and Luke walked back to their hotel, mostly in silence.

"I hate to finish a case," said Lee. "After everything is doped out one feels so flat!"

BEFORE SHIHAB AL ZURI was put into a cell he was searched with the customary thoroughness. The police wished to deprive him of his turban, but he protested so vehemently that this was an intolerable insult to a Mussulman, that, having made sure there was no poison nor dagger hidden in its folds, he was allowed to keep it on his head. After all, he was only under charges as yet.

As soon as he was left alone he unwound the turban and, standing on his cot, tied one end of it to a cross-bar of his cell, the other around his neck. He jumped off the cot. A wild cry rang through the corridors: "La Allah illa Allah!" and his body thudded against the bars. A keeper was at the door almost instantly, and the body promptly cut down, but his neck was broken. The prison doctor said that he must have climbed up to the top of his cell and let go in order to make sure of the job.

When Lee was informed of it he said: "Poor wretch! It was the best thing he could do. He imagined, of course, that he was leaping straight into Paradise."

That same night H.M.S. *Banbury* sailed for distant Shihkar with the body of Ahmed bin Said, his three servants, and Shihab al Zuri's servant, the disconsolate Cheragh Ali. A case might have been made out against Cheragh, who was undoubtedly privy to his master's doings, but Major Walkley and the District Attorney agreed that the public interest would be better served by letting him go.

CHAPTER TWENTY-THREE

THE DEATH OF SHIHAB AL ZURI cast a damper on the Ambassador's dinner. No Anglo-Saxon could feel much sympathy for the poisoner who had prepared his plans so patiently and secretly, still, in the end, he had paid his shot like a man, and all the men at the table were sobered by it.

Not so Mrs. Morven. Secure in her position on the right hand of an Ambassador, she launched forth in her usual style. She was wearing a flamboyant red evening dress and in her coiffure (which looked as if it had been cast in brass) she sported a jeweled aigrette that trembled and sparkled with every beck and turn of her busy head. The aigrette, it was felt, was in particularly bad taste, since it was undoubtedly a gift from the late Ahmed bin Said.

"Let us forget that horrible Shihab," she said, brightly; "let us forget the whole East. Of course poor dear Ahmed was awfully good to us, and I shall never forget *him*. But after all, nothing could have come of it. Diana couldn't have married him." (Luke looked at her in wonder. Was it possible that she expected anybody to believe this?) "As for Shihab, I always felt that there was something wicked in his soul. Didn't I, Diana?"

Diana made no answer.

Her mother didn't require any. "My skin always prickled uncomfortably when he came near," she rattled on. "I am very sensitive that way. Shihab was too meek, too humble, too anxious to please. I have a kind of sixth sense that always warns me when people are not what they seem. It is quite uncanny, really. After a diplomatic dinner my husband always asked me what my impressions were of the different people present. And as it would turn out in the end, I was never wrong!"

And so on indefinitely.

The men listened with polite smiles, longing to gag the woman. They looked at Diana with the softened air that the sight of perfect beauty brings out in men and thought: Why isn't she an orphan? Diana herself said little, but there was a new quietness in her face that made her appear more beautiful than ever.

Sir Bertram, for all his delightful manners, was not quite all there. His attention wandered from his guests. One might have suspected that he was thinking: What on earth induced me to ask this mob to dinner? At the other end of the table his sister, Mrs. Dartrey, who was a famous hostess on two continents, could not quite hide her fear that Diana was about to do her out of a job. Lee Mappin, looking perfect nineteenth century in his black stock and pleated shirt bosom, was doing the best he could, but Mrs. Dartrey gave him only one ear. She was trying to hear what her brother was saying to Diana. It was not a good party.

For Luke Imbrie, in particular, it was a long ordeal. Everything seemed to rub fresh salt into his wound; the exquisite simplicity of the establishment which is the purest form of swank; the casualness of everything; the beautiful order, the agreeable servants. Though there was no parade, one never lost the consciousness that the wealth and power of an empire were supporting the prestige of this Ambassador. It beat the young man down. Who could expect a beautiful woman to turn all this down? he asked himself. Anybody could see it was hers for the taking.

At a moment when Mrs. Morven's attention was devoted to something delicious on her plate, Lee addressed the Ambassador: "What is to become of Abu Daud, Sir Bertram?"

Their host smiled grimly. "I can foretell that with some exactness, Mr. Mappin. The French will land him in Syria and convoy him in safety through mandated territory to that part of Shihkar which lies in the desert beyond the mountains. There the *soi-disant* Sultan Abu expects to raise a small troop of Arab horsemen, who are always ready for a foray, and ride through the pass which is called el Tubja down to the city of Shihkar on the sea. Shihkar is an ancient walled town, but under the latest treaties the fortifications have been dismantled. Abu Daud expects to ride into town unopposed and to receive a tumultuous welcome from the populace. The British Resident has no force at his disposal. He is expected to run away."

Sir Bertram paused to sip his wine. "However," he continued, his smile a little grimmer, "as soon as Abu Daud rides into the desert where he will be out of touch with the telegraph, a fast British cruiser will be dispatched to Shihkar from Aden. Her guns will be landed and mounted on the walls in preparation to receive Abu and his wild Arabs. They won't stand against gunfire, of course; they will retreat through el Tubja. Meanwhile a landing-party of bluejackets with machine guns will have made their way through a pass to the northward, called el Houl, and will be waiting at the other side of el Tubja. Abu Daud will be captured."

"Good Heavens!" said Lee. "How did you learn about his plans so soon? The *Richelieu* is only halfway across the Atlantic!"

"I have it from a charming friend of mine who is making the voyage," said Sir Bertram. "Abu Daud appears to have—what is your expressive phrase?—appears to have fallen hard for her. He has asked her to be his Sultana."

Lee glanced at Luke. "God save us from the Embassy charmers!" he cried. ". . . What are you going to do with Abu Daud?" he asked Sir Bertram.

"Oh, we'll build him a marble palace in the Maldive Islands, or some such retired spot. Plenty of wives and servants, of course. He'll be happy and grow fat."

"And who will rule Shihkar?"

"Young Hussein el Faiz has already been invited in the name of the people."

"But Hussein is the candidate of the Scimitars, the Green Turbans, all the violent nationalist elements."

"Surely," said Sir Bertram. "Why not? He can be separated from his fanatical friends. Hussein is a nice boy. We learn that he has been kept too close by the priests. Too many lessons from the Koran and not enough fun. He's crazy to see the world. We'll send him to Paris and London to complete his education. Meanwhile the British Resident will carry on in Shihkar."

Lee glanced around the fable. "Aren't the British wonderful?" he murmured.

After dinner the little company sat in one of the drawing-rooms, still discussing the case which had brought them together. Luke Imbrie affected an interest in this post-mortem that he was far from feeling. All his faculties were focused on Diana where she sat by herself on a little sofa near the front end of the room. Near by sat Sir Bertram with his back to the windows, and on his left in a big sofa, Lee Mappin, Major Walkley and District-Attorney Bassett in a row. Opposite Luke, Mrs. Morven was telling Mrs. Dartrey a story with endless tossings of the jeweled aigrette.

Once when Luke stole a glance at Diana he found her looking at him. She smiled at him with her eyes, though her lips were immobile, and looked down at the vacant half of the sofa. She then addressed a question to Sir Bertram. Luke felt the blood rushing to his face. He helped himself to a cigarette and lighted it. After a moment he got up, with his hands in his pockets, and moving behind the sofa where the three men were sitting, stood admiring the portrait of an eighteenth-century beauty by Sir Joshua Reynolds, of which he could not distinguish a single lineament. After a while he moved on behind Sir Bertram's chair to some other *objet d'art* between the windows, and so at last reached the little sofa and sat beside Diana.

She greeted him with a drawing-room smile, but her eyes conveyed something more. "That was well done," she murmured.

"Wasn't it indiscreet to ask me over," said Luke, scarcely moving his lips.

"Nobody could possibly have got my message but you."

"Still, they saw me come."

"They couldn't blame me for that."

"You're a deep one."

"Mother and I will be leaving here tomorrow," she said.

"Why?" asked the startled Luke.

"Don't show surprise or anything. Look bored, like an English-man. . . . We're going to the Hotel James Madison for the present. What are you going to do?"

"Lee and I are returning to New York tomorrow."

"Oh! . . . I thought you had a month's leave."

"That was to attend upon Meddy. My excuse is gone."

"Oh . . . !"

"Why are you leaving the Embassy?" he asked.

"It would be impossible!"

"Hasn't he spoken?"

"Yes, he has."

"What was your answer?"

"No."

"Oh my God!" murmured Luke.

"Careful! He's continually looking this way."

Luke's voice was husky. "Do you mean to say that you can give up all this?"

"I hate it!"

"What do you want, Di?"

"A simpler life."

"Have you told the old lady you've turned him down?"

"I'll tell her tonight. There will be a fearful row, but I'll stick it. I've learned my lesson. I mean to run my own show from now on."

"Oh, Di . . . !"

"Careful! If you get emotional I'll have to go over to the other women. . . . How do you feel about the jewels now?"

"As long as they were a free gift it's all right."

"Yet you said you never doubted me!"

Luke was silenced.

"We have to have the jewels on Mother's account," said Diana. "So she can have a home of her own. We couldn't have her with us. I love her, but I will never live with her again."

"Bravo!" murmured Luke. He wiped his hot face. "I can't take this before all these people, Honey. This talk about 'us.' Can't we stroll down a corridor or something?"

"No. He's looking at us. I don't want to hurt him." A note came into her voice that thrilled him. "Can't you wait until tomorrow, Luke?"

"Are you trying to tell me in this nonchalant manner between your teeth that you're in love with me, woman?"

He dared not look at her. He heard her draw a long breath. "Oh, with all my heart, Luke! Somehow you have taught me to be myself; to let myself go! I have gone all, all out for you! I want to live with you. I don't care how poor we are. I'm a useless person, but I could learn if you were patient with me at first. I long to lead a real life, Luke, like other American women, and have you come home every night. . . ."

"My God! this is awful!" he murmured.

"What!" said the startled Diana.

"To have to sit and listen to such things with my hands at my sides and my face ironed out. I'm bursting!"

"It's only until tomorrow," she said.

As in a daze, Luke became aware that Lee had popped up from the sofa and was bowing to Mrs. Dartrey. "I must be off. This has been most enjoyable, Mrs. Dartrey. Good-night, Sir Bertram. . . . Coming, Luke?"

"Go," whispered Diana. "I'll be waiting for you tomorrow afternoon at the hotel."

LEE MAPPIN, true to his amiable eccentricities of character, refused to take any credit for the solving of the Sultan Ahmed case, and tossed all the bouquets in Major Walkley's direction. In this manner Lee had made himself solid with the leading police officers of the country, who were of great aid to him in his profession. Whereas in the beginning he had courted the reporters, now he went to any amount of trouble to keep out of their way. Not that he was overburdened with modesty; quite the contrary; but he indulged his vanity in more subtle ways than other men.

Luke Imbrie decided that somewhere within the convolutions of his astute and humorous brain, Lee had figured that the most enduring publicity was to be had by those who rejected it. In any case, he didn't want to be praised as a detective, but as the author of serious studies of crime. The account of this case that he subsequently wrote was masterly, and Lee himself was scarcely mentioned in it.

This peculiarity was illustrated next morning, when Luke accompanied him to Union Station in a taxicab to put him on a train for New York. As they drew near the cab entrance, Lee caught sight of a number of reporters waiting, and said agitatedly to his driver:

"Don't stop! Don't stop! Drive right around the circle and go out again!"

The driver obeyed.

"Phew! that was a narrow escape!" said Lee. "Driver, are you free to take me to Baltimore? I'll get on the train there. You can bring my friend back, and make a fare both ways."

"You ain't hearing any kick from me, mister," was the reply.

1

HULBERT FOOTNER
THE ADVENTURES OF
MADAME STOREY

ISBN 978-1-61646-236-9

COACHWHIP PUBLICATIONS

COACHWHIPBOOKS.COM

ISBN 978-1-61646-255-8

COACHWHIP PUBLICATIONS

ALSO AVAILABLE

ORCHIDS
TO MURDER

HULBERT
FOOTNER

ISBN 978-1-61646-262-8

COACHWHIP PUBLICATIONS

COACHWHIPBOOKS.COM

WHO KILLED THE
HUSBAND?

HULBERT FOOTNER

ISBN 978-1-61646-256-6

THE MURDER
THAT HAD
EVERYTHING!
HULBURT
FOOTNER

ISBN 978-1-61646-258-2

COACHWHIP PUBLICATIONS

COACHWHIPBOOKS.COM

THE
DEATH
OF A
CELEBRITY

HULBERT
FOOTNER

AN AMOS LEE MAPPIN MYSTERY

ISBN 978-1-61646-263-5

Coachwhip Publications

Also Available

AN AMOS LEE MAPPIN MYSTERY

HULBERT FOOTNER

UNNEUTRAL
MURDER

ISBN 978-1-61646-266-6

COACHWHIP PUBLICATIONS

COACHWHIPBOOKS.COM

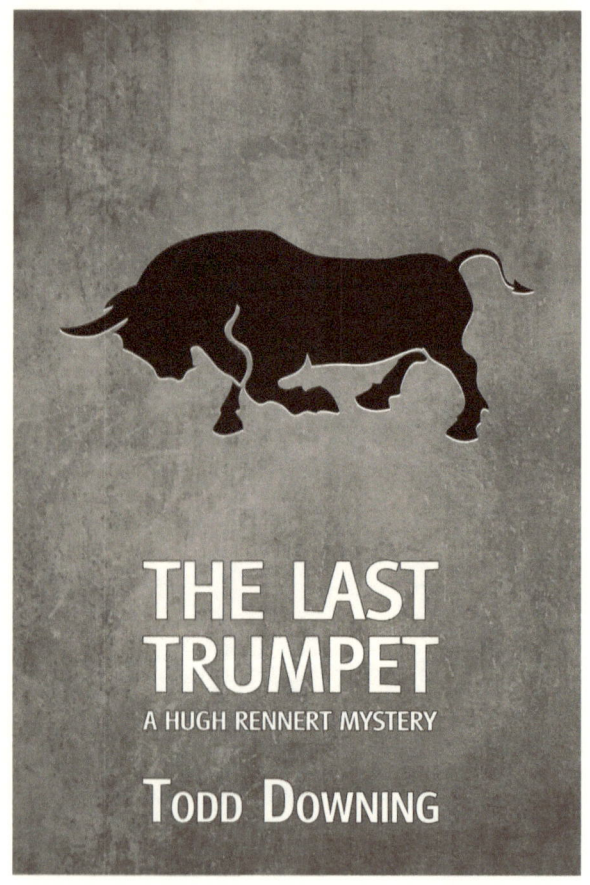

THE LAST
TRUMPET

A HUGH RENNERT MYSTERY

TODD DOWNING

ISBN 978-1-61646-152-2

THE QUINNY HITE
MYSTERIES
CHINESE RED · HERE LIES THE BODY

RICHARD BURKE

ISBN 978-1-61646-247-5

COACHWHIP PUBLICATIONS

COACHWHIPBOOKS.COM

MURDER OF
THE HONEST BROKER

WILLOUGHBY SHARP

ISBN 978-1-61646-211-6

COACHWHIP PUBLICATIONS

ALSO AVAILABLE

THERE IS
NO RETURN
THE ADELAIDE ADAMS MYSTERIES
ANITA BLACKMON

ISBN 978-1-61646-223-9

www.ingramcontent.com/pod-product-compliance
Lightning Source LLC
Chambersburg PA
CBHW032115020726
47494CB00007BA/2073